MW00576891

TRUTH PROMISED

A DR. SAMANTHA JENKINS MYSTERY

STEPHANIE KREML

HIPE BOOKS PUBLISHING

This book is a work of fiction. Names, characters, places, and incidents are the product of the author's imagination or are used fictitiously. Any resemblance to actual events, locales, or persons, living or dead, is coincidental.

Copyright © 2023 by Stephanie Kreml

All rights reserved.

No part of this book may be reproduced in any form or by any electronic or mechanical means, including information storage and retrieval systems, without written permission from the author, except for the use of brief quotations in a book review.

ISBN: 978-1-955921-03-9 (ebook); 978-1-955921-05-3 (paperback)

www.stephaniekreml.com

 Created with Vellum

1

The early morning fog faded during Samantha Jenkins's drive to Redew Biosciences. She'd been overwhelmed when she'd become an advisor to the startup a month before, but as she learned more about the company and how she could help it succeed, her initial anxiety had subsided—for the most part. She turned onto a street leading to a cluster of industrial parks in north Austin, then into the lot for Redew's building, one of many in a row of cookie-cutter concrete structures. Since it was a Saturday, she had her choice of spaces, so she pulled into a spot right next to the front door.

She was meeting with Erik Milsom, Redew's chief science officer. They'd emailed back and forth during the week, while Sam had been seeing patients in clinic, and this was the first chance she had to stop by the offices and speak with him in person. Through his messages, he'd addressed some of her concerns about how Matt Purcell, the CEO, had represented the company's progress during a presentation at the South by Southwest pitch competition.

He'd said that although Matt may have stretched the truth a bit, the company's foundation was solid.

But Sam still had a few lingering questions—questions that Erik promised he would answer in greater detail that morning.

As the sun arched higher in the sky, clearing away the remaining mist and heralding a lovely spring day, she swiped her ID to enter the office. The badge gave her a sense of belonging, even though she wasn't technically an employee—yet. Here, she was a valued member of the team, and here, her opinions mattered. If the promises made to her were fulfilled, she could help exponentially more patients than she ever would as an individual doctor practicing medicine. And that's all she'd ever really wanted to do—help as many people as possible.

Once inside, she stopped by Erik's desk tucked amongst a quartet of cubicles, but he wasn't there. The lamp was on, highlighting an orderly arrangement in a matching office set: a cup packed with all the same brand pens and highlighters, journal articles alphabetized in an organizer, paper clips neatly nestled in a tray as if on display in a showroom. The only thing revealing any hint of personality was a mug, half full of black coffee, declaring: "Fueled by mitochondria and java."

He'd told her he'd likely be in the lab, so she stepped over to the entrance on the back wall. Through the vertical window on the door, the lights from inside cut into the dimness of the office, but when Sam tried to enter, the handle wouldn't turn.

She peered through the window. It didn't look like anyone was inside.

She knocked.

No response.

She glanced around the office, the walls of the cubicles

casting shadows from the sunshine breaking through the blinds on the windows overlooking the parking lot. Erik's car sat out front, a couple of spaces away from hers.

Sam knocked again, this time calling out Erik's name.

Still no response.

She made her way along the back wall to the short hallway where the restroom was located. Perhaps she'd arrived just when he'd needed a biological break. But the door was open, the bathroom dark.

She hoped nothing had happened to him. He was in his late twenties and healthy, as far as she knew.

But what if he'd fallen and hit his head? There was a fume hood in the lab—had he been exposed to a noxious chemical?

Sam quickly returned to the lab door and tried opening it again.

The handle didn't budge. Still no sounds or movement from inside.

Perhaps his girlfriend Lisa had come by and taken him to breakfast. They would probably be back any minute.

She pulled out her cell phone and called Lisa. They'd known each other since they'd been roommates in college. If it hadn't been for their long-lasting friendship, Sam wouldn't have had the opportunity to advise Redew.

Lisa picked up after a couple of rings, sounding like she'd just woken up.

"Have you seen Erik?" Sam asked.

"No. The last time I saw him was on Thursday, when we went to that movie. It was crazy, with all the media and stars."

"Oh, right," Sam said. "You guys went to the premier for that new Adam McKay comedy. How was it?" She was genuinely interested and somewhat distracted by Lisa's demeanor.

"It was amazing. I'd never been to anything like that before. I'd always wanted to go to the film fest at South by, but it's pretty pricey. Plus, even with a platinum badge, it's hard to get into the big premiers. But Bob pulled some strings, so a few of us from our firm sat in one of the boxes at the Paramount, and we could see everyone in the audience below." She listed all the celebrities they'd spotted, along with the best parts of the movie, and some interesting factoids from the Q & A with the director afterward. It was a little unlike her to go on so much; they must have had a great time.

As Lisa carried on, Sam tried the lever on the door once again, putting her weight into it, thinking it might just be stuck. It still didn't move.

"So you and Erik didn't do anything last night?" Sam said, finally breaking off Lisa's account of the premier and getting back to the point of her call.

"No. I had to put in some face time with another startup—like everyone else, they're raising money. And all those VCs are in from the Bay Area for South by, so we had to join them for dinner." Lisa yawned. "I think he said he was going to pull an all-nighter in the lab. He does that sometimes."

"I'm at Redew right now, and I can't find him," Sam said. "We were supposed to meet this morning."

"Oh. Have you called his cell?"

Sam slapped her forehead. "Duh. I should have done that before I called you. But his car's parked out front, and we'd agreed to meet right now."

"He's not in the lab?" Lisa sounded a little more awake.

"Well, that's the thing—the lights are on, but the door's locked. I can't see anyone inside, and when I knock, there's no answer."

"And you said his car's there?"

"Yeah. Do you know how I could get into the lab? I just want to …" Sam hesitated for a moment, searching for the right way to state things, not wanting to alarm her friend. But she couldn't think of anything better that quickly, and if something was wrong, time was critical. "I just want to make sure nothing's happened—"

"You think something might have happened to him?" Worry crept into Lisa's voice.

"Well…I can't see the whole lab, and the door to the fly room is closed," Sam said as she angled herself and pressed her face against the window, trying to maximize her view. "I just want to make sure he didn't fall or something."

"Oh, God." Lisa, normally cool and collected, sounded scared now. "He hasn't had one in a while…I hope he didn't have one, again…We had to go to the ER the last time."

"Hasn't had what in a while? Why did you have to go to the ER?"

"He couldn't breathe, so I took him. He had an asthma attack."

Now it was Sam's turn to be concerned. The small company's business involved testing drugs on flies, after all. What if one of those drugs had triggered Erik's asthma?

Lisa was babbling now, talking to herself, verbalizing her worst fears. But Sam needed her help.

"Lisa? Lisa?" Sam said, trying to get her friend's attention. "Do you know if there's a spare key around here?" She figured she might since Lisa had also been helping Redew, serving as a part-time general counsel, reviewing contracts and other legal issues.

"Uh…check in Matt's office. I think he keeps a set of keys for everything."

"I hope I can get in," Sam said as she hurried to the small office next to the cubicles.

Fortunately, it wasn't locked. A laser-printed sign with Matt's name was taped to the door, and it flapped in her wake as she rushed by. She went behind the desk and pulled open drawers with her free hand as she continued talking on her cell. "Where would he keep them?"

"Beats me," Lisa replied.

But then Sam found a ring loaded with a variety of keys buried near the back of a side drawer. "I think I found them."

She ran over to the lab door and fumbled as she tried each key in the lock while cocking her head against her shoulder to keep the phone to her ear.

"What's happening?" Lisa squeaked.

"Hang on," Sam said as she continued to work her way around the key ring.

Why did he have so many? Several keys had fit into the lock, but they wouldn't budge when she tried rotating them. The rough metal edges bit into her fingers.

Now there were only a few candidates left on the ring. What if the right one wasn't here?

Then, with a slide and a turn, the second to last key engaged the tumblers. Success.

"I'm in."

The door banged open as Sam sprang into the lab. The company's bulky prototype sat alone on a table in the center of the room. The lights inside the fume hood were off, the freezer in the corner hummed. No Erik. But he typically worked in a smaller space just adjacent to the larger lab area. The fly room. For some reason, that door was also locked.

"What's happening?" Lisa repeated.

"I just need to—"

Sam used the same key for the main lab door to enter the fly room. Thank goodness she didn't have to go through them all again. As she pushed the door open, a pillow of cool air caressed her ankles as the smell of yeast filled her nostrils.

She took a step into the small space, just enough to see around the shelves next to the door. She tensed up, her body now on alert.

Erik lay facedown on the floor.

"I found him," she said into the phone, "but I need to call you back."

Sam cut off the connection as her friend's pleas squawked from the tiny speaker.

She must focus on Erik now.

She knelt down next to him, her phone buzzing as she set it on the floor. She rolled him over to get a better look. He didn't seem to be breathing, his lips cyanotic.

She placed her index and middle fingers under the angle of his jaw.

A thready pulse.

She leaned over him and put her ear on his chest, listening for breath sounds.

There were none.

"Erik!" Sam patted him firmly on the cheek. "Erik! Can you hear me?"

His eyes remained closed, but his body shuddered and twitched. He drew in a small breath.

Then nothing.

She swept her index finger inside his mouth, checking for an obstruction. But his oropharynx was clear, so she smacked his cheek this time.

He drew in another breath and stopped.

She was about to smack him again, but then he

continued to breathe, his respirations shallow and ragged, hitching and pausing, then slowing again.

Chin lift. Head tilt.

No improvement.

Sam ran back into the larger section of the lab, grabbed the AED next to the fume hood, and ripped open the foil packets containing gel pads as she ran back to Erik's side.

She untucked and pulled up Erik's shirt to expose him. She slapped the pads on his chest, and, with some effort, to his back. After she plugged the leads from the pads into the AED, she turned it on.

A measured mechanical voice began instructing Sam to do the steps she'd already completed, so she picked up her phone and grimaced as she declined another call from Lisa.

The voice on the machine prattled on as she dialed, her hands shaking from the adrenaline rush.

Just analyze the waveform already!

The operator answered almost immediately. "911. What's your emergency?"

2

One month before she found Erik unconscious on the floor of the fly room, Sam spent a typical Wednesday morning in the clinic, seeing patients and watching the time. Each day began with what seemed like a reasonable schedule, evenly spaced out with follow-up appointments in precise fifteen-minute increments, but inevitably, what looked good on paper would usually descend into controlled chaos. Some patients would show up late, or their cases were complicated, requiring more time than the idealized quarter hour allowed. Then there were the unexpected phone calls from insurance companies and employers Sam had to squeeze in, along with patients who had new injuries showing up, needing immediate attention, throwing everything else off-kilter.

Fortunately, as the morning ended, she and Jerry Reid, the physician assistant she supervised at the ObraCare clinic where they worked, had caught up with the schedule. She glanced at the grid on the whiteboard and saw only one patient was waiting in a room, a walk-in needing a DOT physical so they could renew their commercial driver's license. They were probably taking care of things during their break, just like she was about to do.

Sam took a deep breath and let it out. *It's time*, she thought. She hung her white coat over the back of her office chair, opened the file drawer next to her computer, and pulled out her purse.

"Off to lunch?" Jerry asked as he looked up from his monitor.

"I'm meeting a friend." Then she winced. "But I might be a little late coming back."

"No problem, Doc," he replied cheerfully. "I've got you covered."

"Thanks, Jer," Sam said, patting him on the shoulder as she stood.

She could always count on Jerry. He was old enough to be her uncle, so despite their professional hierarchy, she often relied on his expertise. He'd been seeing patients almost as long as she'd been alive, after all.

As she left through the back door of the clinic, she waved goodbye to Cynthia, one of the medical assistants, who was escorting a patient into an exam room. She started her car and joined the traffic on I-35, heading north into downtown Austin. Although she'd let Jerry think otherwise, she wasn't actually going to lunch.

Instead, Sam would be meeting with an old friend who had a proposition for her. One that she had repeatedly resisted.

Every time they'd meet for their monthly dinners, Lisa would suggest that Sam consider a life outside of clinical medicine. She'd tell Sam about various opportunities with startups in Austin, many of which had been established to commercialize research out of the University of Texas. She'd try to persuade Sam by telling her these companies used new technologies to improve people's lives, through new therapies or by improving the delivery of care.

And every time, Sam would politely listen before saying she wasn't interested until...well, it's funny how being mistreated can shake the foundation of your worldview and loosen your resistance.

A driver honked, breaking Sam out of her reverie. He whipped his car from behind, around to her left, then slammed on his brakes, almost hitting the car in the lane next to her.

What was his rush? It wasn't like he could go anywhere. All the lanes were packed, filled with cars and trucks creeping along, and Sam silently gloated as her lane crawled forward and she pulled ahead of the impatient jerk.

She glanced at her watch, hoping her friend would forgive her for being a few minutes late. Lisa had arranged a meeting with the CEO of a startup, and first impressions were everything. Even though Sam wasn't sure this was right for her, she felt obligated to be on time for Lisa's sake.

Besides, something had to change in Sam's life.

She let out her breath as she finally inched her way across the bridge over Lady Bird Lake. The name had changed recently to honor the former First Lady—and sounded much prettier, too—but to Sam, it would always be Town Lake, the name she had known her whole life. The body of water was long and narrow, really just a section of the Colorado River, dammed off on either side of Austin, as it snaked through the city. A jumble of high-rises, most of which had sprung up in the years Sam had been away, crowded the northern shoreline, as if they were vying to be first in a competition.

The city had changed so much; it was no longer the sleepy college town of her youth.

Sometimes she wondered if she still belonged.

Right after Sam crossed the bridge, she could see the source of the slowdown—a stalled 18-wheeler—but it no longer concerned her as she exited the freeway before the obstruction. She coasted through the green light on the feeder street, turning left and entering downtown, only to have her progress sputter every couple of blocks, as waves of pedestrians took their time, moseying across the inter-sections on their way to lunch.

At the top of the hour, she pulled a ticket and entered the parking garage of the Frost Bank building. She breathed a small sigh of relief, only to realize she had to climb ramp after ramp, passing row after row of cars, trailing behind a line of drivers also looking for spaces, before she found one on the fourth floor.

She hurried to the elevator, texting Lisa, letting her know she was in the building. She'd thought it would only be a minute before she'd get to the meeting, but the elevator seemed to take forever to arrive. She glanced at her fellow travelers gathered around the silver double doors, all on their cell phones, oblivious to her nerves.

Once she got to the lobby, after stopping on more floors to pick up people on the way down, disorientation overtook her for a moment as she tried to determine where she was. The other elevator riders pushed past her while she hesitated. She was near the coffee shop where she'd met Lisa a few times before. But those occasions had been during quiet early mornings on the weekends—Lisa always seemed to be working—and Sam could park on the street, not in the garage.

The smell of roasted beans and lunchtime snacks filled the air, causing her stomach to growl. She'd just have to make do with the granola bar in her purse later. As she made her way along the side of the cafe, the lobby opened up to a wall of glass with a view of pedestrians and cars passing by on Congress Avenue.

She looked around to figure out where she needed to go next. Since the building was so tall, the floors had been divided into groups amongst several elevators for faster access. It took her a second to find which one would take her to Lisa's floor. When she was finally inside what she hoped was the correct elevator, she checked her phone as the doors closed.

Lisa had responded to Sam's text with a thumbs-up emoji.

The express elevator hurdled Sam skyward, which made her stomach drop, giving her an uneasy feeling that matched her mood.

Even though it had seemed like an eternity since she'd entered the garage, Sam would arrive only seven minutes late. Her face flushed, her heart raced. So much for first impressions. She hoped the CEO would be more understanding than the surgery attendings she'd dealt with during residency.

When the elevator doors opened, the receptionist directly across the office lobby gave her a warm smile, flashing his perfectly aligned teeth. He sat at a grandiose desk, the name of the law firm proudly displayed in gleaming, laser-cut metal along the front of the raised counter.

After she checked in with him, he motioned for her to sit in one of the sleek armchairs flanking the elevator doors. As the pleasant purring of the phone lines kept him busy on his headset, his calm voice answering calls in a low tone, she studied the wall of frosted windows behind him. Shadows emerged and receded against the glowing canvas. The only places she'd seen like this were the offices for the chairman of the department of surgery in Houston, but they were not nearly as luxurious as this.

A door to the left opened, and Lisa emerged. When she saw Sam, she smiled and came over.

Sam stood, brushing off her clothes. She held back from hugging her friend—this was a professional meeting, after all. "Sorry I'm late."

Lisa waved her hand as if it was nothing. "Don't look so worried," she said. "They want you—in fact, they really need you, so you've got this."

Sam nodded and followed Lisa through one of the frosted glass doors behind the receptionist's desk.

They entered a conference room with a wall of windows providing expansive views of the city and the hills to the west. Sam was so stricken with the vista in front of her, she barely noticed the man sitting at one end of the oblong table.

He was turned away from them, nodding as he listened to someone on his cell phone. He glanced over his shoulder, tipped his chin to acknowledge them, then ran a hand through his sandy blond hair. "Okay, honey. I've got to go, but I'll be there on time," he said, then nodded once more. "Love you too."

He pocketed his phone as he stood and turned to Sam, giving her his full attention. He was not much older than her and had the air of a GQ model, with a trim build accentuated by a tailored button-down shirt and dark slacks.

"I apologize. My wife is having an ultrasound this afternoon." He grinned. "We get to learn if we're expecting a boy or a girl today." He extended his hand. "You must be the illustrious Dr. Jenkins. I'm Matt Purcell."

"Very nice to meet you," Sam said as she shook his hand. "And how exciting! Is this your first?"

"It is," Matt said with a slight blush, then he motioned for Sam and Lisa to join him at the table. As the women sat down to flank him on either side, he said to Lisa, "I'm so glad you arranged for us to meet."

"Of course," Lisa said in her usual matter-of-fact manner.

Sam pulled out her *curriculum vitae* from her portfolio and handed it to Matt. "Here's my CV, which includes my education, along with some of the research projects I worked on while I was in med school and residency. Some of these resulted in publications."

As he took it, he said, "Have you ever wondered why these are called CVs instead of resumes?" He glanced back and forth between Sam and Lisa. "I guess it sounds more academic, to call it by a Latin name." He waved his free hand in a curly motion with his pinky finger extended.

Sam smiled at him weakly, unsure whether he was taking a jab at her and the so-called elite or just trying to be funny.

Matt glanced down at Sam's CV and said, "Very good." Then he set the document aside on the table. "Thanks for this"—he swished his hand dismissively— "but, as far as we're concerned, an MD is an MD. What we need is someone who can help us determine the best path for us to take, to help us see where our work has the greatest potential to impact the highest number of patients."

Sam nodded as she took this in. He really didn't seem to care that she hadn't finished residency or that she wasn't board certified.

"I'd like to give you another view of healthcare—I know you're used to the typical model, where you, as a doctor, see one patient at a time. And with your team of nurses and other staff, you could manage a handful of patients in parallel." He leaned back in his chair and pressed his fingertips together, forming a temple with his hands. "How many patients do you see in a day, Doctor?"

Sam thought through the last few weeks. "Anywhere between twenty and thirty, sometimes thirty-five on a really busy day."

Matt nodded appreciatively. "And how many patients do you take care of over a year?"

For this, Sam did not have a ready answer. She looked up at the ceiling for a moment, doing a few quick calculations, trying to take into account the number of repeat visits she saw. Then she shrugged and said, "I don't know, maybe two thousand or so? Twenty-five hundred?"

Matt wrinkled his chin, giving him a contemplative look as he nodded. "That's not bad...not bad at all. But imagine how much good you could do if your work affected not just those two thousand patients, but tens of thousands...or even hundreds of thousands?"

Sam raised her eyebrows, then gave Lisa a questioning glance. Lisa just looked at her encouragingly.

How could Sam possibly see hundreds of thousands of patients? She supposed she might see tens of thousands over the course of her career, especially if she continued practicing urgent care. Unlike primary care, where a doctor had a set panel of a couple thousand patients they saw regularly, performing annual exams and managing chronic conditions over the years, she was continually taking care of new patients, patients with minor injuries and illnesses, patients who usually got better after a few visits, patients she would only manage for a brief period and never see again. But he wasn't talking about taking care of each patient individually, especially since he was the CEO of a startup company.

Matt leaned forward with a spark in his eye as he put his forearms on the table and clasped his hands together. "I know—you're thinking about seeing all those patients, and how the personal connection with each one is important. However, imagine how you could scale your influence in peoples' lives?"

"You're talking about how your work at Redew can impact all these people," Sam said. "That is, if you can successfully use your technology to identify new indications for old therapeutics."

Matt pointed at her, making a clicking sound with his tongue as he did, and said, "You've got it! We need someone like you to help us determine where"—he raised his hands up, as if preaching the gospel—"in the universe of medical conditions, we would have the best chance of success."

The prospect of being involved with such an effort sounded amazing. And Matt was so confident and enthusiastic, she believed he'd be successful. All Sam had ever wanted to do was to help people, and this might be another way she could improve the lives of so many patients, so many more than she could ever possibly do on her own. She wanted to be a part of it, but she needed to know more.

"What exactly are you looking for in terms of work requirements?"

Matt glanced at Lisa, then back at Sam. "I don't know how much Lisa has told you, but we are a tiny startup, and we're a little cash constrained. So we need someone who could advise us right now—you know, be available via email, maybe for some phone calls, stop by every once in a while for a few meetings."

"Okay, so you're looking for someone part-time?" Sam asked.

"Well, not even that." Matt leaned back in his chair. "I can offer a slice of equity for access to someone who could answer our questions about clinical applications and maybe do a little research to help us define the direction we should take for possible market entry points."

"Then you're not looking to hire someone?"

Matt put on a winning smile. "We can't—not right now. But if we can reach certain milestones, we have several VCs who are quite interested in joining our series A."

Sam frowned. "I'm sorry. I don't think I understood what you said."

He held up his hand as he gave a brief nod. "Right. I forget you aren't entirely familiar with the lingo of the startup world. We have seed funding from a few angel investors—"

"High-net-worth individuals?" Sam asked.

Lisa nodded, smiling proudly, as if her pupil was performing well. She'd told Sam about angel investors during one of their monthly dinners a while back.

"That's right. Their investment has allowed us to sublet a small office." He leaned forward conspiratorially and lowered his voice. "We got it for a steal because the startup that occupied it previously bellied up, and they were desperate for someone to take over their contract." He sat up again. "Anyway, we have some seed funding that let us get started, to prove that our approach works. And now we're getting results, so we're raising institutional funding from VCs for our first big round, which is called the series A."

"And VCs are…?"

"Venture capitalists," Lisa said.

"Right. You've mentioned that term before too."

"They are the lifeblood of the startup world," Matt said, then leaned forward in his conspiratorial way again. "Although many people call them 'vulture capitalists.'"

"Why's that?"

Lisa frowned and said, "Because they usually want a large equity share for their investment. In some cases, they obtain enough equity to take control of the company, and, in rare, unfortunate circumstances, the original founders may not be the right fit to grow and scale operations. The investors may have to oust them and install their own executives."

She glanced over at Matt, who shrugged, as if he knew that was the way the game was played.

Lisa continued: "Without these large investments, most startups are dead in the water. And it's not like the VCs aren't taking on risk; they're lucky if a fraction of their portfolio companies even give them a return."

Sam thought she followed all of that, but she would ask Lisa a lot of questions later and read up on this ecosystem she was so unfamiliar with.

Matt cleared his throat. "Anyway, to your point of whether we're looking to hire someone; we'd love to, but we just don't have the ability to do that right now. Instead, we'd like to bring on an advisor—a medical advisor—who could help us navigate the clinical world since that's where any therapeutics we identify will end up. Because we can't pay someone right now—even though we know how valuable a clinician's time is—we can offer a piece of equity in exchange for their time. While I can't guarantee anything, if our little enterprise is successful in accomplishing what we'd like to do, those shares could ultimately be much more valuable than any cash compensation."

Sam nodded as she began to understand. Matt was offering shares of his company to someone who'd be available to answer questions. Lisa also nodded, as if this was all par for the course.

"And certainly," Matt continued, "once we do have the

funds, we'd like to bring on that advisor full-time as our Chief Medical Officer."

He let that last sentence hang in the air for a few moments, then he looked squarely at Sam.

"So the question is, Dr. Jenkins, are you the one to help us?"

3

After Matt left for his wife's appointment, Lisa said, "See, you've got this. It's yours for the taking." She leaned forward, locking eyes with Sam. "So, what do you want to do?"

Sam's mind raced. Matt's offer intrigued her. But was this something she wanted? There was also the fact that he'd said a few things that felt…a little off to her.

"He wants me to work for them, but he can't pay me —" Sam began.

"You'll receive shares in the company, though," Lisa said, "which could be worth much more than any salary they'd pay you. Plus, he wants to hire you once they raise more money from investors."

Sam nodded as she thought this through. It did seem attractive, however…"Say this company doesn't raise the money they need—then what?"

Lisa shrugged. "Well, they have enough funds to continue operations through the fall, and if Erik can prove at least one drug in the libraries they're testing can be repurposed using Redew's approach, there's a possibility that they can pitch their findings to a strategic investor—"

"What's that?" Sam asked.

"A strategic investor could be another company—a much larger company—that Redew might work with later on to bring a drug to market. It could be a contract manufacturer or a pharmaceutical company—another organization that could see its business grow if Redew is successful. That way, everyone wins." Lisa smiled. "There are many options."

"I suppose that's why Erik left his job in San Diego to join Redew?"

"Absolutely. Redew has a lot of potential."

"I don't know," Sam said. "I'm not an expert in anything. I don't have any experience being an advisor. It makes me sound like I'm much more than I really am."

"Don't worry about it," Lisa said. "You can just 'fake it till you make it.'"

"That sounds disingenuous."

"Not at all. That's how you get ahead in this world. You need to extend yourself; men do it all the time." Lisa huffed. "They don't hesitate to take on something they've never done before. They just do it and learn along the way. But we've been programmed to be compliant, to do what we're told to do. To be good little girls." She met Sam's eyes again. "The time for that is over."

Sam squirmed in her seat. "It just makes me uncomfortable."

"If you aren't uncomfortable, you aren't growing," Lisa said firmly.

"I know, but …"

Sam had been exactly as Lisa had said: a good little girl. She followed a well-defined course her whole life. Do well in school. Go to college and get a degree. Apply to med school and get good grades. Get into a strong residency program and graduate. Then join a medical practice.

But Sam had broken from that path; she'd left residency. After all that work and schooling, she'd needed time after her mother died, so she'd left her program with three years remaining in her surgery training.

Now she'd been trying to get back on course. If she didn't get back into another residency program and finish it, she couldn't become board certified. And if she didn't become board certified, she would be stuck working for companies like ObraCare—companies that show no regard for her well-being, making her work when she shouldn't.

"Look," Lisa said, "there's little risk in just giving them a chance, right?"

"Right. But ..."

"You find their approach to identifying new indications for old drugs interesting, don't you?"

"Yes," Sam said as she flipped open her portfolio, filled with journal articles about using genetically modified fruit flies to speed up the discovery of drug targets for repurposing. She rubbed her fingers along the edges of the papers, as if she might absorb their knowledge and gain confidence.

"You're so analytical and creative; you've always come up with distinctive ways to do things. You can see connections that others can't. Like that time you cobbled together a lantern when we wanted to play cards on that camping trip."

"That has nothing to do with biotechnology, though," Sam said. "All I did was use a couple of sticks and a piece of paper with a flashlight."

"But don't you get it?" Lisa implored. "You came up with a solution none of us could see."

She did have a point. Sam looked at the world from a different angle, much to the chagrin of the attendings for her surgery rotations. She constantly wanted to know the reasons behind decisions, but frequently, the answer would be, "That's the way it's always been done."

She'd only asked to understand or to learn if there might be a better way. But they often seemed to think she was just trying to show off, and they would become annoyed.

The two friends sat for a moment, with Sam gazing out the window at the hills extending to the horizon west of Austin. Something was still unsettling for her.

"Why would Matt want me to help Redew as an advisor—putting aside the whole 'fake it till you make it' bit?"

"Honestly," Lisa said, splaying her hands, "since they're such an early-stage startup, they've had trouble finding more established doctors to advise them—at least not without paying out the big bucks. And those well-known docs have their own pet projects, research they've already been conducting in their specialty, so they aren't as open to all the possibilities out there." She pointed at Sam. "You, on the other hand, aren't biased one way or another. You're more open-minded and don't have a hidden agenda." She smiled. "So those are your advantages."

Sam leaned back in her chair and looked out the window again, watching the billowy clouds drifting over the hills in the distance. It certainly was a lot to take in.

Finally, she said, "I'm not sure what to do."

Lisa sat up in her chair. "Look, there's minimal downside here. They take a risk on you, and you take a risk on them. If it all works out, everyone wins."

THEY SPOKE for a few more minutes about the details of being an advisor. Lisa pointed out that if Sam enjoyed helping Redew, there were plenty of other early-stage companies that also needed assistance. Sam could build up a portfolio of companies to advise. Some would offer equity, and some could pay cash stipends. And even if most of the startups failed, a few might go on to be quite successful.

"It's the same approach VCs take," Lisa said. "If they have a decent portfolio and only one or two companies knock it out of the park and give them a huge multiple, it more than offsets any losses they have from the underperformers."

It was something for Sam to consider. A whole new approach to making a difference in the lives of patients.

"HOW WAS LUNCH?" Jerry asked when Sam returned to the clinic. He pushed back from his computer and stood so he could go eat his lunch in the breakroom, as he usually did when she was done with hers.

Sam sat down in her chair and hesitated before answering. She really needed to talk to someone, to have a sounding board for all the thoughts and questions going through her head. And this wasn't something she could talk to her father about—sure, he was a doctor, but he was already disappointed that she hadn't followed in his career path and become a cardiologist.

"Actually, I didn't go to lunch." She motioned for him to sit back down, which he did, and then she filled him in on the meeting she'd come from.

"Sounds like an interesting proposition, Doc," Jerry said as he rubbed his silvery goatee. "I agree with your friend Lisa. You could make a career out of being a consultant for companies. I've seen others do it. You could help these business folks understand how doctors think and make treatment decisions. I don't understand all this new-fangled genetic technology, but you're a smart one—you'll figure it all out." He laughed briefly, then leaned forward and touched her arm. "Plus, you should look out for yourself." He gave her a curt nod. "Especially after the way Dr. Taylor treated you. He doesn't care about you."

It was true. Just a few weeks before, her boss had clearly demonstrated how little he valued Sam.

She'd been feeling poorly for a week with what she'd thought was a bad cold. She'd done what she was supposed to do and tried to let it run its course, but it wasn't clearing up. So when she wasn't getting better, and it seemed what had started out as a viral illness had progressed to a bacterial infection, she'd taken a z-pack—a short course of azithromycin antibiotics. Normally, that would have done the trick, but she just wasn't shaking it.

Unfortunately, she'd used up all of her time off, not only to recover from this sickness, but also because her father had gotten remarried in January, which had eaten up a couple more days. So she went to work, even though she knew she wasn't completely well.

When Jerry came in for the day, he took one look at her and said, "Doc, you shouldn't be here."

She slumped in her chair after she'd seen a couple of patients, trying not to let on how weak she was, each breath making her feel more light-headed.

"Sit up, Doc," Jerry said. "Let me take a listen to you."

He leaned over her, carefully placing his stethoscope in each lung field, taking his time to fully auscultate. Then he stood and said, "You've got rhonchi in your right upper lung field and not a lot of air movement out in the periphery. Let's get an X-ray."

Sure enough, once the image had been processed, Jerry confirmed it: Sam had pneumonia. While the rest of her lungs appeared clear and dark and healthy on the computer screen, her right upper lobe was filled with patchy white.

Thinking back on it, she'd probably developed pneumonitis after cleaning her tiny bathroom in her apartment with a new spray that had been advertised all over the place. She knew there were warnings about only using it in well-ventilated spaces, but she thought she hadn't been exposed to it very long. She'd turned on the exhaust fan and left the door open, but the only window above the tub was frosted and fixed shut.

So much for being a responsible consumer—let alone a responsible doctor.

With X-ray evidence of pneumonia in hand, she called Dr. Taylor, her boss, and told him what was going on.

He paused for a moment, then said, "I'm sorry, Sam, but uh…I don't have anyone to cover for you right now."

He didn't say, "I'm sorry you're not feeling well," or "Go home and get some rest."

No. Just, "I don't have anyone to cover for you right now."

Sam was too stunned to say anything other than, "Okay," and hung up the phone.

Jill, the clinic's operations director, had been standing next to Sam when she'd made the call. "What did he say?"

"There's no one to cover for me."

"Didn't he tell you to go home?"

Sam shook her head. "No."

"Well, that's ridiculous. You need to get better, not see patients."

Sam looked at the list on the whiteboard across from the clinical work area. "The rooms are full right now, though. If I don't see them, then they'll be waiting for hours."

Jill stared at the board for a moment. "You're right." Then she shook her head. "But no, you need to go home."

Sam took a breath as deeply as she could. She could hear the rhonchi herself—no need for a stethoscope—the air rattling in her airways, popping open infected alveoli, the tiny air sacs sounding like Rice Krispies in milk.

She felt feeble and dizzy, but she stood anyway. "I can see a few more. It's not fair to them or you or Jerry."

"But the patients will understand," Jill said. "People get sick all the time—even doctors."

Sam shuffled over to the board and moved a magnet with her name to the next room with a patient waiting to be seen. "Don't worry. I've got this."

Jill stared at her, and when she saw Sam wasn't changing her mind, she relented. "All right. But I'm calling the patients that haven't come in yet and canceling their appointments. Then I'll call Paula and let her know what's going on." Paula was ObraCare's regional operations director and Jill's boss. "She can put pressure on Dr. Taylor to find someone to fill in for you until you're better, even if we have to call the agency to get a *locums*. Jerry can take care of any walk-ins or new injuries after you leave."

Sam nodded. Working *locums tenens*—as a temporary doctor covering shifts—was how she'd started working at ObraCare in the first place, while she was still in residency.

The last patient she'd seen that morning, just before she left, was a man who was recovering from a back injury. "I feel bad that you're taking care of me," he said. "What I have is minor, and if my company hadn't covered this for workers' comp, I wouldn't even be here." He gave her a pitiful look. "I don't need to see a doctor. But you do!"

Jerry patted Sam's arm, bringing her back to the present. "So go for it," he said, then glanced around to make sure no one was listening. "Medicine has changed. It's no longer about the doctor-patient relationship. It's only about how much everyone else can make off of that relationship—screw the doctors and the patients!"

4

As Sam mulled over her decision about whether or not she should advise Redew, she exchanged several emails with Erik—Lisa's boyfriend and Redew's chief science officer. He sent her a video demonstrating how Redew's prototype would speed up the identification of new drug candidates by screening libraries of existing drugs against fruit flies with genes that model various human diseases. The video was professionally produced and impressive, like an episode of *Nova* on PBS, and it explained that most successfully repurposed drugs fell into two categories.

The first category included compounds that had made it through phase I and II clinical trials, which proved the drug could be safely used in animals and humans, but in phase III trials, the drugs did not show enough effectiveness to treat the original condition for which they'd been developed. The second category included drugs that had made it to market, meaning that the FDA had approved them because the drug developer had good results in all three phases of their clinical trials, but the developer ended up discontinuing the drugs because they did not sell well. The sales slump could happen for a number of reasons, such as when a newer, more effective drug came onto the market, or because, even though the FDA had approved the drug, insurance companies had decided not to pay for it.

These circumstances provided an opportunity to repurpose these drugs—that is, to find new health disorders and conditions that they could treat. Plus, the time to get them to market for any newly discovered indications would be much shorter since Redew could use any existing clinical trial data from the original applications to the FDA.

Watching the video sparked Sam's excitement, and she could see how, if Redew was successful, their technology could open the doors for new ways to treat patients—with medications that were already out there, just waiting to be rediscovered. She wanted to help Redew, putting her career on a path she hadn't known existed until she met with Matt. And even though she had no experience, she'd give advising a try.

What did she have to lose? All she'd have to do is respond to questions, and if she didn't know the answers, she'd do research to find the information, or she'd reach out to her old med school classmates and professors for their advice. She'd only need to give Matt and Erik some of her time. Time that she'd previously planned to use for the courses she'd been taking toward a master's in public health. Time that was now free because she'd been ill for so long at the beginning of the semester.

Her plan to fix her career was derailed because she'd gotten too far behind in her coursework and had to withdraw. Now she'd have to delay graduation by a semester, which would delay her applications to residency programs in preventative medicine by a year, and, as a result, delay her independence from ObraCare.

But if things worked out with Redew, she might not have to continue on that path after all.

When Sam emailed her decision to Matt, he responded within minutes and invited her to visit Redew's offices to sign a consulting agreement and get a tour.

Unfortunately, Sam had to fib a little to meet with him. She'd told her boss she had to take the afternoon off for a doctor's appointment. If pressed, she could reason it wasn't really a lie. It *was* an appointment with a doctor—with herself. That way, she could at least eke out a couple of hours away from clinic without taking the whole day off and having her pay docked.

Redew was located in an industrial park on the north side of town. It was one of many tiny startups hoping to make a splash in Austin. But biotech did not have as big a presence as software, where anyone could develop the next industry-shifting app with just a couple of laptops. A biotech startup needed a lab with equipment, and Matt had told Sam the company arranged a favorable deal subletting space from another startup that had recently gone under.

The pebbled prefab walls from the nineteen seventies in front of her car were a far cry from the elegance of the law offices downtown where Lisa worked. But, while considering life in the startup world, Sam had found many stories, almost like folklore, of companies starting in founders' garages. Despite the unimpressive-looking build-ing, something felt magical about the place. Could this be the beginning of a new phase in her life?

Maybe.

Sam entered the office through a glass door. The only

indicator she was in the right place was a plain sheet of paper with "Redew Biosciences" laser printed on it and taped to the glass. There was a small reception area, but there was no one behind the empty desk.

An opening to the left expanded into a work area that was sparsely populated with a few cubicles. As the door behind Sam whooshed closed, a young woman with a blonde ponytail popped her head above one of the gray fabric partitions. She came around to greet Sam, her lab coat billowing out behind her as she approached.

"May I help you?" she asked.

"I'm here to see Matt Purcell."

"Oh, you must be Dr. Jenkins," the young woman said as she extended her hand. "I'm Brooke—with an 'e'—one of the lab assistants. Well, actually, the only lab assistant." Then she leaned forward and said, "Matt told me I should say I'm 'one' of the lab assistants, not the *only* lab assistant, so we seem like we're a little farther along."

Sam smiled and shook Brooke's hand. "Makes sense. Nice to meet you."

"Here, let me take you to Matt's office."

Sam followed Brooke past the cubicles to a walled office with a window overlooking the parking lot. Matt sat behind a particle board desk, topped with a monitor and several stacks of papers.

Just as he'd been when they'd first met, he was on the phone. It was a landline this time, and he leaned back in his chair, the cord tethered to the base on his desk, bouncing as he spoke. When he noticed the ladies at the door, he sat up straight and held up a finger.

"Okay…Okay…Sounds great, Bill. Listen—I gotta go, but we're still on for the Spurs game next week, right?" He nodded, then said, "Alrighty. See you then."

He hung up the phone and stood with a broad, toothy

smile. "Dr. Jenkins! Thank you so much for coming." He laughed. "It must seem like I spend all my time on the phone."

After they exchanged greetings and Brooke left, closing the door on the way out, Matt motioned for Sam to take the seat in front of his desk. As she settled in, he did the same on the other side, with his chair creaking as he scooted it closer to her.

"I'm thrilled you decided to become our advisor." He took a document off one of the stacks of papers on his desk and slid it across the surface so she could read it. "Here's a boilerplate advisor agreement. It basically puts all that we've discussed in writing."

Sam glanced at the contract, skimming over the clauses, although she knew what it contained already. Since Lisa had prepared it for Matt, she'd explained everything to Sam. Basically, in exchange for Sam's time—not to exceed twenty hours a month—she would be granted five thousand shares of the company to be vested twenty-five percent each year to reach full vesting in four years. If this were five thousand shares of Google, she'd be rich. Instead, it was five thousand shares of a company that, as far as she could tell, was worth around $400,000. And, according to the agreement in front of her, five thousand shares was only 0.3% of the company.

So basically, she was agreeing to work four hours a week for Redew for the next four years for a little over $1,000, assuming nothing else changed. But during her research into how startups worked, she'd also found successful companies that eventually went public or were acquired by a larger company. Some ended up worth hundreds of millions of dollars, and if that happened to Redew, her five thousand shares could be worth significantly more.

Lisa had given Sam a caveat, though—the percentage that those five thousand shares represented would change as more investors got involved. Redew would issue more shares during each investment round, and the portion of the company her original shares represented would be diluted. However, if Redew did go public, and if they were able to reach a stock price of $100, then Sam's five thousand shares would be worth half a million dollars. Not bad for a few hours of work a week on the side.

But the potential earnings were not the real reason why Sam was there. Of course, she needed a better job, one where she wasn't forced to work to the detriment of her health, and one where she was valued, not just as a doctor, but as a person. However, the opportunity Redew offered, to be on the ground floor of something that could potentially help hundreds of thousands of patients—or more— was exciting.

After she finished going over the advisor agreement, making sure all the terms Lisa had stated to her were included, Sam signed and dated the last page.

"Fantastic!" Matt said as he took the contract back from her and signed it. "We're so excited to have you join us." He flashed his perfect smile. "And hopefully, you'll consider making a more permanent move once we secure our next round of funding."

Sam nodded. "That would be great."

Indeed, it would. This could be a new direction for her, a completely unexpected way to use her clinical training. And she wouldn't have to figure out how to undo the career damage she'd incurred when she left her surgical residency program early.

"I'll scan this and email it to you for your records," he said as he stood. "Now let's give you a tour of our humble office." He motioned toward the door, indicating

Sam should lead the way, then he followed her as she exited.

"Of course, you've already met Brooke," Matt said as they walked past her desk. She gave them a little wave, then she returned to typing on her computer, with several small succulents surrounding the monitor. "She's helping Erik in the lab, but unfortunately, she'll be leaving to start graduate school in the fall." As they moved away from the front windows of the office space, Erik appeared in a doorway along the back wall. "And speaking of ..."

"Hey, Sam," Erik said. "I'm so glad you've decided to help us out."

Although Lisa had made the connection for Sam to meet with Matt, Erik was the one who'd really moved things along. Sam didn't know Erik very well, only having met him a few times, the last being a double date with Lisa, Erik, Sam, and her boyfriend Alex. They'd gone to dinner before catching a taping of *Austin City Limits* not long after Sam had fully recovered from her bout of pneumonia.

"How's Alex doing?" Erik asked.

"He's good. He's been taking a bunch of extra shifts lately, so I don't get to see him too much." In fact, it had been over a week since they'd gotten together. Alex had been on call the previous weekend, and when he wasn't at work, he'd been studying for his critical care boards.

"Figures. Work always dominates our lives," he said, glancing back at Matt. "But that's what we live for, right, Matt?"

Matt smirked and gave him a nod.

"Shall I show you the lab?" Erik said, extending his arm into the room behind him.

"That would be great."

"I'll leave you in Erik's capable hands to continue the grand tour," Matt said, then retreated back to his office.

The lab space was about the same size as the cubicle area. "Since Matt kept talking about how cash-strapped you are, I'm a little surprised," Sam said. "This lab is pretty impressive."

"It'll do." Erik nodded as he pressed his lips together in a critical expression. "It has the essentials, but once we raise our series A, we'll need to move into a better facility."

"How'd you afford all this equipment?" Sam asked.

"The startup that was here before left most of it," he said. "They'd purchased a lot of the pieces when some of the labs at the university were upgrading. Since that company dissolved, and a lot of this equipment is pretty old, there's not a lot of value. But I'm making it work for now."

Suddenly, despite all the positive vibes she'd gotten from Lisa and Matt about how great it was working for startups, the realization that this office, this lab, was in essence the graveyard of another company hit Sam. "What are the chances that Redew will end up like the company that was here before?"

Erik shrugged. "I don't know. There's always a risk working for any startup, but it's exhilarating, you know? To be at the genesis of a project which could impact so many lives."

Sam nodded. They certainly agreed on that point. "Is that the reason you left your old job to come here?"

"Definitely." Erik's eyes lit up. "Sure, I had a great job out in San Diego at one of the companies that created the biotech industry. Thirty years ago, they started out just like Redew, with a couple of guys working on old equipment. But I learned a lot while I was there, and when Lisa told me Matt needed someone to start Redew, I was confident I could replicate that kind of success here." He leaned toward her and lowered his voice. "In fact, I took a pretty steep pay cut to join, but the upside will be huge if we're successful."

"And if we're not?"

He smirked. "Then maybe Lisa can support me."

5

S am stared at Erik for a moment. How seriously should she take his comment? Sure, she was all for the woman being the breadwinner, but did he secretly think Redew didn't have a chance to succeed?

Then Erik laughed. "All kidding aside, I truly believe we've got something here." He walked over to a large table, beckoning Sam to follow. "This is it. Our prototype."

She recognized parts of it from the video she'd watched, but it didn't look as impressive in real life. It was a collection of different instruments and pieces of equipment cobbled together—almost like a high school student's science fair project.

"So you're using this to evaluate drug libraries right now?" she asked. "Is this what was used to identify the two candidates for repurposing?"

"Well…no and yes—to answer your questions in order. No, we aren't using this prototype to evaluate drug libraries *right now*; however, this prototype *was* used to identify the two lead compounds that we might be able to repurpose."

"I'm not sure I follow." Sam looked back and forth between Erik and the prototype. "So…this doesn't work?"

Erik patted the machine next to him. "It does work— or it did. One of the graduate students in Dr. Galloway's lab used it to identify those compounds, but…let's just say we've had some reliability issues, and we aren't using it at this time."

"What do you mean by reliability issues? Does this thing work or not?"

Erik sighed, then slumped his shoulders a little, as if he realized he needed to come clean. "So the prototype works, but you have to babysit it, since there are so many steps that aren't automated yet." He began to point to different sections of the instrument. "It's a little tricky getting the flies into this chamber, where we take videos to feed our machine learning algorithms that count and classify the little guys. Then these fans here send little puffs of air to separate the flies into new vials, so we can cross them again and produce new progeny." He shrugged. "Plus, everything needs to be aligned just right to make it all work."

"Why can't you fix it?"

"Because I'm not that mechanically inclined. My specialty is in the life sciences, not engineering."

"Then this is all a …" Sam stopped herself because she didn't want to sound so negative. But Erik seemed to understand her concern.

"Is this all a lie?" He shook his head. "No, we're forth-right with our investors. The prototype does what it's supposed to do, but there's still a lot of work required to turn it into a reliable platform we can use consistently, so we can sell our services, or, perhaps one day, sell these machines to other companies. A big chunk of the money we raise from investors will go to pay an engineering firm to help us make this a reality."

He pulled an easel out of the corner, set it up next to the prototype, then placed a large poster on it. "Matt likes to have this front and center when anyone visits, but, honestly, it just gets in the way."

Sam shifted around so she could see it better. The poster had blueprints and a rendering of how the finished platform would look, kind of like a big, boxy Xerox machine.

Erik pointed to a geometric logo above the name Trotman Industrial Engineering in the bottom corner of the poster. "The firm we've contacted has already created plans to turn this initial prototype into a reliable product that we can either sell or use in-house if someone wants to pay us for our services." He explained what was in the plans, pointing to different sections of the diagrams, along with the analogous parts of the prototype. "The engineers are ready to go as soon as we find investors."

"If the prototype doesn't work...consistently, how are you doing things now?"

"The old-fashioned way." Erik walked across the lab toward a side door. "Here, I'll show you."

They entered a much smaller space. A couple of microscopes sat on a counter spanning one wall, along with shelves above them containing trays of vials filled with buzzing flies. Sam had detected a faint hint of yeast in the larger section of the lab, but once they were in this smaller space, the odor filled her nostrils, and not in a freshly baked bread way. It smelled more like a dank basement.

"You took a genetics lab in college using *Drosophila*, right?"

Sam nodded. It had been one of her favorite courses, primarily because she'd had a superb professor who'd meticulously planned out each week for her and her classmates. When they would enter the lab, they'd find vials containing the tiny fruit flies at their workstations, along with detailed instructions on which features to observe under the microscope and how to carry out their experiments.

"Most of my time is spent performing crosses to verify the work of Dr. Galloway's grad student," Erik said. "I'm making sure the compounds he identified actually are good candidates and that we can move forward to small mammal studies—which, of course, is another thing we need money for."

"Really?" Sam asked. This was exciting. She hadn't realized they'd identified any drugs yet. "What kind of compounds?"

"They're both for neurological conditions—Alzheimer's and Huntington's."

"And how does that look? Are you able to replicate the previous results?"

"Well," Erik said, rubbing the back of his neck, "it's still a little inconclusive."

Sam's enthusiasm waned a little. Figures. But it made sense. Erik had only been working at this a few months. It was good he was double-checking everything, but what seemed like initial successes may not pan out.

His expression brightened. "But I'll have a better answer over the next few weeks."

"And what if you aren't able to show that either compound works?"

"I still believe in the principles of the approach, so I know we'll be successful at some point. There are so many compounds with good safety data available, but they just didn't show efficacy for their intended uses, so they were never approved by the FDA. And there are libraries that include those and other drugs that did get approved and make it to market, but their manufacturers abandoned them for some reason." Erik's eyes lit up. "Plus, once we have our platform working, we can also look at drug combinations."

Sam shook her head in amazement. "Before you sent me those videos, I didn't know drugs could be repurposed like this."

"Isn't it awesome? We can help so many people with these existing drugs, but we just need to figure out which ones will work." He pulled out a tray from the shelves above the microscopes, then picked up one of the vials. "And these little guys are going to help us do that."

A couple dozen flies flitted around the glass tube Erik held between his fingers. The bottom was filled with about an inch of yellow paste. That was the source of the yeasty smell, Sam realized. It was the fly food.

"*Drosophila*—that means 'dew lover,' right?"

"Yes," Erik said, "and it's the source of the company's name."

"Redew?" Then it hit her. "Oh, I get it. 'Redo' as in repurposing drugs, along with a play on do and dew. Those are—what's the fancy word for them?"

"Homophones. Same sound, different meaning." He shrugged. "Kind of a silly name if you ask me, but the grad student from Dr. Galloway's lab came up with it, and there's really no point in changing it now." He put the vial back in the tray and replaced it on the shelf. "Anyway, once we develop the prototype further and build more of them, will really speed up that screening process. I'm certain we'll find multiple compounds that will become strong drug candidates."

Erik then went on to show Sam the rest of the setup, much of which she'd seen and dealt with while she had been taking her genetics lab in college.

"And Brooke's here to help you with this?" Sam said.

"For now. She's been accepted to a master's program at Northwestern, so she'll be leaving at the end of summer. But she'll be here for the next few months. Hopefully, by then we'll be closer to that series A, and we'll be able to hire a few more people."

They went back out into the larger lab. Sam had been so focused on the prototype before that she hadn't had a chance to take in the rest of the space. A fume hood occupied most of the back wall, with counters extending along either side. A sink with an eyewash station under an emergency shower sat in the corner. There wasn't much room to get around the table, so they squeezed behind it. Erik stopped in front of an appliance around the size of a microwave on the counter to the left of the fume hood.

"This is where most of our setup costs went," Erik said as he pulled out a small rack, the size of a thick Stephen King paperback, filled with tiny storage tubes. "One of these drug libraries is about ten grand. We also needed this freezer to make sure our investment would last, which was another ten grand."

"That much? It's so small," Sam remarked.

"Seems crazy that it's so expensive, but it's ultra-low temp—goes down to -80°C—and it keeps these drugs stable for up to a year." He returned the rack to the freezer, then he flipped a switch on the side of the fume hood. "We mix these compounds in the flies' food here."

The sound of the vent fan whirling to life filled the room, and a light came on inside the hood. Within the glass enclosure, a nondescript white bag marked "Instant Drosophila Medium" sat in the corner, along with a few measuring cups and funnels, and several packets of yeast.

Erik slid up the glass door to point at another type of rack, this one a bit larger than the ones containing the drugs in the freezer. It was filled with empty vials, exactly like the ones containing flies in the microscope room. "We have to measure everything out by hand now because we add the drugs we're testing."

He picked up a blue micropipette automatically, with the ease of someone who had done it many times before, gripping it in his hand and placing his thumb over a white button on the end.

"Hey, I just realized we hold these the way killers hold knives in slasher movies." Erik laughed, bringing the micropipette down repeatedly at an invisible foe, just like Anthony Perkins had done in *Psycho*. "Wouldn't that be funny? A horror parody that takes place in a lab, but the horror is that our test results are all screwed up because someone dosed the subjects incorrectly."

"Ha, ha." Sam faked a laugh. Nerds and their nerdy jokes. She would enjoy working here.

Erik cleared his throat as he replaced the micropipette under the hood and slid the glass closed. "Anyway, at some point, we'll need to work with a contractor to automate this process as well. It's another rate-limiting step that will prevent us from screening high volumes of compounds." He smiled at Sam and leaned against the counter. "So that's our setup. It's not ideal, but it will do."

"What do you mean it's not ideal?"

"We'll need more space, because when we hire more people—people who aren't familiar with some of the quirks and possible safety issues unique to this lab—we'll be opening ourselves up to liability. And we aren't neces-sarily using GMP—good manufacturing processes—so we'll have to shore up our workflow to comply with what's expected for our FDA applications in the future."

Sam pointed to the prototype. "Would turning that into a reliable machine help?"

"Absolutely," Erik said. "Any way we can remove the potential for human error helps."

"And what do you mean by 'possible safety issues'?"

"I don't mean to cause alarm. There's nothing that's extremely dangerous here, and we even have this," he said, pointing to an AED mounted on the wall. "I convinced Matt to get it since our insurance offers a discount on our premiums for having one, along with this." He opened up the cabinet under the sink and showed Sam a fire extinguisher. "We'll just have to train anyone we hire, since only Brooke and I have a handle on things here right now. For instance—"

"Sorry to interrupt," Matt said. He'd appeared at the door while Erik had been speaking. "Whit is here."

"Of course," Erik said, beckoning Sam to follow as he moved toward the door.

They went to Matt's office, and he rapped his knuckles on the door frame before entering. A silver-haired man looked up from Matt's computer and stood.

"Dr. Jenkins," Matt said, "I'd like you to meet Whit Chapman."

As Sam shook the older man's hand, Matt said, "Whit is one of our angel investors and is our acting CFO. He's graciously volunteering his time to help us make sure our current financials and projections look good for any VCs who may be interested."

"Speaking of," Whit said, "I've worked my connections and arranged for a few VCs to meet with you after the pitch session at South by Southwest in a couple of weeks."

"Thanks, Whit!" Matt beamed. "That's fantastic!"

"Dr. Jenkins, you'll be there, won't you?" Whit asked. "It would make a stronger impression if you were there as well."

When Sam hesitated, Matt jumped in and said, "Dr.

Jenkins is still practicing full-time, and she's already been kind enough to advise us, so I wouldn't want her to disrupt her routine on our account."

"That's a shame," Whit said, shaking his head. "These firms are quite interested in what we're doing here, but with everything that happened to Theranos, they'll want to hear a clinician's perspective to make sure we are on the up-and-up." He squinted at Sam. "Surely you can take a couple of days off?"

"A couple of days?" Sam asked. She might be able to come up with a way to sneak out of the clinic for an hour or so, here and there, like she'd done this afternoon. Jerry and Jill would cover for her, but she didn't think she could take off more than that. Plus, it wouldn't be fair to put them in a bind like that. "Couldn't I just take an afternoon off?"

Whit continued to look at her critically, as if he were assessing an appliance he was considering purchasing. "These VCs have companies lining up left and right to get meetings with them. There are so many events and pitch sessions going on, and their schedules are bound to change, so we'll need you and Matt to be on standby to account for this."

"If it's just the initial meeting," Matt said, "surely Erik and I can handle it. Anyone that's really interested in us can always meet Dr. Jenkins later."

Whit scowled as he slowly shook his head. "I don't know. If they have any qualms at all—since healthcare and biotech aren't the main areas of focus for some of them— they'll balk."

Sam didn't want their chances of getting funding to disappear because she couldn't take a couple of days off. And even though she didn't fully understand exactly how the prototype worked, or if it would ever be reliable, she trusted Erik. He'd shown her the engineering plans, and he'd told her that he'd seen this process before with other companies in the startup world.

Then she thought about Dr. Taylor, her boss. Something in her life had to change. She had to make the situation at ObraCare work for her, not the other way around.

Technically, what Whit was asking was outside the scope of the agreement she'd just signed, so she had every right to say no. But these men, standing in front of her, seemed so earnest, all with expectant looks on their faces— even Whit, despite his stern demeanor.

Sam felt they were on the brink of something great, building a company with so much promise. And it was all up to her.

She took in a deep breath, nodded, and said, "I can do it. I'll make it work."

6

As soon as Sam got into her car outside of the Redew offices, she tapped out a message on her phone. She hesitated for a moment, staring at the send icon. Would this be a huge mistake? Was it worth putting her medical career at risk?

Right now, she had a secure job, even if it wasn't ideal. On the one hand, she was doing what she'd always wanted to do—help other people. The vast majority of patients she saw truly appreciated her, and she really did enjoy taking care of them.

But, on the other hand, how could she continue working for someone who didn't care about her?

Of course, Dr. Taylor wouldn't always be her boss. Someone else might replace him at ObraCare. In fact, if she wanted to, she could probably bring up how she'd been treated with *his* boss. She didn't want to become a trouble-maker, though.

The blinds in the window in front of her car jostled, and she thought of the people inside. They all seemed so confident about Redew's future success. She believed in

Erik's ability. He was smart and organized, and he knew what he was talking about. And although she'd just met Whit, he had an air about him. Like an elder statesman.

Then there was Matt. If she didn't know he had a pregnant wife, she probably wouldn't have trusted him much. He'd seemed like a salesman who'd say anything to close a deal. However, since he was starting a family, he definitely had a reason for this startup to succeed.

She read over her message once again, taking in a deep breath. After everything that had happened recently, she felt it in her bones. She needed to take a chance on herself. This was the right thing to do.

She sent the message.

Within minutes, Dr. Taylor called her.

"Sam, what's going on?"

You know damn well what's going on, she thought. She wanted to lay into him, tell him that after he forced her to work when she could hardly stand, when her oxygen saturation was plummeting, and her patients felt sorry for her because she was the one who needed medical care more than they did, she was ready to quit.

But she needed to be more judicious. There was always the possibility that things at Redew might not work out.

So instead of saying what was really on her mind, she took another deep breath, slowing her heart rate, calming the agitation bubbling up inside her. "I'd like to change my status from full time to prn."

"I see."

Then, nothing.

The silence from Dr. Taylor's end continued long enough that Sam worried the connection had dropped. She was just about to ask if he was still on the line, when he finally spoke.

"Our policy requires you to give us two weeks' notice

before changing status, so you'll need to continue reporting to the South Austin clinic for the time being. Is that acceptable?"

So that was it.

No questions. No curiosity. She'd at least expected him to say, "Why are you doing this?" or "What can we do to make you change your mind?"

But no. This was strictly a transaction for him.

"Yes, that's fine," Sam said.

"Okay. In two weeks, will you be able to continue working forty hours a week, in five eight-hour shifts, at any of our clinics in the Austin area?"

"Yes," she said a little too quickly. Then she paused as she thought through what he'd just said. She hadn't considered that when she switched to prn, he would move her around from clinic to clinic, like a pawn on a chessboard.

But that should be okay, for now. This would only be a temporary situation.

"I can do that," she said, "most of the time."

Sam had to let him know her demands, though. Let him know he couldn't *completely* control her time. That was the whole reason she was talking to him.

She had to have days when she was free from clinic so she could attend to the needs of Redew. "But I'll have weeks where I can't work every day. And some weeks, I won't be available at all."

"I see," Dr. Taylor said again. "Let me remind you that you are bound by your contract's noncompete clause."

Sam had to think back to what that clause in her contract said—something about not being able to practice at another facility within a ten-mile radius of any Obra-Care clinic. And that applied to a full year after she stopped working for them. It pretty much covered all of Austin and any other major city in Texas.

Little did he know that didn't matter to her. And if things worked out with Redew, she wouldn't be practicing medicine at all.

Dr. Taylor only seemed to care if she was leaving for the competition. It was a valid assumption. There had been several other occupational medicine and urgent care clinics sprouting up around town to serve the growing population.

"That won't be an issue," Sam said. She actually rather enjoyed being in this position with him, where he really needed her, and she kind of didn't need him.

"Very well then. I'll let Suzie—uh…I'll let my admin know, and she'll email you the forms to make this change official."

Ha, he can't even remember her name. It's Pam. In the time that Sam had been working for Dr. Taylor, he always had a new admin every few months. Made sense given how he treated his subordinates.

"Thank you. I'll be watching for them."

Sam hung up, feeling relieved, not realizing how much she'd been waiting for a moment like this, where she was finally in charge.

THAT EVENING, Sam met James and Kevin at a food truck park. Her friends sat at a picnic table under the branches of a sprawling live oak, each sipping a locally made cider. Kevin broke off a can from a six-pack, offering it to her as she sidled onto the bench across from them.

"Is Alex coming?" James asked.

"No. The doc who was supposed to work tonight called in sick, so he took the shift." Sam popped the top and took a sip of cider. It was one of her favorites, spiked with blood orange juice. The citrus and apple flavors mingling together with effervescent bubbles felt refreshing on her tongue.

Then she noticed James and Kevin sharing a brief glance.

Sam put her can down. "What?"

"Nothing," Kevin said, pointing to the food truck behind Sam. "You should really try their falafel wraps. The blend of spices paired with their homemade yogurt is killer!"

"Don't change the subject," Sam said. "What are you thinking?"

Both men remained silent for a moment, and when it was obvious Sam wasn't letting it go, James said, "It's just that Alex has canceled the last two times we've gotten together. And we—"

Sam cut him off. "He's trying to show how committed he is to his practice, so he can become a partner. He has to take on extra shifts whenever he can. And on top of that, he's studying for his critical care boards."

"Okay, okay. I get it." James held up his hands. "He's busy."

"Hey," Kevin said, raising his eyebrows as he touched Sam's forearm, "you need to tell me about this new venture. When do you start?"

"Well, I'm not really working for them," she said. "I'll just be an advisor."

"Still, it sounds exciting. What do they do?" Kevin glanced at James, who seemed relieved that the conversation had moved on. "James tried to tell me, but he didn't know all the details."

Sam explained, as best she could, what Redew was working on, and Kevin peppered her with questions, most of which she didn't know the answers to. He'd been working at Facebook for several years, but his goal was to leave someday and join a startup, so he'd been going to pitch sessions for incubators around town.

"Seems like every other week someone gives notice in our building," Kevin said. "But there are too many copycats around—the next Uber, the next Tinder, the next DoorDash, the next whatever. I'm looking for a unique idea to stand out from the crowd. And it needs to be something that can give investors the multiples they're looking for."

"What kind of multiples?" Sam asked.

"It's got to be big. Like several hundred-X." Kevin took a sip of cider, then said, "But from the handful of health and biotech startups I've seen, they're kind of small potatoes compared to the software plays."

Sam thought about what she'd seen so far from Redew, along with the financial projections that she didn't fully understand, but there were a couple of numbers that stood out. "Making investors a few hundred million isn't enough?"

"No, we're talking billions, baby. Everyone's looking for unicorns, 'cause that's the only way to give investors huge returns."

Sam didn't think Redew would get to that point. "But wouldn't investors be interested in a startup with the potential to help thousands of patients? Just on principle?"

Kevin laughed. "Nah, it's all about the multiples. They may say they're excited about improving healthcare and making lives better, but at the end of the day, they only want the returns."

Surely investors in healthcare were a little more altruistic. After all, that's why Sam had become a doctor. Plus, the US healthcare system was in such disarray, she couldn't believe anyone would want to deal with it unless they had good intentions.

James seemed to pick up on Sam's inner conflict. "Hey, it will be a great experience, no matter what happens. You're still a doctor now, and you're just easing into this—"

"I did a little more than ease in." Sam grimaced and blew out her breath. "I told my boss I'm switching to prn."

"What's PRN?"

"Sorry—it's short for *pro re nata*. It's Latin for 'in the circumstances of,' and we write it on medication prescriptions that should be taken as needed instead of scheduled. So, of course, doctors being doctors, we've used it to talk about our work shifts too. Basically, I'll still be working for ObraCare, but on an as-needed basis."

"Like a part-time job?" Kevin asked.

"Sort of."

"Or moonlighting? When cops take on extra work doing security?"

"Yeah, that's kind of what it's like too," Sam said. "I'll float around to the different clinics in Austin to help out where there's a high volume of patients or to fill in if one of the doctors is sick. Some weeks I may work full-time, and some weeks I can work just a couple of days. It will give me more flexibility to help out with Redew since I needed to take time off—they want me to go to South by Southwest for the pitch competition and be available to meet with VCs."

"That's great!" Kevin said, looking just a bit jealous.

"Huh." James didn't seem quite as impressed. "Well, I suppose you could always go back to full time if things don't work out with Redew."

Kevin elbowed him. "Come on, don't be so pessimistic. Sure, there's always that possibility. But they're fundraising right now, which is why they want Sam around—to give them more legitimacy. VCs always want to know what's going to happen with the proceeds of funding. Having people lined up, ready to start working, is smart." Then he looked at Sam. "You just need to make sure they have enough runway."

"Runway?"

"What's their cash position? Do they have enough in the bank to support their cash flow, for the next year or so, until they close series A?"

Sam shrugged. "I think so, but I'm not sure. They've got a couple of angel investors, and one of them is working as their acting chief financial officer."

"Oh, that's good. If he's actively involved, then he'll make sure Redew stays afloat. Who's the angel?"

"Whit Chapman."

"Wow. He's a legend." Kevin grinned, sitting back like a cat who'd caught a canary. "Then you've got it made."

"Why's that?"

"He was one of the early guys at a startup in the telecom corridor, up in Dallas. It was sold to AT&T for some big bucks a few years ago. If he's working that closely with Redew, then he's committed to making sure you find funding."

James frowned. "If he's from Dallas, what's he doing in Austin?"

"I heard he moved here for the startup activity," Kevin said, "but he's slowed down a bit over the last year. His wife isn't doing so well."

"What's wrong with her?" Sam asked.

"I'm not sure," Kevin replied. "I think it's something terminal."

7

S am was buoyed by Kevin's enthusiasm toward her involvement with Redew. Sure, James was a little more realistic about things, but he did have a tendency to look at life with a negative lens at times. The next two weeks were filled with regular clinic days at Obra-Care, and then Sam took her first day off to go to Redew to practice the pitch she and Matt would give at SXSW. It felt strange for her to be in this office on a regular workday, like she was a normal person and not a clinician. She was used to running around the clinic, seeing as many patients as possible, completely focused on each case, with hardly any time to stop and consider the world around her.

Shortly after she arrived, she and Matt went into the conference room and started practicing in front of Lisa. The day before, he'd sent her the pitch deck along with a script, and Sam had run through it a few times after she got home from clinic, so this was their first time going through the material together. Lisa started timing them off the bat, but they kept running over, taking way more than the three minutes they were allowed.

After going through the pitch for the third time, and only shaving off a few seconds, Matt said, "Let's stop using the timer. We need to get comfortable with the material first."

"The pitch session is tomorrow," Lisa said.

"I know, but we have time. It's still early, and since we aren't making any headway in bringing this down under the limit, let's just take a step back, get confident with what we need to say, and then we can start working on the time."

"I agree." Sam held up her printout of the slide deck. "I'm still having to look at my notes, but if I can memorize everything, that will help us go through this faster. Too bad we can't just show a video."

Matt laughed. "That would be nice. But they want to see how we present ourselves, how well we know our company, and if we're worthy of funding. VCs often invest in people more than the product, so it's almost like a job interview. They want to know if we're coachable."

"And they can get all of that from a three-minute canned pitch?" Sam asked.

"That, and the Q & A afterward. They have a feel for people, and they only want to put their money behind those who are open to receiving their guidance."

Lisa tapped her watch. "Well, we need to keep working on this. Whit is stopping by soon."

Matt nodded. "Okay, then."

They ran through the pitch a few more times, tweaking a word here and there, trimming anything that seemed redundant or wouldn't provide the most impact on their audience in their limited time.

On occasion, when Matt wanted to cut something, Lisa would say, "But that's an important point, especially from a legal perspective. It could be misconstrued if you leave it out."

However, as they closed in on their goal, with their pitch almost down to three minutes, Matt finally pushed back. "We have to remember our objective here. We don't have enough time to get into the minutiae, so we just need to hook them, get them interested, get them wanting to know more. Plus, if they have concerns, they can always bring it up during the Q & A."

"Makes sense to me," Sam said. She found it strange she was agreeing with Matt again. Of course, she understood Lisa's perspective. They wanted to be as forthright as possible, but how could they explain all the intricacies of this startup company in just three minutes? They could only hit upon the highlights.

Before they could go through the pitch again, Whit showed up at the conference room door. "Greetings and salutations."

"You look like you're in a good mood," Matt said. "Have you learned something?"

Whit started to speak, but then Matt held up his finger. "Wait, it's time for our weekly meeting—let me have the lab folks join us."

Whit nodded, and Matt buzzed the lab on the speaker phone, telling Erik that he and Brooke should come to the conference room.

While they waited for the others to arrive, Whit and Lisa talked about another company while Matt told Sam she should just jump in when it was time for her to speak. "When we start practicing again, I'm not going to signal you. You know the script, so just say your part when it's time. That's the only way we can get down under three minutes."

"It's almost like this is a performance," Sam said.

Matt pointed his finger, clicked his tongue, and winked at her. "Exactly."

Erik and Brooke arrived, squeezing around the table to take their seats. Lisa and Erik locked eyes for a moment as he sat next to her, their serious demeanors softening a touch with the hint of a smile forming on their lips.

"Okay, kids," Whit said, "here's the plan."

He listed various people he'd planned to meet with the following day. Some were interested in the other companies he'd put money into, but he said he'd assess them to see if they might also be interested in Redew. At one point, he and Lisa got into a deeper discussion about another of his startup investments, so Erik and Brooke started discussing what they were working on in the lab, and Matt took the opportunity to give Sam more pointers for the pitch.

"When I was fundraising for my last startup, investors really wanted to know how we would achieve our revenue goals," Matt said as he flipped to the image of the blueprints in Sam's printout. "So this slide is key, to let any potential investors know we have Trotman Engineering lined up as soon as funding is available. Having a reputable firm on board that's already vetted our concept will give us a leg up on the other companies at the pitch session."

Sam nodded. But she was curious, if Matt had done this before…"What happened to your last startup? Was it also in biotech?"

"No, it was a software play. Even though we had a working prototype, there just wasn't a good product-market fit." Matt flashed his perfect smile. "That happens sometimes."

By then, Lisa and Whit were paying attention to their conversation.

"It's true," Lisa said. "It's the number one reason startups fail, affecting forty-two percent of startups, according to a recent study."

Wow, that was a lot. If Redew had a high chance of failing, maybe Sam had put herself in a bad position by switching her status at ObraCare to prn. While Dr. Taylor had acted like he was going to continue scheduling her full time when she'd spoken with him two weeks before, now that she was officially working part time, he hadn't done that. For most weeks in the following month, he'd only scheduled her to work four days, and in one particular week, he'd only scheduled her twice. That would be fine if she was getting paid for her time at Redew. But she wasn't.

"So, will this product-market fit problem be an issue for Redew?" she asked.

Matt tapped the blueprints in front of her. "No, because we're building a platform, not creating one product. With this design, we'll be able to identify many different compounds with the potential to treat patients." He nodded to Erik and Brooke. "We've already identified two compounds for treating Alzheimer's and Huntington's, and we'll only find more once we build our system."

"About that," Erik said, "we're still trying to replicate the results from Dr. Galloway's lab." He then went on to explain in technical terms the ins and outs of the experiments he and Brooke were performing. While Sam could comprehend some of what he was saying, she got lost pretty quickly.

Whit looked frustrated as he held up his hand. "Hold on there a minute. I don't understand any of this. Give me the thirty-thousand-foot view."

Erik began his explanation again, but he didn't really restate things much differently than he had before. Brooke added a comment here and there, but Whit continued to frown.

Finally, Matt cleared his throat and interrupted. "I think what Erik is trying to say is that he thought he'd have results for both of these compounds before SXSW, but he needs a little more time."

Matt glanced at Erik to confirm. Erik seemed like he wanted to say more, but after a moment, he nodded.

"Okay, then," Whit said as he slapped Matt on the back. "I can always count on you to cut to the chase. So, we're close to moving these compounds to the next stage, right?"

Erik flipped through his notebook and started to go into another technical explanation, but Matt interrupted him again. "I think we're where we need to be at this point, and Erik will have more data for us soon."

Erik looked satisfied with Matt's response and closed his notebook.

Matt's and Lisa's phones buzzed on the conference table at the same time, so they both picked them up. "Holly wants to have the baby shower the second weekend in April," Matt said. "Does that work for you?"

Brooke stood and said, "I forgot, I need to check on …" Her voice trailed off as she left the room.

"Let me see," Lisa said as she flicked and swiped her phone. "Should be."

"You're throwing a baby shower for Holly?" Sam asked. "That's very nice of you." She didn't know Lisa and Holly were that close.

"Well, we've known each other since our first year of law school."

"So she's a lawyer too?"

"No." Matt laughed. "She got an offer to be a pharma rep, so she quit law school after one year. It just wasn't her thing." He flashed a smile. "And then she met me."

"Okay, enough of the chitchat," Whit said. "Let's get

back on course. Why don't you run through your pitch for me?"

After Erik left to return to the lab, Sam and Matt presented to Whit, who gave them helpful pointers. Lisa began timing them again, and after a few more run-throughs, they got their pitch down under three minutes. Then Whit started throwing questions at them to simulate the types the judges might ask, with Matt fielding most of them. At the end of the day, Whit and Lisa seemed satisfied that they would do well during the pitch session, and Sam felt like she was on the verge of something monumental.

She went to Alex's apartment for dinner. He'd been able to leave the hospital at a decent time, so he'd gone shopping and made chicken marsala. After they finished the succulent meal—Alex sure could cook—they cuddled on the couch, sipping a Barolo as they watched *Casablanca*. When Bogart said, "Here's looking at you, kid," Sam took a deep breath, feeling complete.

Things couldn't get any better than this.

8

S outh by Southwest was like no other conference that Sam had ever attended. Not that she'd been to very many events like these, but the ones she'd taken part in were usually a little formal and stuffy, even if they were at fabulous locations. When she'd been in residency, she'd presented case reports at academic surgery conferences in California and Hawaii, and while those venues allowed the attendees time to have fun in the sun, the subject matter and the seriousness of the senior surgeons had made it feel like study hall on the beach.

While SXSW had a touch of that seriousness, for the most part, it maintained a party-like atmosphere. It had evolved over the years, starting as a music festival in the late 1980s, then adding a film fest, and finally incorporating a tech showcase. During March every year, startups from around the world descended on the Texas capital, vying for publicity, hoping to be the next Twitter—which had found its footing at SXSW when founder Jack Dorsey tweeted the name of the bar he was hopping to. Now, it was not uncommon to have big-name companies and organizations contribute to the carnival-like aura. In past years, the *Mr. Robot* TV show had erected a Ferris wheel on Congress Avenue, NASA had displayed a full-sized mock-up of the James Webb telescope on the lawn of the Long Center, and in a parking lot across the street from the Austin Convention Center, a life-sized TIE Fighter from *Star Wars* had landed, to the delight of thousands of fans.

It was a week-long celebration of creativity, with sessions about every expressive medium one could imagine. Even college kids skipped ski trips during Spring Break in order to volunteer at the conference, hoping for the chance to literally rub elbows with a celebrity, be it a movie star at a film premier or the latest tech billionaire.

That's how Sam found herself at the JW Marriott in downtown Austin, just a couple of blocks from the convention center, surrounded by countless bars where thousands of international bands played nearly 24/7 during the week of the conference, aspiring to make their big break.

Energy emanated from everyone around her, all the way from the volunteers in their bright SXSW T-shirts, manning the entrances to the conference rooms, to the people with the money—the venture capitalists wearing stylish European-cut outfits, carrying around their cross-body bags that cost more than Sam earned in a month.

Matt fit right in, though, as he thanked people exiting the ballroom who'd stopped to compliment him and Sam on their pitch.

Once the crowd thinned a little, Matt said, "You did great, Sam! I think we've definitely garnered interest from some of the big names in the room."

"Thanks," Sam replied. She started to ask about a comment Matt had made during the Q & A, one that was a little unsettling to her, when Whit walked up, slapping Matt on the shoulder and nodding to Sam.

"Great job, you two," Whit said. "I had to duck out after your pitch, but there was a positive buzz in the room."

"What was your read on the guys from Mundy?" Matt asked.

"Well, we'll just have to see when you meet with them later this afternoon." Whit flashed a smile.

Matt's eyes lit up. "So you did it, then? You got us time with Mundy Capital?" He looked back and forth between Whit and Sam. "They want to talk to us?"

Whit nodded. "But *you're* the one who hooked their interest with that fantastic pitch. The meeting I've secured is only fifteen minutes. However, if you can repeat that performance, I'd say we have a good chance we'd move to the next stage."

"Do you mean they'd fund us?" Sam asked.

Matt laughed.

"It could open the door a little wider," Whit said, "with the possibility of a lengthier conversation. From there, if they like what they see, then we will proceed to due diligence."

"What's that?" Sam asked.

"That's when they take a closer look at our books and our technology," Matt said. "If we pass muster, then we might get a term sheet."

"After some negotiation," Whit added.

"Right. After some negotiation," Matt repeated.

Sam squinted. "And a term sheet is…?"

Matt stood up straighter. "It's the terms for the investment: how many shares they would get, how much money they'd invest, over what time frame—"

Whit waved his hand. "We'll get to that point, eventually. What we need now is an encore of your pitch."

"You said we'd have fifteen minutes with Mundy Capital," Sam said. "But the pitch we just gave was only three minutes long."

"That's okay," Whit said. "You'll just repeat your part, and Matt has a slightly longer version of the presentation for just this situation. Then you'll both answer any questions they have."

Matt grinned. "You'll be fine, Sam. I'll be right there with you, so you can defer to me if you get stumped."

She was glad for that. During the five-minute Q & A session after their pitch, Matt was the one who'd answered all of the judges' questions. They were mainly about revenue projections and addressable markets. All business stuff that she knew nothing about.

In fact, Sam wondered again why they needed her for the pitch competition at all. She'd only just learned the very basic ins and outs of Redew's process over the previous couple of weeks. Other than the minute when she'd spoken during the presentation, she'd stood there on stage, doing nothing. Except...there was one question that she'd started to answer, but Matt had jumped right in and cut her off before she could say anything.

"Actually, there's something I want to...clarify. When the judge from Johnson & Johnson asked how many drugs we've already identified, you answered that we have two candidates for neurological disorders." Sam shifted her weight, pushing aside her unease and her uncertainty in her own knowledge. "But Erik is still making sure the results are repeatable before we can confidently say that. Plus, there's the part about the automation; Erik and Brooke are still manually counting flies in the lab."

Matt held up his hand. "I know, I know. There wasn't enough time to go into a detailed response—"

"But don't you think your answer was a little...disingenuous?"

"Not at all. We've identified those two possible drug compounds. And we do have a working prototype for screening—"

"Erik says it's not completely reliable."

Matt nodded. "True. Not yet, anyway. Once we get funded, we can contract Trotman to take our design further, to build a more robust platform and—"

Sam started to have a bad feeling about this. "Is that why you didn't want Erik to present during these pitches? Because he would have said something to dampen the judges' impression of you?"

"What?" Matt stepped back, as if he'd been punched. "No, not at all. Erik understands, at these early stages, the prototypes that got you started aren't always scalable."

"So, while you're telling potential investors that we have an automated way of sorting flies to screen these drug libraries, in actuality, you have Erik and Brooke counting flies under a microscope the old-fashioned way." She shook her head. "It's the whole fake-it-till-you-make-it mentality."

Whit stepped in, holding up his palms. "Now, now. Everything Matt told the judges is true, given the time constraints. Investors know that small startups have very limited resources. They've all cobbled together devices and machines for their proofs of concept. All of them have issues around reliability and scalability. Those problems are nothing that can't be solved with the right amount of capital."

Sam still wasn't so sure, and when she didn't respond, Whit continued, "So, during the longer presentation, if the investors have questions, they'll ask them. If they're still interested, then they'll have ample time to clear up any concerns they have during due diligence."

"How much time?" Sam said, furrowing her brow.

"Because this isn't something that can be explained with a couple of well-rehearsed sound bites. I mean, I barely grasp what is possible, and I've spent over two weeks studying this."

"Investors usually take at least a couple of months to perform diligence," Whit said, his voice calm and steady. "They'll want to know about any possible pitfalls or potential setbacks. Plus, they'll have their own subject matter experts fully examine our technology and processes."

"That's right," Matt piped in. "Additionally, they'll want to know contingency plans should our initial assumptions prove incorrect."

"Okay," Sam said, somewhat placated.

Whit's expression softened. "I like your mettle, kid." He smiled, patting her on the shoulder. "You've got a fire inside you, just like my daughter." He looked up, focusing on something down the hallway behind Sam. He stepped back and the features on his face brightened, as if he'd seen the most wonderful thing in the world. "Speaking of …"

A young lady wearing a Day-Glo orange volunteer tee scampered up to Whit and embraced him. "Hi, Daddy."

"How's your day going, pumpkin?"

"It's been great! I just saw Olivia Wilde on my way over here!"

Sam could tell that Whit didn't know who his daughter was talking about, but he beamed at her nonetheless. His daughter then rattled off the names of other famous actors and musicians she'd seen or wanted to see, and all the while, Whit smiled and nodded.

He finally interrupted her as she slowed down reciting the litany of names. "Pumpkin, I'd like you to meet Dr. Jenkins." He turned to Sam and said, "And this is my daughter Allison."

Sam shook Allison's hand. "A pleasure to meet you."

Allison looked at Sam appreciatively. "So you're the doctor Dad's been talking about? Awesome! My best friend is premed." She shook her head. "But I'm not that great at science."

A slight grimace flashed on Whit's face, ever so briefly, then he turned on his smile again. "You have a lot of other talents, pumpkin." To Sam, he said, "Allison is very artistic. She's studying set design."

"Which is why the film fest is amazeballs!" Allison looked sheepishly at her dad when he frowned. "I mean, it's great. Anyway, I gotta go." She tipped her head back in the direction she'd come from. "I'm assigned to a room down there." She pecked her father on the cheek and ran off.

Whit continued to glow as he watched her disappear in the crowd.

"You seem quite proud of her," Sam said.

"She's the light of my life."

While they'd been talking to Allison, Matt had been pulled aside by a young man who could have been a carbon copy of Matt. Sam recognized him as one of the other CEOs who'd been in the same pitch session.

As Whit and Sam moved closer, the young men were gesturing animatedly with excitement lighting up their faces, as if they'd just won big teddy bears from a board-walk game. Matt made introductions all around, then the other CEO, whose name was Brett, congratulated Matt and Sam on giving a strong pitch before leaving to meet up with the rest of his team.

Sam couldn't help but feel somewhat buoyed by the enthusiasm surrounding them. So much hope and possi-bility filled the air, with the attendees around her high off the potential to create something spectacular, to have a massive impact on the world.

Once the three were alone again, Whit picked up the conversation they'd started before his daughter had appeared. "To allay your doubts about why we wanted you to present today instead of Erik, it goes to the types of crucial questions you asked. We need someone like you, a critical thinker, to probe for any possible issues before we get too far along so that we don't have another debacle like what happened with Theranos. And having you—a doctor who's analytical—with us during these meetings will definitely alleviate some of the concerns potential investors may have."

This made Sam feel a little better. Theranos had been a blood-testing startup that claimed it could perform hundreds of tests on a single drop of blood—something that Sam had thought was far-fetched and not even clinically necessary. The only exception was in the ICU where labs were drawn on patients daily, and in some cases, multiple times a day. For these patients, the amount of blood drawn for testing added up to a significant volume and could lead to anemia.

But Theranos claimed they could perform these tests with an instrument they'd developed that was the size of a toaster oven. They'd even convinced Walgreens that the pharmacy chain could run these tests in their drug stores. Still more unsettling was that Theranos had persuaded the Arizona state legislature to change the laws requiring a doctor's orders for these blood tests.

Sam had wondered how patients could understand many of these tests when, after years of training, she still had to seek guidance from other doctors on occasion to interpret them and figure out how they should affect her clinical decisions.

In the end, it had all been a sham.

The machine Theranos had developed never worked, and to provide test results to thousands of patients depending on them, the company had diluted the tiny blood specimens and processed them on standard laboratory equipment, often yielding erroneous results.

Theranos ultimately folded, and the founders were tried for fraud and found guilty.

All along, the company famously had impressive board members and advisors—including a former Secretary of State and a future Secretary of Defense—but no doctors. Doctors who would have asked critical questions.

Sam was glad that Whit, at least, appreciated her line of inquiry.

Matt patted her shoulder. "You see, we aren't pulling the wool over anyone's eyes. With your help, we'll make sure we can deliver what we promised."

What they'd said made sense, but Sam still wanted to talk it over with Erik. He, being a scientist, was a straight shooter. He would let Sam know if Matt was promising too much.

9

Sunday. One day since Sam had found Erik facedown in the lab at Redew on that fateful morning.

After the paramedics had arrived, they'd resuscitated him, moved him out to the parking lot on a stretcher, and loaded him onto the ambulance, with one of them manually squeezing a bag-valve to help him breathe. Sam chased behind the speeding vehicle in her car, calling Lisa on the way to the hospital.

At the emergency center, the doctors connected Erik to a ventilator. But his pulse ox never climbed above sixty percent, and not long after, his heart stopped.

In the waiting room, Lisa called Erik's parents to let them know what had happened. Sam was amazed at how well Lisa handled the call—she'd only met Erik's parents one time, when she and Erik had gone up to Dallas for the annual Texas–Oklahoma football game. She'd spoken with empathy, but in a professional manner. However, as soon as Lisa hung up the phone, she lost her composure.

"They're driving down now," she said between sobs.

Sam could only imagine the devastation Erik's parents must be feeling, hearing that their son had just passed away. How awful that four-hour drive must be, suffering through the shock, every mile dragging them closer to the inevitable, the proof their son was dead.

The next morning, Sam sat numbly on her couch in her apartment, flipping through the channels on her TV mindlessly. Normally, on a beautiful spring day like this, she would sip coffee on her balcony overlooking the green-belt, but she'd kept the vertical blinds over the sliding glass doors closed. She didn't deserve to enjoy it. Not after what had happened to Erik.

Now Sam waited as politicians blathered during the Sunday talk shows. She'd received a call from an investigator in the medical examiner's office asking if she could stop by. Apparently, Lisa had shared her number because the investigator had a few questions regarding Erik's death.

Sam had thrown on some clothes, but she hadn't showered. If she hadn't been expecting someone, she would've stayed in her PJs, wallowing in her guilt, even though, logically, she knew that she'd done everything she possibly could've to help Erik.

"Thanks for letting me come by to speak with you," the ME investigator had said when she'd arrived. She'd opened a pocket on the outside of her bag and extracted a business card when she introduced herself. Below the seal for Travis County, her name, credentials, and title were listed:

Miranda Curran, RN
Medical Investigator I

"Please call me Miranda," she'd said. She was a lithe

brunette with olive skin, probably in her mid- to late-twenties, which would put her around the same age as Sam.

"Not a problem," Sam said as she motioned for Miranda to have a seat at the dinette table. "Would you like something to drink?" Sam's mouth suddenly felt dry.

"No thanks, I'm fine," Miranda said as she set her shoulder bag on the chair next to her and pulled out a notebook and a folder.

Sam filled a glass with water from the tap in the small kitchen, then joined Miranda at the table.

"I just have a few routine questions." Miranda opened her notebook to a clean page. "When you found the decedent, where exactly was he?"

"He was lying on the floor in the lab."

"This was at the company where he worked?"

"Yes—it's a small startup that licensed some technology from UT."

Miranda nodded as she jotted down some notes. "And this was yesterday morning? Why were you there?"

"Yes. I was meeting with Erik to—" Should Sam share the details? She'd wanted to make sure he was okay with Matt's statements from the pitch competition, with his exaggerations about how far along Redew was in identifying repurposed drugs. And during the meetings with the potential investors—Whit had arranged two more, in addition to the one with Mundy Capital—Matt had continued to make the same potentially misleading statements.

But it didn't matter anymore. Erik was dead.

She had no idea what would happen next.

Sam cleared her throat and took a sip of water.

Miranda sat there all the while, watching expectantly.

"I was meeting Erik to go over the results of some experiments he'd been doing."

Miranda nodded. "Could you walk me through what happened when you arrived?"

"Well, I found it a little strange he wasn't waiting for me. I couldn't find him anywhere around the office, and the door to the lab was locked. The lights were on, so I figured he must have been inside, but I couldn't see anyone. I checked the restroom—there's only one in the office space because it's so small—and when I didn't find him, I called my friend Lisa since they are…they were dating."

Sam paused as a wave of remorse washed over her again.

Miranda waited patiently. She looked like she'd dealt with this type of situation many times before, appearing emotionally detached, but understanding. She reached into her bag, pulled out a pack of tissues, and handed one to Sam.

"Thanks." Sam took it and dabbed her eyes. She blinked a few times, then said, "Where was I?"

Miranda gave Sam a sympathetic smile. "You had called Lisa because you couldn't find the decedent."

Sam took another deep breath. "Right. I couldn't find Erik, and I thought Lisa might know where he was, but she said she'd been busy with her work the night before and Erik had spent a late night at the lab—he was known to do that sometimes. When I told her about the situation, she then worried that maybe something had happened to him."

"And why was that?"

"Because she'd taken him to the ER once before when he'd had an asthma exacerbation."

"I see." Miranda thumbed through her notes. "Yes, she told me that was in November." She looked up at Sam. "So, then what happened?"

"I was about to hang up and call Matt or Brooke—they both work at Redew—to see if I could find a way to unlock the door, but then Lisa said there was a key in Matt's office, which I found, and that's how I got into the lab."

"And the dec—Erik was on the floor."

"Yes, I couldn't see him through the window on the door because he was in a smaller room off to the side."

Miranda nodded. "Was he breathing when you found him?"

"No. He was cyanotic, but I thought I felt a weak, thready pulse, so I hooked him up to the AED, called 911, then initiated CPR."

"Did the AED discharge?"

Sam shook her head. "He didn't have a shockable rhythm."

Miranda nodded again as she flipped through the folder. "EMS arrived seven minutes after you called. You continued CPR that whole time?"

"Yes, but I had to stop when they arrived so I could let them in."

"And I see they inserted an LMA, but they had some trouble seating it, so they ended up intubating him. But even that required a couple of tries, with an esophageal intubation on the first pass."

Sam nodded. *Thank goodness for CO_2 detectors*, she thought.

She remembered standing by helplessly in the cramped space of the fly room, not wanting to impede the EMTs, but fully aware of every step they took. They had tried inserting the LMA, or laryngeal mask airway, a device that looked like a dish wand, with a triangular head on the end of a long tube. They had become popular since it was easier to insert than an endotracheal tube. Because LMAs sit like a tiny mask on top of the larynx—hence the name

—they are less traumatic, with a decreased risk of injury, as opposed to intubation. Plus, LMAs could be placed blindly, whereas intubation required visualization of the vocal cords with a laryngoscope so that an endotracheal tube could be threaded in between.

If done incorrectly, the tube could end up in the esophagus—which is what happened to Erik, delaying the delivery of much-needed oxygen to his lungs. After the head EMT inserted the tube, inflated the cuff, and pulled out the laryngoscope, the other EMT attached a clear boxy CO_2 detector and the bulky plastic bag, which looked like a clear blue football. But the paper in the detector stayed purple after a squeeze, and Sam did everything she could to hold herself back from jumping in, wanting to help. Fortunately, the head EMT realized his misplacement immediately, pulled the tube out, and tried again.

After another squeeze of the bag, the $CO2$ detector turned yellow as the air exited Erik's lungs, and the tension decreased a notch in the tiny room. Now that Sam had the distance of time, it made sense that establishing an airway would be difficult—Erik was having bronchospasms from his asthma.

"EMS bag-ventilated him," Miranda continued as she scanned the medical records, "and they started a neb treatment, bolused atropine, and initiated epinephrine. His rhythm and pressure improved for a while, but it appears his sats never did, even after he arrived at the hospital, and they placed him on a vent with one hundred percent oxygen." She looked up at Sam. "It looks like you did everything you could." She turned to another page in her folder. "How long have you known the decedent?"

Sam looked up at the ceiling as she tried to recall when she'd first met Erik. She knew he and Lisa had been friends for a while, but Sam hadn't met him until the two of them had started dating more seriously. "A few months."

"Have you been working at Redew very long?"

Sam shook her head. "No. I'm not actually working for them. I'm advising them, and I've only been helping them for about a month."

"That's right," Miranda said. "You're a doctor."

Sam nodded.

"Which is why I was able to spout all that medical jargon and you didn't ask what I was talking about."

Sam held up her hands. "Guilty as charged."

A slight flicker, like the start of a smile, crossed Miranda's face, but then she looked intently at the papers in front of her for a moment before she asked her next question. "Did you know the decedent had asthma?"

"Not until Lisa told me yester—" Sam stopped because now that she thought about it, she had known before then. "No, wait. She'd mentioned the incident where she had to take him to the ER a while back. So I suppose I had known about his condition."

"How much time did you spend with him over the last month?"

"Probably a few hours a week."

"And in that time," Miranda said, "did he exhibit any symptoms of asthma?"

"No, which is probably why I'd forgotten that he suffered from it," Sam replied.

Miranda flipped through a couple of pages, then said, "The hospital inventory of the decedent's personal effects shows that, other than his wallet, his pockets were empty. No rescue inhaler. Did you happen to notice if he had one nearby? Like, was there any evidence that he'd tried to use it?"

"Now that you mention it, no, I didn't see one." Sam closed her eyes as she tried to replay what had happened the day before. "But I could have overlooked it."

Had there been anything on the floor? Just his glasses, but she couldn't remember anything else. Perhaps his inhaler had been on one of the counters. Then once the EMTs showed up and started working on Erik, stuff was strewn everywhere—packaging from the disposable equipment, syringe caps, vials, bits of other plastic. It was probably still a mess.

"That's okay if you don't remember," Miranda said. "Do you know what types of chemicals or other compounds are used or stored in the lab?"

"You mean, were there any respiratory irritants that may have triggered his asthma exacerbation?"

"Exactly."

"Honestly, I don't know." Sam grimaced. "But probably so, because they're screening a lot of different drugs." Even though they mixed the flies' food inside the fume hood, there was always the possibility Erik had been exposed to something. "I could find out."

"That would be very helpful," Miranda said. She tapped her business card, which Sam had put on the table. "You have my contact information. You can call or email me once you have that information, or if you think of anything else that may be important."

"Like what?" Sam frowned. "Erik's death seems like a pretty straight-forward case, doesn't it?"

"It does." Miranda closed her notebook and gathered the papers back into her folder. "But I just want to be thorough." She tucked everything into her shoulder bag and stood.

"That makes sense."

They walked to the door.

"I appreciate your time." Miranda turned and placed her hand on Sam's shoulder. "And I'm so sorry about what happened to your friend."

"Thank you." Sam took in a deep breath. "I'll be in touch once I find that list of compounds."

10

Right after Miranda left, the possibility that Sam had overlooked Erik's rescue inhaler gnawed at her. She truly didn't remember if the inhaler had been nearby, and now she chastised herself for not searching for it, because if she had found it, she could have given Erik a dose to open up his airways. It certainly would have made CPR more effective. At least she remembered he'd had asthma and told the EMTs, so they started a nebulizer treatment once they intubated him. But not giving him a dose from his inhaler before they arrived might have been the difference between life and death.

Even though it wouldn't change anything now, it bothered her like a thorn in her side, so she grabbed her purse and keys and headed to Redew to find the inhaler. Plus, Miranda had asked for a list of chemicals and compounds used in the lab. One of them may have triggered Erik's asthma attack.

When she arrived, Brooke was kneeling on the floor of the fly room with a whisk broom and dustpan, sweeping up all the debris from the incident the day before. Sam pulled a trash can over so Brooke could empty the dustpan.

Brooke thanked her, then stood. "This is not how I planned to spend St. Patrick's Day." She gave her head a little shake. "I'm sorry, that was…awful. I'm being so…self-ish. I can't believe he's gone." She leaned on the counter, slumping her shoulders.

"Neither can I," Sam said. This certainly wasn't something either of them had expected, and she didn't fault Brooke for being upset.

"It must have been pretty crazy finding him, right?"

"Yeah, it was."

"I'm glad you knew exactly what to do. I would have freaked out and …" Brooke looked down, shaking her head. "And then, I don't know."

Sam patted her on the shoulder. "I'm sure you would have done the same as me, which wasn't much. Just call 911 and start CPR."

"I guess."

Brooke put the broom and dustpan away in the cabinet under the sink in the larger section of the lab, while Sam packed up the AED and replaced it in the holder next to the fume hood.

They returned to the fly room, and after picking up a stray wrapper she'd missed earlier, Brooke slumped against the counter next to the microscopes, becoming still again, a stunned look on her face.

Sam took the wrapper from Brooke, tossed it in the trash, and slid the can back to the end of the counter where it belonged. "Are you going to be okay?"

Brooke nodded dumbly. "I think so. I just…I've never known anyone who died before. I mean, other than old people. Like my grandpa. And my great-aunt."

Sam wanted to give her a hug, but she'd only known Brooke for such a short time.

Heck. The girl needed one, so Sam opened her arms for an embrace. Brooke accepted, and Sam gently rubbed her back. "I'm so sorry. It's always a shock."

She could feel Brooke stifling her sobs, and after a moment, Sam pulled away, found a tissue, and handed it to the younger woman.

"I don't know why I'm so frazzled. It's just…he's not that much older than me."

"I know. I'm pretty upset too."

"I mean, what if that had happened to me?" Brooke's pupils dilated, compressing her blue irises. "Sometimes I work alone in the lab. What if I had passed out, and no one was here to help me?"

She has a point, Sam thought. *And now if I ask about the list of compounds, it might upset her even more. Better tread lightly.*

"Here, let's go sit down," Sam said, "and I'll get you something to drink."

She led the young woman to the conference room, then got some water from the breakroom and joined her at the table.

"You going to be okay?"

"Yeah. I'll be fine." Brooke shrugged. "I guess that's just life."

They sat in silence for a moment, then Brooke said, "I don't know what's going to happen, though. I mean, Erik was the main person here doing all the scientific work."

"Do you know what he was working on?"

"Sure I do. But not to the level that he understood it. Maybe someday, after I finish grad school." Brooke shrugged again. "I guess the only person who'd really be out of a job right now is Matt." She looked at Sam. "At least you're not really working here, since you're an advisor."

A pit formed in Sam's stomach. Sure, she was just an advisor, but she was kind of banking on landing a full-time position, since she'd switched to part time at the clinic.

"So there's no one else who could replace Erik?" Sam asked casually, trying to keep any note of concern out of her voice.

"Well, there's Greg." Brooke made a face. "But I don't know if he'll agree to join Redew after everything that's happened. And Matt's also worried about liability since Erik collapsed here at work. He hopes Erik's family doesn't make a stink and sue. He was here earlier with Whit, trying to figure out what might happen."

Sam grew more unsettled. She had made a huge mistake rearranging her clinic schedule, banking on the promise of a job at Redew. Her mind was racing so much that she hadn't noticed Brooke had spoken.

"I'm sorry. What did you say?"

"I was just wondering why you came back this morning," Brooke said as she wrapped her hands around her glass of water.

"Oh. An investigator from the Medical Examiner's Office asked me about Erik's rescue inhaler—she wanted to know if it was nearby when I found him and if there was any evidence that he'd tried to use it."

"Why's that?"

"It looks like he had an asthma attack," Sam said. "He'd had one last fall, bad enough that he went to the ER. It would make sense if he'd had his inhaler with him. Did you happen to see it while you were cleaning up?"

Brooke shook her head. "There was only trash on the floor—the wrappers from all the stuff the paramedics used."

"Did you ever notice him needing to use the inhaler?"

"No. I didn't even know he had asthma."

So, his condition must have been pretty well-controlled, Sam thought. It would make sense. She'd expect that after he ended up in the ER, his doctor would have either started him on maintenance meds or adjusted them if he was on them already to prevent another attack.

"Also," Sam said with some trepidation, hoping that Brooke wouldn't start worrying about her mortality again, "the investigator asked me for a list of the compounds used in the lab. Do you know where that would be?"

"Sure," Brooke said as she stood. "We've got a binder with a master list and all the MSDSs."

From her past work in labs at school, and from taking care of a few patients with occupational exposures, Sam knew that MSDSs were Material Safety Data Sheets required by OSHA to be readily available in any workplace with the potential for contact with harmful chemicals.

She followed Brooke back into the lab, glad that the younger woman's momentary epiphany about her own mortality had passed. Brooke went to one of the work-benches, pulled a binder off the shelf above, then set it on the counter in front of her and flipped to the front page.

"Here's the list of all the substances we use. As you can see, there are quite a few. Most of the compounds are the drugs we're testing." She slid the open binder to Sam. "Feel free to make copies if you need to." Then she looked at her watch. "I've gotta get back to my parents—they drove down from Dallas yesterday after they found out."

Sam was confused. "Did they know Erik?" It was possible. He was from the Dallas area, too, but the whole Dallas–Fort Worth metroplex was massive, so it seemed unlikely. Still, you never knew.

"No, but my mom insisted." Brooke leaned closer to

Sam and said in a conspiratorial voice, "She looks for any chance to see me, especially since I'll be moving to Chicago in the fall."

"Yeah," Sam said wistfully. "Moms are like that."

At that moment, a small hollowness opened in her chest. Her mom had been exactly like that, making up any excuse to visit Sam while she was going to school in Houston. That was, until her mom had passed away.

After Brooke left, Sam checked the master list in the front of the binder to make sure it included every chemical for which there was an MSDS, just in case it hadn't been updated recently. It was all there.

She made a copy of the list on the machine next to the coffee maker in the break area, then put the binder back where Brooke had gotten it.

She turned and scanned the larger section of the lab, where the prototype and other equipment sat. Then she peered into the smaller room with all the flies. The smell of yeast continued to linger in the air, but she'd grown more accustomed to it.

Where would Erik keep his inhaler?

She focused on seeking out the colors of the most common inhaler brands—bright red or teal. But she didn't see those shades amongst all the items in either space. The colors in the lab were muted, except for the required warning signs on the equipment. And everything was as orderly as Erik's personality had been, so a bright inhaler certainly would have stuck out.

There didn't seem to be one anywhere. At least not lying around.

Perhaps, after Erik's visit to the ER and the presumed adjustments to his medications, he'd felt well enough that he didn't need to have his rescue inhaler with him all the time. Which would have been his fatal mistake.

She wanted to call Lisa. Maybe her friend would know about Erik's medications and his mindset. But Sam didn't want to add to Lisa's grief by asking about something trivial. Because, after all, it wouldn't make a difference in anyone's situation. It wouldn't change the fact that Erik was dead.

Sam started opening cabinet doors and drawers, on the off chance that Erik had tucked his inhaler into one of them. They were filled with the usual lab supplies, pipettes, forceps, and storage tubes.

In the smaller room, flies buzzed around in their vials. They were carefully arranged in racks nestled inside tubs, each labeled with the compounds being screened.

She was almost done with her search when her phone buzzed. She needn't have fretted about disturbing her friend after all.

"Hey, Lisa," Sam answered as she continued to pull open drawers. "How are you doing? Is everything okay?"

"I suppose I'm as well as I can be. I'm still in shock."

"Yeah, so am I," Sam said. "Do you need anything? Can I bring you something?"

"No, no. I'm okay…Well, not okay. But I don't need anything. I just…well, I—where are you right now?"

"I'm at Redew. The investigator from the Medical Examiner's Office came by my apartment to ask me some questions about Erik's…I mean, about what happened yesterday. She asked me about his rescue inhaler. He carried one with him, right?"

"Yes. He did, although he didn't need to use it much after his doctor adjusted his meds, after that visit to the ER." Sam could hear Lisa sniff on the other end of the line. "A lot of good that did him."

Sam waited, to give her friend some time.

After a few moments, Lisa said, "Why do you want to know about his inhaler?"

"The ME investigator asked if I'd seen it," Sam said. "I didn't remember, but things were pretty chaotic, so I came here today to see if I missed it or if he even had one here."

"It should be there somewhere—unless he had it in his pocket. Sometimes, he would carry it with him."

"But the investigator said it wasn't with his belongings at the hospital, and I don't see one around—"

And then she found it. It was in a drawer right next to the spot where she'd found Erik. Maybe he'd been trying to get to it, but he hadn't had enough time.

"What's wrong?" Lisa's voice sounded concerned.

"I just found it. It was in the drawer right next to ..."

Sam's insides felt like they were melting. She shouldn't be talking about this with Lisa. The loss was too fresh.

She swallowed, then said, "So why did you call? If you don't need anything, do you want me to just come over?"

"I'd appreciate that. I'm supposed to see Erik's parents a little later this afternoon, and I don't think I could ..." Lisa sucked in a faltering breath. "It would be nice to have someone else there."

"Of course. I can be there for you."

"And there's something else," Lisa said. "I found one of Erik's notebooks. He's always...he *was* always so meticulous, so it was surprising he'd forgotten it and left it here. He'd called me on Friday asking if I'd seen it, but I didn't find it until just now." She started sobbing. "That was the last time we spoke."

11

Lisa lived in the Triangle, an aptly named development on a plot of land exactly that shape, where Guadalupe Street merged with Lamar Boulevard, two main traffic arteries through the heart of Austin. It was just a stone's throw away from the original location of Threadgill's, a gas station-turned-diner, where Janis Joplin had performed before heading west to San Francisco in the 1960s. As Sam drove past the landmark on Lamar, she imagined what Austin had been like back then, when Lamar was a dusty farm-to-market road, and Threadgill's stood just outside the city limits. Now the old art deco building sat abandoned, covered in graffiti, swallowed up by urban sprawl, its fate in limbo.

After entering the Triangle and driving along a couple of streets lined with restaurants and shops, she found a spot on the street outside Lisa's building. When Lisa opened the door, her eyes were bloodshot, her nose and face flushed. She'd always seemed pretty unflappable in college when they'd roomed together after they'd met at freshman orientation.

Lisa's apartment was the outer manifestation of her desire for excellence, with clean lines and tones of gray. It had the same vibe as the lab at Redew, the way Erik had made sure everything was labeled and in its place, leaving nothing to chance—except for the prototype. It was no wonder that they'd made a great couple.

Sam had grabbed coffee and kolaches on her way over, but when she offered them to Lisa, her friend declined. She wasn't hungry. It made sense.

Sam wasn't really either. However, after everything that had happened the previous twenty-four hours, she'd forgotten to eat. Her last meal had been on Friday, yet again with James and Kevin, since Alex had been on call. Once she took a bite of her kolache, her body suddenly signaled to her brain that she was indeed in need of sustenance. She scarfed up the rest of the sausage-filled pastry, trying to avoid sprinkling crumbs on the couch.

Lisa was too lost in her own thoughts to notice. She sat with her legs curled under her and picked at a tissue wadded up in her lap as she stared blankly at the floor.

Sam took a sip of coffee, then held the paper cup in her lap as it warmed her hands. "When are you supposed to see Erik's parents again?"

"They want to meet later this afternoon. Since they don't know how long it will take for the medical examiner to release his body, they want me to help with arrangements, in case it's after they go back to Dallas."

Sam nodded, not knowing what else to say. She knew that Erik had two younger sisters, with one still in high school, so she figured his family would need to leave sooner than later, to be there for her.

After a moment, Lisa continued, "Ellie, his sister at NYU, is staying up there for now—there's no point in having her come home before there's a set timeline—then she'll fly to Dallas once the funeral plans have been finalized. And, of course, there's Bethany. Well, she's already there. She's staying with Erik's grandparents right now."

Lisa was babbling, something that Sam hadn't seen her do in all the time they'd known each other. Sam sometimes babbled as she thought through things, but Lisa—never.

She supposed her friend's focus on the logistics of how Erik's family would manage things was better than dealing with her own feelings right now.

Then Sam noticed the lab notebook on the coffee table.

"Is that Erik's?" she asked.

"Yes, that's the one I told you about. It's so unlike him to forget something that important. He's always so conscientious."

"Where did you find it?" Sam asked.

"Down there." Lisa pointed behind Sam's feet, nestled up against the couch. "It must have fallen while we were watching a movie last week." Then Lisa stopped, her gaze unfocused, lost in a memory.

Sam imagined that maybe things had been more serious between Lisa and Erik than they had let on. Perhaps her friends had been engaged in a steamy moment, unknowingly knocking the notebook off the table, kicking it under the couch. This couple, normally so structured and composed, might have been overcome by passion.

Sam picked up the notebook, filled with documentation of Erik's work. She opened it to a page that Erik had used to catalogue designations for various strains of *Drosophila*. The next page had lists of compounds prioritized for testing. From what Erik had taught her during her short tenure at Redew, she could only understand a little of what he'd written. But as she flipped through the pages, amongst the neatly written records, a comment was scribbled on a sticky note. It was clearly in Erik's handwriting, just not as tidy: "Verify counterselection."

"Do you know what this means?" Sam asked.

Lisa glanced at the words, then shook her head. "No idea. But, you know, he's the reason I connected you to Redew."

"Sure, that makes sense."

"But what I mean is," Lisa said with a serious look, "he had questions about the clinical language Matt's been using, about the certainty in his claims. He'd hoped you could temper these assertions."

"I think I know what Erik had been concerned about. In fact, that was why we were meeting yesterday morning."

Lisa shifted on the couch, sitting up straighter. "Is that so?"

Sam filled Lisa in on the details of the pitch session at SXSW and the uneasiness she felt about Matt's statements.

"That's how Erik felt, too." Lisa hugged herself. "He wanted you to give them a dose of reality."

"Whit had said the same thing to me when I brought up my concerns. He wants me to really challenge our assumptions—internally, at least. But it seemed like Erik may have changed his perspective a bit, at least in the emails we'd exchanged last week." Sam sighed. "I suppose Redew will probably fold now, just like the startup that used to be in their office space."

She didn't want to let Lisa know how she might have tanked her career with ObraCare. Lisa was too practical and would chastise her for making such a short-sighted move. In fact, she probably would ask Sam why she hadn't gotten her involved. Lisa might have negotiated some type of leave so Sam could stay full-time with ObraCare and still have the flexibility to take a week off for all the meetings during SXSW. Maybe she should have asked her friend for help, instead of being so impulsive.

But then Lisa said, "No, I don't think Redew's done yet. Matt will find someone to replace Erik." She shook her head. "Unfortunately, everyone is expendable. In fact, Erik wasn't the only one they considered for his position, but the other candidates may have moved on. Someone from Dr. Galloway's lab pushed really hard for the job. I think his name was Craig?"

"If this guy worked in Dr. Galloway's lab, why didn't Matt hire him? Wouldn't this guy have worked on the prototype?"

"I think so," Lisa said. "But Erik was clearly the better candidate. He was already working at an established biotech and had more industry experience. After being there a couple of years, though, he realized he didn't want to be just another worker bee."

"So Erik moved here from San Diego just for this job?"

"Well, yes, and …" Lisa grabbed a Kleenex from the box on the end table, next to a pile of scrunched-up tissues contrasting starkly with the ordered angles of the apartment.

At that moment, Sam knew that Erik had also moved to Austin to be with Lisa.

12

S am was scheduled to work in the clinic for the first few days the following week, and despite the trauma of the weekend, she didn't want to cancel those shifts for fear of upsetting Dr. Taylor. She had a feeling that she might need to grovel, to ask him for a full-time job again, especially now that Redew's future was uncertain.

For almost every single shift since she'd switched to part-time status, she'd been sent to a different ObraCare clinic around Austin, as well as the clinic in San Marcos, which was an hour drive south. She didn't complain, though, and did as she was told.

However, on this particular Monday, she'd been scheduled at her old clinic again. She'd been expecting it to be a regular day, where she would be working with Jerry. But instead, another doctor showed up at 10:00 a.m., the time Jerry usually started his shift.

She was around Sam's age, her frizzy dark hair pulled back from her face into a bun, and she wore light blue scrubs under her white coat. "Hello. I haven't met you before. I'm Dr. Anita Cresswell."

Sam stood up from her desk, where she'd been typing up a patient note in the clinic work space, shook Anita's hand, and introduced herself. "Are you working *locums*?"

"Yeah," Anita replied as they both sat down in front of the computers. "My husband and I just moved from Houston for his new job, and I'm interviewing at a couple of OB practices right now."

"Oh? How's that going?"

"Okay. They definitely need more doctors here, which is why we felt comfortable making the move. It's just…I'm kind of burned out. I knew doing OB was going to be hard, even before I applied to residency, so I don't mind taking a break right now, doing *locums* here."

Sam laughed. "I can see that. The main thing I remember from my OB rotation in med school is that the residents were angry all the time."

"I know, right?" Anita also laughed as she shook her head. "That's not how I wanted to be. I thought it would be better in private practice, but it's tough. I don't like being on edge all the time." She shrugged. "Plus, this break's given me time to study for my boards, and after weeks of waiting, I found out I passed yesterday."

"Congratulations!" Sam said.

Anita didn't seem to be reveling in her achievement. "It's ironic, though." She scrunched her nose. "I don't think I want to practice OB anymore. Your life is not yours, and the liability is crazy."

Sam nodded. It was true. Obstetricians had some of the highest rates of medical malpractice lawsuits, mainly from unintentional complications that sometimes happened to newborns during delivery, some of which could lead to lifelong disabilities, like brachial plexus injuries or cerebral palsy.

Anita shrugged again. "Anyway, I kinda like working in these urgent care clinics." She leaned forward and lowered her voice. "Of course, I haven't seen these types of injuries since I did my ortho selective in med school." She smiled as she sat up in her chair. "But at least it's all low acuity and not too difficult to figure out."

Sam returned the smile. That was also true.

"So, what's your story?" Anita asked.

"Oh, I'm just working prn to fill in, here and there, while I do some work for a startup."

Anita's face lit up. "Wow! That's great!" She leaned forward conspiratorially. "You're so smart, doing something else outside of medicine."

ON WEDNESDAY, Sam went back to Redew. Matt had asked her to come by so they could discuss the future of the startup, and her worst fear was that he would no longer need her. She was certain any hopes of a full-time job with them had disappeared with Erik's death.

As she crossed the cubicle space toward Matt's office, he called out to her from the conference room next to it. He was sitting at the table with Brooke, Whit, and a man who looked to be in his late twenties. The newcomer slouched in his chair near the door and was a bit disheveled, with tattered cuffs on the sleeves of his hoodie and his dark brown hair unkempt. He appeared to be ignoring the others in the room, but at the same time, it was like he was evaluating everything around him and disapproving of it all.

"Dr. Jenkins," Matt said, "I'd like you to meet Greg."

"Nice to meet you." Sam extended her hand, and after Greg appraised her for a moment, he reluctantly shook it and grunted.

As Sam squeezed between Brooke and the whiteboard to get to an empty chair, Matt continued, "Greg is quite familiar with everything we've been doing here at Redew. He's a graduate student in Dr. Galloway's lab. He's agreed to come onboard with us since he's completing his dissertation and will be defending it in a couple of weeks."

"That's great," Sam said, relieved that her expectations for the day had been incorrect. "Good luck with your defense."

Greg grunted again.

"Dr. Jenkins has been helping us as an advisor for the past month or so," Matt said, "and she's been instrumental in advancing our talks with several VCs." He nodded at Whit as he said this. "Now that you're joining us, I think we have a good shot at securing our series A, isn't that right, Whit?"

"Indeed," Whit replied. "There's a lot of excitement about what's possible with this approach—and how this technology can uncover the untapped potential of existing drug libraries."

Sam glanced around the room. While Matt and Whit had hopeful expressions on their faces, Brooke seemed a bit uncertain, and Greg continued to look dower.

"You realize I'm not starting until after I defend my dissertation," Greg said. "The only way this will work is if I don't have to be here until I'm done with my defense." He checked his watch. "And this is taking up too much of my time. I need to get back to campus so I can finish my last experiment and write it up. If it doesn't give me the results I need, I'll barely have enough time to redo it. If I can't get it to work, I won't be graduating."

"Remember," Matt said, "we'd be happy to work with you if you need more time to finish. We don't care if you have a PhD before you start—"

"But *I* care," Greg snapped.

Everyone blinked at the outburst, stunned.

"I gotta go." He stood and left.

Wow, Sam thought, *he's going to be difficult to work with.*

Now Whit appeared uncertain, and Brooke looked worried.

But Matt put on his winning smile as the banging from the front door carried into the conference room. "As you can see, Greg's a bit stressed right now, and rightfully so. His years of hard work are culminating in his defense." He shook his head. "I can't imagine the pressure he's under. The closest I've come to anything like that is pitching to VCs." He let out a little laugh.

Frowning, Whit leaned back in his chair, interlacing his fingers across his abdomen. "Are you sure he's the right person to pick up where Erik left off?"

"Oh, absolutely," Matt said. "We were considering him at the start, but he was still busy with his PhD. And Erik was more experienced, especially with industry practices." He broadened his smile. "In fact, Greg is the one who developed some of the algorithms for the prototype and used them to identify the two drugs that we'll bring to market."

Sam squirmed in her seat. *How can he say that with any confidence?* As far as she knew, Erik hadn't confirmed those results.

Matt turned to Brooke. "You've worked with him before, so you can vouch for his capabilities, right?"

Brooke nodded, but she didn't seem like she completely agreed with Matt. However, she also seemed like she knew this was not the time to say anything.

Whit squinted at everyone as he looked around the room, his nostrils flaring as he assessed the situation. Finally, he said, "Okay. Let's see how he does. Will this mean we'll fall behind on our timeline?"

"No, I don't believe so." Matt gave Brooke an encouraging nod, indicating she should share what she knew.

"Before Erik ..." Brooke closed her eyes for a moment, took a deep breath, then began again. "Before Erik passed away, he'd initiated crosses to screen the library that Greg used in Dr. Galloway's lab, to try to reproduce his results. But this time, he'd used titrated dosing to better understand the effects of the agents on the progeny resulting from the crosses."

She continued to explain the experiments in detail, and after a few minutes, Whit's eyes glazed over. He held up his hands. "Okay. I don't really understand all of what you said. Just give me the thirty-thousand-foot view."

Brooke stammered as she began again, but she didn't really say anything differently this time.

Sam could tell Whit was getting frustrated. She cleared her throat. "I'm sorry, but may I interrupt for a moment?"

"Yes, please." Brooke looked relieved.

"So basically," Sam said, "Erik had already started several experiments to investigate the drug library that includes the two compounds Matt says Redew will take to market."

"Okay," Whit said.

Since Sam had his attention, she decided to gently bring up her concerns. "But Erik hadn't completed the experiments yet. He was trying to repeat what Greg had done previously, where he'd identified the possible treatments for Alzheimer's and Huntington's. So, it's still not clear that we can confidently advance the drugs to the next phases of testing."

Sam couldn't tell if the men understood exactly what she was saying. They both had benign smiles on their faces. Brooke, on the other hand, was nodding in agreement with Sam's statement.

However, since Sam's own understanding was still a bit shaky, she figured it was best not to belabor the issue. At least not yet. She'd just need to learn more from Brooke—and Greg. Not something she looked forward to.

Sam sighed and pushed on. "It sounds like Erik gave Brooke detailed instructions on what to do next. So once Greg starts working here, there will be essentially no slip in the timeline—no work lost." To confirm what she said was correct, she looked at Brooke, who nodded again, with a relieved look on her face.

Whit sat back in his chair, seemingly satisfied.

Matt grinned. "That's why we need Dr. Jenkins to join our team."

"Get that series A secured," Whit said, "and you can hire her and anyone else you need."

13

After the meeting had ended, Sam joined Brooke in the lab, her mood a bit more buoyant since it didn't seem like the company would fold, at least not immediately. And from Brooke's explanation, she thought she understood the work that Erik had done a little better.

Nothing was certain, though, at least not until Matt convinced some VCs to fund them. However, from the meetings she'd been to with Matt at SXSW, he'd done a great job selling the future of drug discovery, and the investors they'd spoken with seemed rather impressed. They also seemed to appreciate how Sam described the various neurodegenerative disorders and the potential for changing the lives of thousands of patients. And if they could find better treatments for something as common as Alzheimer's disease, their work could possibly impact millions.

So Sam wouldn't be groveling to Dr. Taylor. At least not yet.

But there was the issue of Greg. Would he be someone

she could work with after Brooke left in the fall? Matt said they would hire more scientific personnel once they secured their series A. But with Erik gone, Greg would be the technical lead, and she didn't really know what to think of him, especially after that less-than-promising intro-duction.

However, Matt did have a point. Defending a PhD dissertation had to be quite stressful, so she'd hold her conclusions for now.

Then again, Brooke seemed like she'd had something more to say. Maybe she'd divulge it, away from the men.

"What do you think about Greg?" Sam asked, once she and Brooke were alone. They were in the fly room, sitting next to each other on the stools in front of the micro-scopes. "What's it like working with him?"

Brooke shrugged. "He's okay."

"Is he always like that?"

"He tends to drag on things. But a lot of sciency people can be like that."

"Yeah, I've met plenty." Sam had worked with quite a few who complained and criticized a great deal. From her experience, as long as you showed them you were compe-tent, they were fine to work with. She hoped that would be the case with Greg. "It sounds like getting his PhD is really important to him, so why did he want to work here?"

"Sure, he's like that now, but when the whole idea for this startup came about, he was all in." Brooke pulled a tray of flies down from the shelf and placed it next to the microscope in front of her. "Matt and Whit wanted someone with more experience outside of academia, someone who'd run a lab that had to meet milestones in a corporate environment. So they brought in Erik, and Greg was miffed about it." She smiled. "And then he was even more miffed when I decided to work here—he said I only got the job because Whit's my uncle."

"Really?" Sam hadn't noticed any familial warmth between them, but Whit seemed like someone who would keep things professional in a workplace setting.

"Yeah, he became an investor because of me. I was working in Dr. G's lab, and I was the one who told him about Redew." Brooke opened up her notebook to a page where she'd clipped a pen to mark her place. She ran her finger midway down it, nodded, then pulled a rack of flies out of the tray. "But they eventually allowed Greg to become an advisor—kind of like you—only he hasn't been around much. They have Dr. G as an advisor, too, of course, but he insisted Greg be a junior advisor since he was the one who'd done a lot of the work building the prototype in Dr. G's lab. It hasn't really mattered that Greg hasn't been around much, 'cause we aren't using the proto-type anyway."

"And how did Matt get involved?"

"He'd met Dr. G during one of the MBA mixers at UT —you know, to foster an 'entrepreneurial environment,'" Brooke said, making quotations with her fingers. "Every university wants to be like Stanford and churn out a bunch of startup companies, hoping they'll create the next Google or PayPal." She rolled her eyes. "Anyway, Dr. G told him about the prototype, and Matt thought it was a great idea for a startup. But Dr. G didn't want to be actively involved, so he let Matt head the company." She removed a vial from the rack, inverted it, and tapped it gently on the counter to move the flies away from the gooey food in the bottom. "Anyway, Greg will be fine. I think he's just upset because he's not a founder, like Erik was."

"Sounds like you're not completely on board the entrepreneurial bandwagon."

"It's fine, but I'd like to do something in academia, which is why I'm off to grad school soon." Brooke laughed as she rubbed her wrist, encircled with an intricate ivy tattoo like a bracelet. "My dream job would be to work at a botanical garden, but my parents don't think it's a good idea. They want me to do something more prestigious."

"I know how that goes." Sam's dad had wanted her to be a cardiologist, like him.

Brooke picked up the vial of flies, looked back and forth between the info on the label and her notebook, then scribbled something in it.

Sam looked around the room, feeling a bit useless. Then she said, "Hey, since I'm not due in clinic until tomorrow, I can help out around here if you need it."

"That would be great!" Brooke's face brightened. "Without Erik here, there is a ton of stuff to do." She disconnected tubing from a round pad under the microscope and inserted it alongside the foam plug in the vial. "Every day we have tons of progeny to sort, count, and cross again, in addition to setting up new crosses for each of the drugs in the library. Erik created a tight schedule, so we could try to collect as much data as possible on these drugs and hopefully get some positive results." She looked up at Sam. "You said you worked with flies before, right?"

Sam smiled. "It's been a while. I took a genetics lab in undergrad where we performed experiments every week on *Drosophila*."

"Great." Brooke motioned to the vial on the counter next to her. "So you know how to anesthetize them with CO_2?"

"Yeah, it's a lot better than using FlyNap, like we did in high school."

"Oh, that stuff's disgusting. Plus, you risk killing your flies if you want to use the progeny for further crosses. Then again, you can also kill them with too much CO_2."

The flies had stopped moving in the vial, so Brooke pulled out the tubing and reconnected it to the ceramic pad under the microscope. Then she poured the sleeping flies onto the pad.

"Anyway, if you could help me count these flies, then I can do the same with this other batch that needs to be crossed today. It would save me a ton of time. Yesterday I was here until midnight."

"I'm happy to help," Sam said, "although you'll need to show me what I'm looking for."

Brooke did just that, and they worked side by side, each at a microscope, with Sam occasionally asking a question here and there since she was a bit rusty. But after Sam counted the flies in her first vial—using a paintbrush to carefully sort red eyes from black eyes and separating males from females—she felt more comfortable. The details were coming back to her.

"Dang it," Brooke said as she sat up from her microscope. "We're out of CO_2." She quickly, but gently, scooped the flies up and put them back into their vial.

Sam looked down at the pad under her microscope. Several of the flies were beginning to twitch, since there was no longer a constant flow of CO_2 through the tiny pores in the pad. She followed Brooke's lead, putting the flies back into their vial and replacing the plug.

Brook went over to the CO_2 tank at the end of the lab bench. It was skinny and silver, with the valve peering up just over the edge of the countertop. "It's empty. I swear Erik said he'd replaced it last week." She tapped on the glass covering the gauge. "This is a fifty-pound cylinder—it should last months. Maybe I misunderstood him, and he hadn't gotten around to it yet." She sighed. "Oh, well. We'll just need to get another one. And I need to find Erik's notebook anyway. I have the one he was using the day he…well, I have the one he was using. But I know he had another one where he was working out which drug titrations we should do next."

"Oh, I think I have it." Sam reached down and pulled the notebook out of her bag on the floor. "He left it at Lisa's apartment." She handed it to Brooke.

"Thanks." Brook flipped through it and stopped on the page with the Post-it. "Huh, that's funny. Why'd he write this?"

"I noticed that too. Everything is so neat and orderly, but this note seems out of place."

"It's his handwriting, all right. But I've never seen him write like this in his notebooks, only when he was drawing stuff on the whiteboard during some of our meetings, mainly when he was getting frustrated trying to explain something to the nonscience people."

"Do you know what it means?"

"Not really, but we use counterselection to make sure we're only doing experiments with the disease models of interest. I don't know what he wanted to verify, though." Brooke shrugged as she put the notebook on the counter. "I'll have to figure it out later. I need to find out where to get another CO_2 tank."

"Is there anything else I can help with right now?"

"Not really," Brooke said a bit absentmindedly as she glanced at the notebook. "I'm just hoping we can get another tank before the end of the day." She pulled a binder off a shelf and started flipping through it. "Fortunately, Erik kept all the information for suppliers in here."

"Well, give me a call if you do need help, once you get

more CO_2. I'll be in clinic the rest of the week, but I can come by in the evenings and this weekend."

"Thanks. I'd appreciate that."

"Hopefully it won't be too bad until Greg can start."

"Yeah, Grumpy Greg."

"You really think he can pick up where Erik left off?" Sam hoped she could get Brooke to open up even more about him.

"I suppose so. Greg certainly is bright, but he's definitely not as organized as Erik." Brooke tapped on the binder. "Erik made sure everything was documented. He kept saying that even though we are a startup, we'll eventually be handing off some of the work, probably to a CRO—"

"A contract research organization, right?"

"Right, so once we identify those drug candidates, the CRO will take what we've done with *Drosophila* and perform preclinical studies on larger animals, like mice. This will ensure what we've learned is still true for mammals with the diseases we're testing. So Erik kept saying that even though we're small, we need to act like we're big, because if everything goes well, it's our initial data that will be the foundation for anything we submit to the FDA. And we don't want to give them any reasons to deny our application."

"That makes sense."

Brooke smiled wistfully. "It was great working with Erik, to see how a lab really should be run—not that Dr. G's lab isn't run well, but there are differences, you know, between an academic lab and a commercial lab. And even though I want to be a professor someday, I hope I can set up my lab with a little more precision."

Sam nodded. "So you still have some reservations about Greg, then?"

"Yeah, because he comes from that academic environment, and, well, you saw how he was dressed today. That's kind of how his whole life is, at least what I've seen of it." Brooke shrugged. "But it doesn't really matter much to us, does it? I'll be gone in the fall, and you're still seeing patients, so if Redew fails, it's no big deal for us, right?"

And there it was. With Brooke's nonchalant comment, Sam's trepidation returned.

Once again, she found herself regretting what she'd done. Not that she had been rude when she'd informed Dr. Taylor that she wanted to work prn, but she didn't know if he would even consider bringing her back to a full-time status.

From what she'd seen, though, there had been a lot of doctors cycling through ObraCare's clinics in Austin and Houston. She could think of only two or three who had made a career out of working for them. Most of the other doctors she'd met had practiced in other areas, from family practice to emergency medicine—even one doctor who'd been a plastic surgeon—all of whom were working at ObraCare part-time in their semiretirement. So maybe he still needed her.

She wished she could return to the track she'd been on. Everything had seemed like it was going to work out before she'd gotten sick. Back then, her plan was to get her MPH, do a modified residency in preventive medicine with an occupational focus, become board certified, and keep working at ObraCare.

If she'd already completed her objectives at the time she'd developed pneumonia, she could have quit and easily found somewhere else to work. But not now. She was incomplete in the eyes of most hospitals and clinics; even other doctors treated her as if she were deficient.

14

T he day after the meeting with Greg, Sam was back at her old clinic again, not at a random one around Austin. It gave her the chance to probe Jill and find out how easy it might be for Sam to ask Dr. Taylor for her old job back.

"I don't know, Dr. Jenkins," Jill said in response to Sam's inquiry. "Since you switched to prn, we've mainly been using *locums* to fill in on the days you aren't here."

"Really?" Sam shook her head. "That's crazy, because they're sending me all the way up to Round Rock and down to San Marcos. It's almost like Dr. Taylor's purpose-fully trying to make my life more difficult."

"Could be, but I'm not supposed to have an opinion." Jill shrugged. "I do know that even with the growing popu-lation and the greater need for clinics like ours, the compe-tition is tougher with all of the consolidations. A lot of big healthcare systems—including a couple from outside Austin—are opening up clinics around here, trying to capture the urgent care and occ med markets. And the problem is, they've got a lot more money to spend on ads than we do, with the additional benefit of being directly connected to a hospital. Several employers have told me they prefer that setup—there's more continuity of care since the doctors managing injury cases are using the same EHRs that the ER docs and the hospitalists use. There's none of this faxing requests and waiting for records to be faxed back."

Sam could certainly see how that would be an advantage.

Jill sighed. "Anyway, I've heard from some of the other operations folks that if we continue to lose business, there's talk of a hiring freeze."

FRIDAY EVENING, after not seeing each other the previous couple of weeks, Sam and Alex finally met for a quick dinner at Torchy's Tacos near his apartment. Queso always made things better, and the Trailer Park taco was Sam's favorite, even if it wasn't the healthiest. Just one taco was a meal for her—a perfectly fried piece of chicken covered in cheese, bacon, and pico de gallo, all wrapped in a fluffy flour tortilla.

As Sam munched on her taco, with the occasional swig of beer, Alex filled her in on his plans to become a junior partner in his critical care practice.

"Chuck told me that if I pass the boards, he'd nominate me to be eligible for partnership in two years. Wouldn't that be great?"

"Yeah, that's awesome," Sam said. "So, remind me again, what are the benefits of partnership?"

"The biggest part would be that I'd receive shares in the practice along with a percentage of the annual profits. And I'd get priority for choosing slots on the schedule, so I could avoid taking overnight shifts all the time or having to double up, like I'm doing now."

"You'll need to hire more doctors to cover everything, right?"

"That's true, but since the new medical school opened with its critical care fellowship, we'll have a nice stream of candidates. It seems everyone wants to move to Austin right now."

Alex tore into his taco and followed it with a scoop of queso.

"Man, I never thought I'd be double-boarded!" He grinned at her.

A glob of queso had dribbled onto his chin, so she picked up a napkin and wiped it off as she returned his smile.

Sam was happy for him, but she wasn't really feeling it.

She was even further away from her own chances of becoming board certified now. If things didn't work out at Redew, she was thinking about doubling her coursework in the summer to try to catch up. Or maybe she'd apply to some combined residency and MPH programs, even though her chances of getting accepted would be better if she completed her MPH beforehand.

Alex looked at her curiously. "What's going on in that head of yours?"

"I'm just …" Sam started, then quickly stopped. Now she felt guilty worrying about her own career, when she should be excited, celebrating Alex's opportunities. "Never mind."

"You're ruminating on something. What is it?"

She hadn't talked to Alex about her concerns, about her future. Things seemed like they might be back on course with Redew, but Greg was still an unknown.

"I'm just thinking about where my career will end up."

Alex shrugged. "You seem to be in a pretty good spot. You're helping that startup. They've all but offered you a job, once they're able to pay you. You still practice at ObraCare, so you always have that."

"But now that Erik's…gone. I don't know …" She took a deep breath. "They have someone else they're bringing in, so it might be okay."

"These things happen," Alex said. "I'm sure it will work out." He reached across the table and took her hand. "And, really, you don't need to work. Once I make partner, we can get married, and then——"

He sat up and pulled his phone out of his pocket. "It's the hospital. I've got to go in."

"But I thought you weren't on call."

"I'm on backup, and they need me."

It was then she noticed he'd only been drinking iced tea.

He stood. "Sorry, but I'm going to have to cancel our movie night." He leaned over, gave her a perfunctory kiss, then flashed an aw-shucks smile. "Forgive me?"

Sam nodded.

"Good," he said as he returned her nod. "See ya."

Then he rushed off, leaving her sitting with a red plastic basket of half-eaten chips.

SAM REALLY NEEDED to talk to someone, to process everything Alex had said, so once she got to her complex, she headed over to James's apartment. But he wasn't there, even though his car was parked in front of his building. Maybe he was with Kevin.

She sauntered back to her apartment and flopped down on the couch. Who else could she call? She didn't want to bother Lisa; she was still grieving the death of her boyfriend. Maybe Millie? She got along well with her new stepmother, but she was of a different generation. However, she would have immediately called her mom, if she'd still been alive. So maybe it wasn't just a generational thing.

But then there was a knock on the door, and it was James.

"I'd gone for a walk, and on my way back, I saw you leaving my building." Once he got a good look at her face, he asked, "Are you okay?"

As they had done many times over the years, they sat on her couch, and she filled him in on everything going through her mind. James seemed fully engaged and interested.

When she finished, he said, "It's tough. Sure, your plans are delayed a bit, but it doesn't mean that you have to give up on residency. You can do it, and someday you'll gain your independence when you get board certified. It's just going to take time."

He paused, then cleared his throat. "Now, Alex, on the other hand…Well, you know how I feel about Alex."

"You were the one who told me I should go out with him in the first place."

"Just because he's hot doesn't mean he's a good boyfriend."

"But you know what he told me tonight?" Here was the meat of it, what had confused her, what had knocked her emotions off-kilter. And Alex had said it in such an offhanded way. "He told me I wouldn't have to work. That once he became a partner in his practice, which he said could be in two years—"

"Two years? That's pretty fast."

"Yeah, well, it's a relatively new practice," Sam said,

"and it's been growing with all of the new hospitals opening up here. He's not a founding member, but he's one of the first group of doctors the founders hired. Anyway, he told me I don't have to work once he makes partner…once we're married."

James frowned. "What? He's talking about marriage? I know you've been dating for a while, but …"

"Yeah, I don't know exactly how I feel about it. It's like every little girl's dream, right? Grow up, meet a handsome doctor, get married. Be a wife…and then a mom."

"That's just the dream you've been sold by a lifetime of marketing." James shifted in his seat to face her. "Do you know why they started selling blue baby clothes for boys and pink for girls?"

Sam shook her head, wondering where this was going.

"So they could sell more clothes. Because mothers would reuse the clothes they already had when the next baby came along. But that doesn't help manufacturers or drive the economy." He smirked. "So some evil marketing genius came up with the idea that boys should be dressed in blue and girls should be in pink. Didn't help if a boy was followed by a boy or a girl was followed by a girl, but it did force at least some of the moms to buy all new clothes."

"What does this have to do with what's going on between me and Alex?"

"Don't you get it, Sam? You, me"—James stretched his arms out—"all of us have been programmed since birth to expect and want certain things." He shook his head. "And it's all been manufactured, so we'll keep buying what they're selling."

Sam leaned back on her couch for a moment, thinking everything through. James had a point, but deep down, part of her really wanted to have what Alex was offering. To just get married, have a happy family. Once Alex made partner, he'd be able to pick the best shifts and wouldn't have to be on call so much. They could live the life of the American dream.

"I see what you're saying," Sam said, "but I don't think you understand—"

James squinted at her. "Why? Because I'm gay?"

Sam sat up, aghast that he would say such a thing. "No, I just—"

"Because I want the same things everyone else wants," he said as he stood. "I want someone who loves and respects me, someone who always believes in me. What I don't want is what everyone thinks they want—the fantasy story that's been shoved down our throats all our lives, that's been fed to us, to keep us docile and compliant."

He stormed toward the door with Sam chasing after him.

"I'm sorry if I—" Sam began to say as he rushed down the stairs. But she didn't really know what had set him off, or exactly what she was sorry for.

15

S am ran down the stairs, chasing after James, calling out to him. But he ignored her. He got in his car and drove off. She texted him a few times, and he finally responded with a curt reply stating he'd be busy the whole weekend. She'd have to figure out what was bugging him later.

The next morning, Alex also texted her, letting her know he, too, would be tied up the whole weekend, working in the ICU. Maybe a little time away from him would be good. So Sam continued helping Brooke at Redew, using the mundane work with the flies to distract her.

A few days later, despite her friend's cynical view of her relationship with Alex, Sam went to Alex's hospital to meet for lunch. He said he could spare just thirty minutes or so, as long as there wasn't a patient crashing.

Sam arrived a little early, stopping by the Starbucks in the hospital lobby to wait for Alex's text; he hadn't known exactly when he'd be available. She had a stack of protocols and articles on using *Drosophila* disease models to screen drug libraries.

The papers helped her understand how Redew's proto-type—when it worked—used the movement of the tiny flies to sort them. So, instead of manually sorting flies under a microscope, like she and Brooke had been doing for days, machine learning algorithms would process videos of flies affected by neurodegenerative disorders that had received treatment. The theory was that flies crawling up the wall of the chamber were responding to the drug they'd been given. On the other hand, flies that couldn't were continuing to have movement problems, and thus, also continuing to exhibit symptoms of the neurodegenerative disorder. The algorithms also used identifying marks on the flies to tell them apart, like the slight differences in the patterns of the stripes on their bellies or the branching patterns on their wings, each of them unique, like finger-prints. This meant that one of Redew's technological breakthroughs was that it used movement, instead of an indirect indicator like eye color, to more precisely sort the flies.

Sam was so engrossed in what she was reading, trying to make sure she understood the implications of this approach, that she hadn't noticed someone was next to her until she heard a cough.

She looked up to find Miranda, the medical examiner investigator who had interviewed Sam right after Erik's death, standing beside her table.

"Fancy seeing you here," Sam said.

"I had to stop by the hospital morgue for a case, and well, you know—gotta have coffee." Miranda held up her cup. "Thanks again for sending the list of compounds in the lab so quickly."

"You're quite welcome," Sam replied. "I suppose

everything is consistent with a severe asthma exacerbation, then?"

"That's what the medical examiner believes. There are quite a few respiratory irritants on that list that could have triggered it."

"But...you say that in a somewhat skeptical tone."

"Really?" Miranda shrugged. "The ME's the final authority, so it doesn't really matter what I think."

"But...what do you think?"

Miranda shook her head. "I can't say."

"You still have questions, though," Sam prodded, her curiosity now piqued. She motioned to the free chair on the opposite side of the table. "Why don't you sit down?"

Miranda shook her head again. "I shouldn't. It's an ongoing case—even though the ME is about to close it. It's not proper for me to discuss it with you."

"I understand." Sam nodded. "Well, it was good to see you again."

Instead of saying goodbye, Miranda lingered for a moment. She glanced around the coffee shop, then she finally sat down.

"Okay," Miranda said, as if she'd just convinced herself of something. She leaned closer to Sam, lowering her voice. "Like I said, I really shouldn't discuss the case with you, but could I ask you a few general questions?"

"Sure."

"Did you ever find that inhaler?"

"Yeah, I did, actually. It was in the drawer right next to where I found Erik on the floor."

"So he must have been trying to get to it and just didn't reach it in time." Miranda shook her head. "How tragic."

Sam nodded.

"But I'm wondering—did you notice anything else unusual or strange that day?"

"Honestly, everything was a blur that morning." Sam paused for a moment while she tried to remember the details. "Now that you mention it, it did feel kind of cold in the lab." She shrugged. "But I don't know what that means."

"And you said the door to the lab was locked. Wasn't that a bit unusual?"

"I suppose so. Actually, both doors were locked—the outer door to the main lab and the inner door where Erik had been working with the flies. I can't think of a reason they should have been locked, since there are only a handful of people who even have access to the office to begin with."

"When you finally found the key, entered the lab space, and discovered the decedent on the floor, you stated you immediately called 911 and initiated CPR, correct?"

"Yes." She frowned, leaning back in her chair and crossing her arms. "You aren't suggesting that—"

Miranda held up her hands. "No, no. I just wonder if —" She cut herself off and shook her head. "I really can't discuss this."

"I understand," Sam said for the second time. She waited, because clearly Miranda wanted to talk.

She followed Miranda's gaze out into the hospital lobby as a mix of people bustled about—staff in scrubs, patients in gowns, visitors in street clothes.

Miranda wasn't leaving, so Sam gave her time to sort through her thoughts.

Finally, Miranda turned to her and said, "Okay. You're a doctor, so you understand—please keep mum about this, even though once the ME closes the case, all of this information will be available to the public anyway."

Sam nodded.

"There's one thing that's not totally consistent with

what the ME believes is the cause of death. The primary cause is clear: asphyxiation. But the ME thinks it's clear-cut that the secondary cause was a severe asthma exacerbation. The pathology slides do show signs of inflammatory changes from chronic asthma, but the serology doesn't show a corresponding rise in IgE."

"So, he didn't have an acute exacerbation?"

"Maybe, but I'm not certain."

"Did you mention this to the ME?"

"Yes, but he brushed it off. Plus, he's getting slammed by the increased number of homicides, since—well, you know, just because the city's growing so much."

"Why don't they hire more staff?"

Miranda scoffed. "It's like any government organization; we're underfunded, and the politicians are always reactionary. Things don't change until it's absolutely necessary—or there's negative publicity from something that happened because we didn't have enough money."

"If the ME's already made a decision, then what can you do about it?"

Miranda looked down at her coffee and picked at the cardboard sleeve. "I don't know. I just want to find the truth, but who am I? Just a low-level investigator in the office."

Sam knew exactly how Miranda felt, but she didn't know what either of them could do. Then she thought about Erik's notebook—the one Lisa had found in her apartment. Everything was so carefully written and recorded in it, except for that note scrawled on the Post-it. Did that have anything to do with Erik's death?

Should she tell Miranda about it? What would she even say? She had no idea what that note meant.

Her phone buzzed. It was Alex: *I'll be ready in 15.*

"I've gotta meet my boyfriend for lunch."

At the mention of Sam's boyfriend, Miranda brought her hand up to the necklace peeking out from her open collar and touched a ring with a modest-sized diamond hanging from the chain.

"Funny, I used to do that too," Sam said. "When I was a surgery resident, I would wear my engagement ring on a chain since I had to scrub my hands and wear gloves all the time."

"Yeah, constantly pulling on and off gloves doesn't work well with rings." Miranda cocked her head, glancing at Sam's ringless left hand. "You just said you're meeting your boyfriend. I don't mean to pry, but …"

"It's okay," Sam said. "My engagement didn't work out."

16

During their lunch in the oh-so-romantic setting of the hospital cafeteria, Alex talked about the cases he had in the ICU and didn't bring up his plans for partnership or marriage again. Sam was too preoccupied with what Miranda had told her anyway. Was it possible that there was something unusual about Erik's death? Of course, she didn't dare discuss this with Alex after his reaction the last time she'd started snooping around when someone had died mysteriously, so she didn't say anything to him. But she was dying to talk to someone about it.

She'd promised Brooke she'd continue helping in the lab that afternoon, and there was no way she'd mention Miranda's concerns to anyone at Redew. So she just had to wait.

That evening, as soon as she got back to her complex, she headed to James's apartment, even though he'd left hers abruptly a few days before.

When he saw it was Sam at his door, he had a sheepish

look. "I thought you wouldn't want to talk to me after my little…tantrum the other day."

"It's okay. I figured something else was bothering you and—"

"I've been so irritable lately," James interrupted, turning away from her. He began pacing around his living room. "And I've been trying to figure it out."

She followed him inside and shut the door.

"I have so many things on my mind. I'm getting better assignments at the paper, but the fate of the whole news industry is up in the air. And then Kevin asked me to move in with him—"

"Wait—what?" No wonder James was on edge. "You just got back together a few months ago. You've certainly seemed happier…that is…until the other day." She found a comfy spot on his couch and motioned for him to join her, which he did. "Tell me about it."

"The other day, when you said Alex was talking marriage, and that you wouldn't have to work, it kind of hit me the wrong way." He met her eyes directly. "Because Kevin essentially said the same thing to me. He's got a great job, and he said if I moved in with him, I wouldn't have to piece together wedding gigs and depend on free-lancing with the paper. He said I could focus on my photography."

"That sounds great," Sam said, "but…you have reservations."

James nodded. "I mean, I love the guy—even though we've had some ups and downs—but I don't know if I'm ready for a commitment. Who says we all need to couple up?"

"I know what you mean. I had lunch with Alex today, and it felt like…I don't know. Like he's already expecting me to be at his beck and call. His interest level keeps going up and down. He was super charming when we first dated, but then he backed off once we got to a steady state." She took James's hand. "But you're worried about something else, too, aren't you?"

"I think we've got the same issue. I don't want Kevin to take me for granted, just like you're feeling about Alex. I see myself as an independent guy, and I've made things work—although this rent increase has me a little nervous."

Sam shared some of his anxiety.

Their apartment complex was older, and the rents had been reasonable, even though they lived in a great location. But the owners saw the increased demand for rentals as an opportunity, and last week, they'd sent their tenants a notice: for the coming year, they were upping the rent by twenty percent.

Now that Sam had stopped working full-time, she had to take that into account. Fortunately, her student loans were minimal—unlike some of her medical school class-mates, who were hundreds of thousands of dollars in debt. Even though her father was a cardiologist, he wasn't a financial wizard, so she'd had to take out loans for med school. And then her mother's illness drained the rest of her parents' savings, so she was on her own.

She shook her head as the full realization of the mistake she'd made sunk in.

"What's wrong?" James said.

"I screwed up again in my career decisions. I basically told Dr. Taylor to stuff it—"

"But he deserved that after treating you like crap, making you work when you could hardly breathe."

"I was too brash and made my move too soon. I should have made everything work around my schedule at the clinic, and once I actually received the job offer from Redew, then I could have quit without any concerns."

James grimaced.

"What?"

"Well, not to make you more insecure, but I heard something about Matt. One of Kevin's coworkers had joined Matt to form a startup while he was getting his MBA. She said he'd keep making grand statements and promises about the capabilities of the software she'd developed. He convinced a few angel investors to fund them— partly because of his salesmanship—but the market never materialized. The few customers they had kept asking why the software didn't work exactly as he'd promised, and he was pretty good at placating them, but eventually they left once their contracts ran out. So the company had to dissolve."

Sam rolled her eyes. "Great."

"Sorry to be so cynical." James patted her hand. "Kevin didn't think it was that big of a deal, since lots of startups never make it past that early stage. He also says CEOs oversell what their companies can do all the time; it's the whole fake-it-till-you-make-it mentality that's common in Silicon Valley."

"You really can't do that with anything health related," Sam said.

"I know. These software guys can mock up whatever they want and claim they've got something that works, even if it does it only once, hacked together, with a lot of human intervention. Sometimes they can find someone to actually build that software product once they've secured enough funding, but ..."

"If you do that in medicine, people can die. Literally. The science always wins." Sam sighed. "Even though Matt may be a talker, I don't think that's what's going on with Redew. I've been learning as much as I can about what the prototype is supposed to do, and all the steps they need have been reliably replicated at other research institutions. The difference is that Redew's prototype will bring all these processes together in one system. And the good news is that they are bringing in someone to replace Erik."

"That quickly? He just died."

"Apparently the new guy—his name is Greg—is a grad student who worked on the original prototype. He's about to defend his dissertation, and as soon as he's done, he'll join full-time."

"That's good news. So why do you look worried?"

"I met him earlier this week, and let's just say, he doesn't seem to be the most agreeable person. Brooke—the lab assistant who was working with Erik—knew him from her undergrad days, and she says he's almost always like that. She calls him Grumpy Greg."

"Aren't there lots of brilliant people who don't have the best personalities? Like Steve Jobs, for instance."

"Yeah, I've known plenty." She took a deep breath. "I guess I should just see how things work with him."

Then Sam remembered why she'd wanted to talk to James in the first place. "But I've got something to tell you. I ran into the investigator from the medical examiner's office at the hospital right before I had lunch with Alex. And she said something kind of strange to me, that she thinks there's something that doesn't make sense about Erik's death."

"How so?"

"She said he definitely died of asphyxia, but if it was because of a severe asthma exacerbation, his blood work didn't completely support that conclusion."

Sam went on to explain the logic behind Miranda's suspicions, and then James asked, "Didn't she tell the medical examiner?"

"She did, but she said he's old school, and he just wants to close the case because he's swamped."

"I can imagine. We've got a story almost every day about another homicide. This city isn't the sleepy college town we grew up in anymore."

"You can say that again."

"Did she think there was foul play?"

"She didn't say. Just that the evidence doesn't line up like it should."

"Seems like she's bothered by unresolved questions, kinda like you." James gently punched Sam on the shoulder. "But who would want to kill Erik?"

Sam shrugged. "I don't know."

17

The next day, Sam found it hard to focus on helping Brooke. Her mind kept creeping back toward her discussion with Miranda the day before. Maybe it was nothing, just a lower-level tech second-guessing the medical examiner's determination. Sam liked Miranda, though, and she had a feeling that she might be right.

Sam finished counting yet another set of flies, sat up, and raised her arms above her head to stretch. This really was tedious work, and as each hour passed, she wished the prototype was functional. Tension in her neck along with eyestrain and throbbing in her temples signaled a headache was not far in her future, and she worried she might make a mistake or injure one of the little guys, even though she was using a soft paintbrush to push them around on the fly pad under the microscope.

Before he'd passed away, Erik had told her to listen to a podcast episode by the science journalist David Pogue, discussing how Google engineers had devised a way to sort mosquitoes for population control. He'd told her that

Redew's approach was similar, using puffs of air to direct flies into different vials. The system used machine learning algorithms to detect unique patterns on the flies from videos inside the prototype's chamber. Then the whole chamber would shake, causing the flies to drop from the sides, funneling them into a tube where puffs of air would send them down different chutes, like switches sending trains to various tracks on a railroad. It was one of the ways he'd convinced her that Redew would be successful, if only they could raise the funds to work out some of the design issues on Dr. Galloway's prototype. It seemed like a dream compared to the manual way she was sorting flies now.

Occasionally throughout the day, she'd attempt to prod Brooke and Matt on the subject of Greg, aiming to learn a little more about him. She really hoped he'd be a good replacement for Erik.

But Matt was on the phone most of the time, trying to set up meetings with more potential investors, answering questions from the Mundy Capital associates they'd met at SXSW, and pitching to potential customers.

Matt had explained to Sam that, even before Redew had a working prototype, they might be able to screen small drug libraries as a service to bring in some revenue. If they could get a contract with one of these companies, then he could go ahead and hire some lab techs as a stopgap and extend Redew's runway until they raised enough money to build the more robust automated system.

While he'd been telling her this, he'd confirmed Greg was a member of the scientific board with Dr. Galloway, since Greg had worked on the prototype the most. But that was the only information she'd been able to garner from Matt, other than the fact that Greg had stopped by the

Redew offices a couple of times to meet with Erik before Sam had joined as an advisor.

As for Brooke, she didn't really seem to want to talk about Greg much. Plus, it was hard for Sam and Brooke to chat, even though they sat side by side at matching microscopes along the counter in the smaller lab. Both women needed to focus on the task at hand; otherwise, they'd lose count and have to start over again.

One time, when they both were in between counting batches, Sam commented, "This is a pretty tight space. Seems kind of strange to do all this work in here. It's more like a storage closet."

"I agree," Brooke said. "Erik didn't like the setup either. He thought it could be a potential safety hazard, but Matt insisted on keeping the larger space less messy. He wanted it to look how it will in the future—when the next generation prototype is ready—so that prospective investors could see his vision."

Something Brooke had said perked up Sam's ears. "What did Erik mean by 'potential safety'—"

A knock on the door frame interrupted Sam, and the ladies turned to find Matt. Brooke immediately straightened up in her chair.

"How's everything going?" Matt asked.

Brooke gave him a brief summary of all the work they'd accomplished, which Sam was more than happy to have her do. Sam could count the little insects, but she was still grappling with keeping track of all the fly lineages and drug compounds they were screening.

Apparently, Matt wasn't that enthused either, as his eyes glazed a bit while Brooke spoke. When she finished, he said, "So we're on track? Does it still look like our lead compounds will advance to phase II?"

"I think so," Brooke replied. "I need to recheck some

of these results. The data may not be as strong as we originally thought for one of the compounds."

"Oh, really? Is that so?"

"Uh…yes." Brooke looked a little sheepish. "But like I
said, I need to go over everything again."

"Very well," Matt said. "I'm going to be out for the rest
of the afternoon. Holly's having her glucose tolerance test,
and she wants me to be there."

After he left, they continued their work with the flies,
but Sam noticed the younger woman didn't seem so perky.
At least, as far as she could tell for someone who was bent
over a microscope. Brooke's shoulders seemed to slump a
little more, and her movements were slower, less efficient
than they had been.

Sam wondered why. Maybe it was because Matt
seemed to question Brooke's ability to analyze the data. Or
it could just have been that it was getting late in the day,
and doing a monotonous task for hours on end was making
Brooke tired. Sam was certainly exhausted.

Before Sam left for the day, she filled a box with the
personal items from Erik's desk—they'd been left there
since he'd died, along with his car. To help out Lisa, she
was going to drive his car to his apartment; his parents had
arranged for movers to pack everything up and bring it to
their home in Dallas the next day. Sam had assumed Erik's
keys were still at the office, but she couldn't find them.

"You're sure they weren't with his personal effects
collected at the hospital?" Sam asked when she called Lisa.

"I'm sure. In fact, there's an itemized list of everything
he had with him. No keys."

There was always a possibility that the keys had been
lost, but Sam knew that the ER nurses would have taken an
inventory when Erik arrived. In fact, Sam had signed patient

inventories many times during her trauma rotations, as the nurses had to count money found on a patient in front of a witness to affirm that the amount documented was correct.

"You're sure they aren't at Redew?" Lisa asked. "There's a silver double helix on the keychain."

"Let me look again." As Sam continued to hold her cell to her ear, she poked around inside the box. No keys there. She fully pulled out the desk drawers, bending over to peer all the way to the back of each, then sweeping with her free hand, her fingertips finding nothing against the cold metal. "I don't see any keys in his stuff I just packed, and I double-checked his desk."

A sigh came from the other end of the connection. "Okay. He had a spare set of keys for his car, so I'll bring them to you. It's just…I was hoping I wouldn't have to go into his apartment. It's still so painful."

"I could do it," Sam offered.

"No, no…it would take too much time, for you to run around—"

"But that's what friends are for."

"You're doing enough for me already. I'll be by as soon as I can."

While Sam waited, she read a few more journal articles, extending her understanding of how the flies were categorized. Since Redew was focusing on neurological conditions, flies with the genes for a particular disease, like Parkinson's, would also have problems moving. If the drug they were given helped, then they would have fewer movement issues and could climb the wall in a chamber inside the prototype more easily. Those same machine learning algorithms that identified each individual fly could also sort the flies based on how the drugs affected them. She was starting to see how everything fit together.

After forty-five minutes, Lisa arrived with the spare set of keys.

Sam placed the box she'd packed in the passenger seat of Erik's car, then she drove behind Lisa, following her back to his apartment. At one of the intersections, her friend had stopped short, so Sam had to jam on the brakes. She put her hand out to keep the box from sliding off the seat, but Erik's planner flipped onto the floorboard.

While the light remained red, Sam leaned over to pick it up. It had opened to the week after he'd died.

He'd blocked off time for each of the crosses he'd never get to count and evaluate—the same crosses that Brooke and Sam had been working on since his death. Interspersed with these chunks of time were a few meetings with Matt, and there was one meeting he'd set up with Dr. Galloway. Underneath, he'd written, "Re: counterselection."

The car behind Sam bleeped. The light had turned green, and Lisa had already gone through the intersection. Sam tossed the planner back in the box and accelerated to catch up.

Once they got to Erik's apartment complex, Lisa indicated where Sam should park his car.

"The movers will be here first thing in the morning," Lisa said as they got into her car so she could take Sam back to Redew to retrieve hers. "Thanks for helping me with this."

"Of course. Like I said, that's what friends are for."

"With all this traffic, I thought I was going to lose you, especially at Burnet," Lisa said. "What happened?"

"Oh, nothing. The box with Erik's things from the office slid forward when I stopped, and I was trying to pick up something that had fallen out."

Sam considered what she'd seen in the planner. Something was up. And now she wondered even more what Erik was going to tell her that fateful morning. She didn't think it would be right to talk to Lisa about it, though. But she knew how she could help.

"Since I'm still coming up to speed on everything going on at Redew, do you think I could meet with Dr. Galloway?"

"Oh, sure," Lisa said. "I can reach out to him and set up a meeting."

"Thanks. That would be great."

18

A week and a half later, after several email messages ping-ponged back and forth amongst everyone to settle on a good time, Sam and Lisa finally got on Dr. Galloway's schedule. Sam picked up Lisa from her office downtown and parked in one of the many garages on The University of Texas campus, then they made their way to the new Engineering and Education Research Center. Like the city it called home, the university had undergone many changes over the years, with old buildings torn down and replaced by new, state-of-the-art structures, replete with open spaces and nooks to help foster student inspiration and collaboration.

"I don't even recognize this place anymore," Sam said as they joined a group of students entering the building.

"Same here," Lisa replied. "But if the school wants to continue to attract the best students from around the country—and the world—they've got to keep up."

Once they were inside, Sam stopped and lowered her voice. "Are you sure you're up for this? I mean, I really do appreciate that you came with me since you already know

Professor Galloway." She put her hand on Lisa's shoulder. "But are you ready to talk about Erik right now? Is it too soon?"

Sam could have met with Dr. Galloway by herself, but Lisa insisted she wanted to join in. Without Lisa, it certainly would have been easier for Sam to probe the professor about why Erik had made an appointment—and if it might have contributed to his death. Plus, it had only been two and a half weeks since Sam had found Erik on the floor of the lab. Was her friend done grieving yet?

Lisa straightened up and took in a deep breath. "I'm ready. I want you to figure out what Erik was working on so Redew can be successful. He had so much potential, and if his work can live on to help others, then I think that will be the best way to honor him and his legacy."

"Okay, then," Sam said. "Show me the way."

They took the elevator up to the third floor and found Dr. Galloway's office, but the door was closed. The brightly lit hallway was empty, save for a couple of students chatting as they passed by the end of the corridor.

"He might be finishing up a meeting with someone," Lisa said as she glanced at her watch. "But we're right on time." She rapped lightly on the door.

When there was no answer, Lisa tried the lever, but it didn't budge.

"Do you know when he teaches?" Sam asked. "Maybe he's on his way back from class."

Just then, Greg came around the corner with a purposeful gait, his focus on the floor. He didn't even notice them as he turned to enter the room next to Dr. Galloway's office.

"Let's see if Greg knows where he is." Sam followed him, with Lisa trailing behind.

It wasn't just a room; it was a lab like the one at Redew,

but larger, much larger. Several black bench tops held parts
of machines just like the prototype at Redew.

A few students were busy around the lab, each at their
own station. A girl working next to the door set down a
screwdriver and said, "Can I help you?"

"We're looking for Dr. Galloway," Sam said, "but we'd
like to talk to him for a moment." She pointed to Greg,
who had just sat down in front of a laptop in the back
corner of the lab.

The girl looked over her shoulder, her brown ponytail
swaying counterpoint to her head movements. When she
turned back to Sam and Lisa, her nose was scrunched.
"Are you sure you want to talk to *him*?"

"Yeah," Sam said. "I'll be working with him more in a
few weeks."

The girl's face brightened. "Wait, are you Dr. Jenkins?
You work at Redew?"

"Well, I'm just advising them right now," Sam said.

"Brooke says you're super nice—for a doctor." The girl
blushed as soon as she realized what she said might not
have been phrased in the best way.

"Thanks," Sam said.

The girl stuck out her hand. "I'm Nicole. I'm hoping to
be like you someday—a doctor, that is."

Sam smiled. "That's great. Where are you in the
process?"

"I'm studying for the MCAT now, and then I'll start
working on my applications this summer."

"Well," Sam said, "I'd be happy to answer any questions if you have them."

Nicole's eyes widened. "Really?"

"Of course." Sam dug into her purse. "Here's my card.
You can email me, and I'd be happy to help as much as I
can."

"Wow. Thanks!" Nicole beamed. Then she looked over her shoulder again. "But you might not want to bother Greg right now. He's grumpier than usual. Do you really need to talk to him?"

"We came here originally to speak with Dr. Galloway, but Greg might be able to help us too."

Sam glanced over at Lisa, who shrugged.

Nicole leaned closer to them and whispered, "Good luck."

Sam and Lisa made their way back to where Greg was sitting at a desk littered with crumpled Cheetos bags and empty Monster Energy cans.

After a few moments, when he didn't even acknowledge them, Sam said, "Good afternoon. You may not remember me, but we met at Redew a couple of weeks ago."

Greg didn't look up from the laptop. "I remember."

"We're here to talk to Dr. Galloway, to ask him some questions I have about the work Erik was doing. But I thought maybe you might be able to answer them too. Do you have a minute?"

When Greg didn't respond and continued typing, Sam pulled Erik's notebook out of her bag and turned to the page with the Post-it. "Do you know what he meant by this? It says 'verify counterselection.' Brooke and I were trying to figure it out, but we don't know what he intended to do."

Greg sneered. "Like Brooke—with an 'e'—could help." He glanced dismissively at the notebook, then went back to typing on his laptop.

Sam raised her eyebrows as she glanced at Lisa. Her friend shrugged again.

"Look," Sam said, her voice more firm. "Could you just take a second to talk to us?"

He finally stopped typing and looked up at them.

"Listen. I need to get this done. I'm defending my dissertation on Monday. I have to get this bullshit paperwork finished by the end of the day, or someone may balk and reschedule the committee meeting." He glowered at her. "Then I won't be able to help you at Redew it all."

Sam took a step back. "Okay, fine."

She and Lisa made their way out to the hallway, waving at Nicole as they walked by.

Once they were alone, Lisa said, "Not surprising."

"What?" Sam asked. "Is he always like this?"

Lisa nodded. "Yeah. And he originally wanted Erik's job at Redew."

"Well, he's getting it now that Erik's …" Sam faltered. "I'm sorry."

Lisa took in a deep breath. "It's okay."

"So you already knew Greg?"

"He's the one who did a lot of the research under Dr. Galloway that led to the formation of Redew, and he wanted to be a founder."

From where they stood in the hallway, they could see across the lab to the corner where Greg typed furiously on his keyboard.

"As you can see, he's not the most pleasant person to be around."

Sam nodded. "Unfortunately, it sometimes goes with the territory. History is filled with geniuses who were difficult to work with."

"That's true," Lisa agreed.

"And I suppose he's under even more stress now with his defense coming up." Sam hoped he would be less of a jerk once that was out of the way. But maybe not.

The fact that he'd wanted Erik's job prickled the back of Sam's neck. She hadn't told Lisa about Miranda's suspi-

cions. And if it was true that Greg had wanted Erik's job...
then maybe there was something to Miranda's theory.

"Oh, goodness, ladies, I'm so sorry." An older
gentleman had appeared from around the corner. He was
followed by two young men. "I forgot that you had set up a
meeting with me." He glanced back at his entourage, then
stepped into the doorway of the lab. "But would you mind
waiting a few minutes more? I need to help these students,
but perhaps Nicole can show you some of the work that
we're doing."

Nicole looked up and smiled. "Sure, I'd be happy to."

"I shouldn't be too long." Dr. Galloway disappeared
into his office with the students.

While they waited, Nicole excitedly rattled off the
different types of projects Dr. Galloway's graduate students
were working on, with disclaimers that she really didn't
know much, since she was just an undergrad. She introduced Sam and Lisa to two other students in the lab, who
went on to give brief explanations of their research. Greg
sulked in the corner, looking very annoyed as he continued
to type on his laptop. Nicole and the other students
ignored him.

Sam could see how these projects were related to the
prototype that sat at Redew. Then she realized something
was missing. "Where are the flies?"

"That's Dr. Hawthorne's domain," Nicole said. "He's
in the biology department, and even though this is an
interdisciplinary lab, Dr. Hawthorne understands the
genetics behind fly research much better than—" She
stopped herself, as if she realized she was about to say
something that might get her in trouble.

"Better than who?" Sam prompted.

Nicole glanced around at the other students in the lab,
then she lowered her voice. "I shouldn't say, because I love

working with Dr. Galloway, and I feel like it would be bad-mouthing him. He really is a great professor and does everything he can to support *all* of his students." She looked over her shoulder again in Greg's direction.

"It's okay. We'll keep whatever you say between us." Sam peeked at Lisa to make sure she agreed.

"That's right," Lisa confirmed. "She's a doctor, and I'm a lawyer, so we know how to keep things confidential."

The young woman relaxed a little. "Well, it's just that Dr. Galloway focuses on the engineering challenges. You know, automating the screening and evaluation process?"

Sam nodded. "That makes sense."

Lisa cleared her throat. "Dr. Galloway is the one who's filed for the patents on the work his lab has produced and, through UT's tech transfer office, has licensed out the intellectual property to Redew."

Sam wanted to press Nicole further, to get her to say more, but Dr. Galloway reappeared.

"Okay, ladies. I'm ready for you now."

They thanked Nicole for showing them around, and Sam reiterated her promise to answer Nicole's questions about the medical school application process. Plus, maybe she could get her to open up more if they talked away from the lab.

Once they were in the professor's office, and Lisa had introduced Sam, he said, "What can I do for you today?"

Sam opened Erik's notebook and turned it to the page with the Post-it. "Do you happen to know what this means?" She handed it to Dr. Galloway.

"Is this Erik's?"

Sam nodded.

"I was so sorry to hear that he passed. I'd only met him a couple of times, I'm afraid. He seemed to be an upstanding young man."

The professor spent a few moments looking at the notebook, flipping back and forth through a few pages, then he slowly shook his head. "I'm sorry. I'm not the best person to help you interpret this. The genetics part isn't my area of expertise. Sure, I understand the basics of the screening process, but not the nitty-gritty details. Our lab specializes in building the mechanisms for handling the flies, including the algorithms to sort them using visual guidance."

"Oh, I see." Sam began to understand the full picture. Maybe this is what Nicole had alluded to.

"That is correct," Dr. Galloway said. "We've collaborated on numerous projects, but I'm sorry to say, he's the one who knows more about the crosses Greg had performed. I have a rudimentary understanding, but Dr. Hawthorne is the expert, I'm afraid."

"Can you tell us where his office is?" Sam asked. "We could stop by and talk to him, since we're already on campus."

"That won't be possible," Dr. Galloway said. "He's on sabbatical and won't be returning until the fall semester." He handed the notebook back to Sam. "You could always email him, but I'm sure Greg can figure it out once he starts working at Redew—or Brooke could. She may be young, but she is rather bright and has a ton of potential."

Sam looked down at the columns of data, printed in Erik's exacting script. "She and I spent some time looking at this, trying to make sense of it all. She said the data is from flies in the Huntington's line. She recommended that I talk to you about it, actually."

"I see," he said. "Yes. Greg and Brooke have a lot more cross-disciplinary experience than I do." He sighed. "Things certainly have changed a lot since I was in school."

After they said their goodbyes and left the building, Sam sat down on a bench under a large oak, feeling deflated. "Well, that was a dead end."

Lisa joined her, and they watched as a couple of squirrels fought over an acorn at the base of the tree. It was midway through the hour, so the crowds had disappeared into classrooms, and only a few students sauntered by. Then again, perhaps the fact it was a Friday afternoon contributed to the stillness around them.

"Do you think it's gonna be a problem with Greg at Redew?" Sam asked. "Can he really pick up where Erik left off?"

"I don't know," Lisa said. "Erik was certainly more involved with the biological side of things. When Redew was first formed, and Matt was looking for a technical expert, Greg seemed to be the obvious choice. But he and Matt clashed, and Erik was available, so I made the introductions. Plus, Whit really liked that Erik had industry experience. So Greg lost out."

"And now he's getting a second chance."

19

Once Sam got home to her apartment that evening, she couldn't shake the convergence of thoughts in her head. At the forefront was Miranda's suggestion that the facts didn't line up, that Erik's death may not have been caused by a typical asthma exacerbation.

Then there was Erik's note to "verify counterselection." Counterselection of what? Sam had learned from the scientific articles she'd read that researchers use selection and counterselection techniques to ensure the *Drosophila* strains they work with contain only the genetic markers they're interested in. Was this something Erik was going to discuss with her the morning he died?

And Professor Galloway really hadn't been much help, despite the fact Erik had scheduled a meeting with him, presumably about that counterselection issue. Dr. Galloway had said he'd only met Erik a couple of times, so they didn't really know each other that well. Perhaps Erik would have discovered the person he really needed to talk to was Dr. Hawthorne, had he lived.

Even though Brooke hadn't known what the Post-it meant when she'd seen it the first time, Sam decided to press her again. Dr. Galloway seemed to think highly of his former student, and presumably, she already knew Dr. Hawthorne. Since Sam was scheduled for clinic at the beginning of the following week, she went to her desk and sent Brooke an email about the visit to UT, asking her to reach out to Dr. Hawthorne regarding Erik's counterselection note.

As a last resort, if Dr. Hawthorne proved to be another dead end, they could always ask Greg. But she really didn't look forward to talking to him about anything, for a variety of reasons.

And in Sam's mind, if there'd been foul play with respect to Erik's death, it seemed to come back to Greg. Plus, she now knew he'd been upset when Erik had become a founder of Redew—a company using technology based on Greg's work in Dr. Galloway's lab. Sam could understand why he'd be disgruntled—she'd be jealous, too, if she'd been in his situation. But she'd never resort to murder.

Perhaps Erik had reached out to Greg, to ask him about this counterselection issue he'd found. What if Greg had met with Erik at Redew and killed him?

But how? Who could help her sort through this?

Miranda. She'd been the one who'd set Sam's mind on this track in the first place. Maybe she would know what everything meant.

Sam dug through the pile of papers next to her laptop, mostly printouts of scientific articles with a few bills scattered throughout, and found Miranda's card buried at the bottom. After she dialed the number on her cell, it rang several times and went to voicemail.

"Hi, Miranda. It's Sam. I have—uh—" What should she say? She has a suspect?

No. Not on a message. Plus, who did she think she was? Nancy Drew?

She'd decided it was just best to leave a message to call her back, when her phone started buzzing. It was Miranda. Sam clicked "End and Accept."

"Sorry, I didn't get to the phone in time," Miranda said. "I just got out of the shower—it's so hard to get rid of the smell of death!"

"Isn't that the truth." Images of gangrene from Sam's residency days crowded into her mind, along with the memory of the unique, fetid odor of dead tissue, permeating her nostrils, lingering long after she'd left her unfortunate patient's rooms.

"I'm so glad you understand!" Miranda laughed. "So, what do I owe the honor of this call? Has something come up?"

After Sam spent a few minutes explaining her hypothesis about Greg, Miranda said, "I'm sorry, but I shouldn't have said anything to you. I never should've suggested there was anything untoward about Erik's death." She went on to explain that based on the list of compounds that Sam had provided, the ME sent samples of Erik's blood for further testing. He wanted to determine if there were elevated levels of the drugs known to trigger bronchospasm. Additionally, the ME had finally addressed Miranda's observation regarding the IgE levels in Erik's blood. "He told me IgE has a short half-life, so that could be one explanation. Plus, there's new research that's found asthmatics may have different phenotypes regarding IgE response, and Erik might have naturally expressed lower levels of IgE. So it really does look like his asthma did him in."

At first, Sam wanted to argue her point, but then she took a deep breath and thought better of it. "You're right. That's how conspiracy theories arise, from someone trying to tie a bunch of disparate events together with a common cause, when it's all just coincidence." She huffed. "It's funny how the mind keeps looking for more evidence to support those things. And now I'm one of those kooks."

"No, you're not," Miranda said. "We're all guilty of it at times, using confirmation bias to find clues to support what we want to believe."

"Well, thanks for hearing me out," Sam said. "I'm sorry to have bothered you."

"It wasn't a bother. It was good talking to you again, and I was wondering ..." Miranda paused.

"Wondering what?"

"I know it's a little awkward to ask, but you said you were a surgery resident, right?"

"Yeah, why?"

"And that's a field dominated by men, right?"

"It is, even though they keep trying to increase the number of women going into the residency programs. But many times, they end up like me and leave surgery for something else."

"Then you know what it's like to be working with a bunch of men; it's a bit of a boys' club. Sure, they include you, but it's hard to have close friendships."

"Totally," Sam agreed.

"And have you ever noticed how sometimes when you mainly make friends with men, other women give you the evil eye, like you're up to something, even though the relationship is completely platonic?"

"Yeah, I sure have." Sam had certainly had her share of intense stares from women when she'd been speaking with male friends and colleagues, especially those who were in committed relationships. It was as if the women observing these conversations thought she was a tramp, trying to lead these men astray. When all she'd been doing was having an engaging discussion about something related to work or about some shared interest.

"So, like I said," Miranda continued, "I know this is a bit awkward, but I thought we got along pretty well, and I was wondering if you'd like to get together for lunch sometime?"

"That would be great," Sam said. "And I don't think it's awkward; that's how friendships start."

Plus, Sam really needed a friend right now, especially since James's relationship with Kevin was getting more serious. Actually, she supposed her relationship with Alex was also getting more serious, since he'd mentioned the "m" word, although she wasn't really sure how she felt about it. Then she realized Miranda was engaged as well. It made sense; they were all at that age, when couples start settling down.

Then she thought of Lisa. How awful it was, that she'd never know what would've happened with Erik.

It was tragic…but as they say, that's life. Horrible things happen to good people, and, as the evidence was showing, Erik most likely died from an asthma exacerbation.

Sam needed to stop digging into things when there really wasn't anything to be found.

"So when would you like to meet?" Miranda asked.

They volleyed around a few dates, then finally settled on Monday the following week, when Sam was scheduled to work at her old clinic located in a strip mall, with numerous fast casual restaurants nearby.

Once they hashed out the details, Miranda said, "I'm looking forward to it."

"Same here," Sam said. "Then we can talk about something other than death."

20

After Sam hung up with Miranda, she pulled Erik's notebook out of her bag. The more she thought about it, the more she realized how ridiculous it was that she was being so suspicious. Nothing was going to change the fact that Erik was dead, and they still needed to decipher what the Post-it note meant. She hoped Brooke would figure it out with Dr. Hawthorne's help.

Sam flipped through the notebook yet again, while consulting the protocols that Erik had put together, with each pass through his tables of data giving her a better understanding of the scientific case he was building. But an explanation for the note on the Post-it wasn't revealing itself, so she was jotting down a list of questions to ask Brooke the next time they saw each other, when someone knocked on her door.

She peered through the peephole. James stood on the other side, bouncing on the balls of his feet. As soon as she opened the door, he blurted out, "It's Matt. He's the one!"

"What?" Sam had already moved on from her

conspiracy theories, her mind now deeply focused on genetics experiments, so it took her a moment for her attention to resurface, to understand what he meant. "Wait…are you saying you think Matt killed Erik?" She shook her head. "He needed Erik, so that doesn't make any sense."

"Hear me out," James said as he walked past her and plopped down on her couch. "I've been doing a little bit of research, and I got a chance to talk to Katie, Kevin's coworker. You know? The person who worked with Matt at his previous startup?"

Sam closed the door and joined him on the couch. "The one you told me about."

"Right. After talking to her, it sounds like Matt is one of those tech bros who's all about chasing unicorns."

"Billion-dollar startups? Like Kevin was saying?"

James nodded. "Yep. That's what all of these startup boys want, to create the next unicorn that's valued over one billion so they can cash out and make a ton of money."

"Wasn't Kevin saying the guys who are most successful are in the software industry?"

"That's the thing: Matt had been trying to do that, but because of what happened with Katie, he earned a reputation for overpromising, so nobody in the software scene wants to work with him anymore—at least not here in Austin." He shrugged. "He's moved on to biotech, which is not as easy, but based on what I've learned with my non-sciencey brain, it seems like what Redew's doing has a lot of potential—so he's latched on and found his pony to ride."

"But Whit seems to have full trust in Matt. And he's a tech guy."

"Ah, but not really. Whit made his name in the telecom

industry, and he's a bit older. He's relatively new to the
software world, from what I can tell, so he probably doesn't
know about Matt's reputation. And he doesn't have any
experience in biotech, so that might be why he trusts
Matt."

Sam wasn't completely sure about James's reasoning.
"But why would Matt kill Erik? That puts the company at
risk."

"They replaced Erik almost immediately, though, so it
doesn't seem like there's any real setback, right? Especially
since the guy coming in did the initial research the company's technology is based on."

Sam tucked her legs under her and turned to face
James. "I think if anyone had a reason to kill Erik, it would
be the guy who's replacing him—Greg. He wanted to be
one of the founders of Redew, but he and Matt didn't get
along for some reason, and now that Erik's dead—"

"He's getting Erik's job," James finished.

"Exactly." She then went on to lay out what she'd
learned during her visit to UT, and as she spoke, her suspicions blossomed again, despite her earlier conversation
with Miranda. "Plus, the couple of times I've met him, he's
been a total ass."

"But if he did it, how?"

"Greg's been an advisor for the company, just like me. I
have a badge to access the offices and the lab, so he probably does as well. And he's familiar with all of the
compounds that they are screening, so he might know
which one could kill Erik." As Sam said this, doubt crept
into her mind again. She was creating a convoluted narrative that seemed implausible. "That is, if Erik was even
murdered."

"Why do you say that?"

"Before you came over, I was on the phone with

Miranda, the investigator from the medical examiner's office."

"The one you mentioned before, who told you she had suspicions about Erik's cause of death?"

"Right. I called her to share everything I just told you, and she said she never should have let on about her misgivings that something might be amiss. The ME finally listened to her concerns about the IgE levels, and he sent off Erik's blood for more extensive testing. So now Miranda doesn't think there was foul play involved in Erik's death."

"Well, I'd still watch out around Matt," James said. "He seems to say anything he needs to get what he wants."

"Yeah, I saw some of that during the pitch session at South by."

"South by? So you're trying to be a hipster now?"

Sam laughed as she felt her phone buzz in her pocket. She pulled it out and saw it was just a news notification. But there was also a text message from Brooke that she'd missed. She dialed Brooke's number and put her cell to her ear.

"What's up?" James asked.

"Brooke says she thinks she knows what Erik's Post-it meant, so I'm calling her."

James looked confused, but the ringing on Sam's cell had stopped, and Brooke's bubbly voice came on, requesting the caller to leave a message. "It's Sam. Just got your text. Call me back when you get a chance."

"What's this about a Post-it?"

Sam got up, retrieved the notebook from her desk, and showed James the yellow square.

"Oh, so that's what you were talking about earlier; that's why you were at UT. But you said you didn't learn

what Erik meant by"—he pointed to the note as he read—
"'verify counterselection,' did you?"

"No, not from Dr. Galloway. Turns out genetics is not
his area of expertise."

"Still," James said, his eyes widening, "it's a clue."

"Don't get too excited. It's probably no big deal, especially since Miranda doesn't think there was anything
nefarious about Erik's death."

James looked deflated as he checked his phone. "I gotta
go." He stood. "That new horror movie is out, and Kevin
got tickets. Let me know if Brooke has anything interesting
to say."

Right after he left, Sam received another text from
Brooke. She couldn't talk just then, but could Sam stop by
her condo in the morning?

Sam texted back: *I'll be there.*

21

B rooke lived in a high-rise condo downtown. Pretty nice digs for a college student, but her parents had bought it as an investment, one that they could stay in when they came to town for UT football games, even after their daughter moved away.

Sam parked in the garage under Austin City Hall since she knew there would be plenty of space on a Saturday morning. She was dying to know what Brooke had figured out.

As Sam walked toward the condo building, the atmosphere changed, with a stillness she didn't normally associate with this place. But maybe it was just because it was a Saturday morning.

Usually, when she came to the Second Street District, it was at night, and there would be a vibe of excitement, fueled by the audience lining up to see the latest musical act at ACL Live, the venue where Austin City Limits was taped. But when she crossed the street to the block housing Brooke's building, somberness filled the air.

Instead of happy banter, people passing her on the

sidewalk were whispering and mumbling. A couple had their heads lowered, tilted toward each other, with looks more suited for a funeral.

What was going on?

When Sam got to the side entrance of Brooke's building, she found a police officer standing in front of the recessed passageway. Brooke had sent her a code, so Sam had pulled out her phone to retrieve it for the keypad next to the steel mesh door. As she approached, the officer held up his hand.

"I'm sorry, ma'am. No one is allowed in right now."

"But I'm supposed to meet someone who lives here."

He shook his head. "Sorry, I can't let you in."

"Why not?"

"We're in the process of investigating an incident."

"What kind of incident?"

"I'm not at liberty to say, ma'am. But you can't enter the building."

"O-okay," Sam stammered. "Thank you."

She backed away onto the sidewalk, bumping into a man passing by. He frowned at her.

"Sorry," she muttered.

She dialed Brooke's number on her cell. It went directly to voicemail. "Hey, Brooke. It's Sam. I'm outside your building, but there's a police officer here. He's not letting me in. Call me back."

She had a bad feeling about this.

Further down the block, a crowd had formed, extending to the intersection, with everyone's attention focused on something she couldn't see—around the corner, along the side of the building. She ambled down the sidewalk to find out what was going on.

As she got closer to the corner, she noticed blue and red flashing lights reflecting off the buildings on the other side of the street. It was blocked off with crime-scene tape, holding the crowd at bay, with several police vehicles scattered about, as if a child playing with his toys had left them abruptly. She joined the back of the crowd, full of murmurs, but she couldn't see over the heads of the people in front of her.

Then she spotted a familiar face. It was Kevin.

She squeezed between the onlookers, inching her way toward him. He was standing on his tiptoes, straining to see over the crowd, and as she got nearer, he glanced her way. When he saw her, he beckoned her to join him.

"What's going on?" Sam asked.

"Someone jumped."

"Who?"

Kevin shrugged. "I don't know. They said it was a girl who lived here." He pointed upward to the side of the building.

Sam's gaze followed his finger to a balcony several stories up. She could see figures moving about on the balcony, including a police officer, poking his head between a couple of hanging plants to look down at the crowd below. A few other people in the surrounding units had come out onto their own balconies and were also looking down at the amassed spectators.

She used her eyes to count the floors, to find out where the person had jumped from. It was the eighth floor—that's where Brooke's unit was. Her heart began to race as she checked her phone to see if she'd missed a return call from Brooke. There was none.

She dialed Brooke's number again, and again, it went straight to voicemail. "Brooke, this is Sam," she said urgently. "I'm still outside your building, and…it seems like someone fell. I just want to make sure you're okay. Please call me as soon as you get this."

After she hung up, Kevin asked, "You're meeting someone?"

"Yeah, a girl who works at the startup I'm helping out." Then Sam looked up at Kevin. "What are you doing here?"

He pointed to the building. "That's where I live."

"Oh." She laughed nervously. "I guess I knew you lived downtown, but I just didn't know exactly where."

"Yeah, it's a nice building." He motioned to the high-rise caddy corner to them. "And I work right there."

"Oh, that's great." She was still concerned that Brooke hadn't called her back yet, but she wanted to get Kevin's side of the story about his relationship with James. "I hear you asked James—"

She stopped when she saw a familiar figure. A couple of men wearing suits, one with a salt-and-pepper crown, the other with dark hair, walked to the yellow tape and flashed their badges to the officer keeping watch. The one with dark hair, whose gait had drawn her attention, turned his head. It was him.

Kevin nudged her arm. "Are you okay? You were asking me something about James."

She turned to him and said, "Yeah, I'm sorry, but I see someone I know. Be back in a sec." She pushed past a few people to make her way to the crime-scene line.

As she approached, a police officer held his arm out to keep her back, but she called out, "Dylan!"

The dark-haired man turned her direction, a questioning look on his face, then a flash of recognition. He held up his finger to the older man with him and came over to Sam.

"Hey, Dylan, what happened?" Then she looked him up and down. "And why aren't you in uniform?"

"I just made detective." The corners of his mouth curled up ever so slightly before he became serious again.

"Congratulations."

"Thanks." He let a small smile escape. "Look, I can't talk right now. I've gotta work this case. But it's good to see you." He turned to walk toward a tarp on the pavement covering the form of a body, but then he pivoted and came back. "What are you doing here?"

"I'm supposed to meet someone who lives in this building, but when I couldn't get in, I tried calling her, and she's not calling me back."

Dylan gave her a curious look. "What's her name?"

"Brooke Delaney."

"Can you wait here?" He blinked, trying to conceal his emotions. "I need to talk to you."

Sam pointed to the tarp. "Is that Brooke?"

"I'm sorry," Dylan said. "I can't discuss this case right now. But I do need to talk to you." He turned to the police officer. "Make sure she doesn't leave."

The officer nodded.

Sam watched as Dylan joined his colleague, who was squatting on the ground next to the tarp. She couldn't see very well since there were investigators and technicians from the medical examiner's office milling about, but with the tarp raised, she could see the arm of the deceased lying on the pavement, the palm open, and on the wrist, a tattooed band of ivy, like a lacy bracelet.

22

After a few moments, Dylan and his partner lowered the tarp back down onto the body and stood. Sam couldn't move, could hardly breathe, her body like concrete, her mind grappling with the reality of what she'd just seen.

Then Miranda appeared, wearing a badge on a lanyard, joining the detectives next to the deceased. Dylan's partner started talking—gesturing and pointing to the shape under the tarp—while Miranda jotted notes on her clipboard, nodding as she listened. Another person came over to ask a question, and when the older man turned to answer, Miranda dropped her arm to her side. Dylan reached over, giving her hand a surreptitious squeeze.

A voice next to her said, "What's going on?"

She turned to see that James and Kevin had joined her. "Someone fell. I think it's Brooke, the girl I was supposed to meet."

"What?" James said. "You're kidding, right?"

"Dylan told me to stay here. He said he needs to talk to me."

"Where is he?"

Sam pointed at the group gathered around the tarp, and her friends leaned over the crime scene tape to get a better look.

"Stand back," the police officer barked.

The trio jumped and stepped back.

"Why's he wearing a suit?" James asked.

"He just got promoted to detective," Sam replied.

James looked over at Dylan again. "Wow. He's moving up in the world. So, who is this girl you were meeting? Is it the one who texted you last night?"

"Yes. She couldn't talk then, but she said she'd figured out what Erik's note meant and wanted me to come by this morning."

"Wait—do you think this is related to Erik's death?" James said, his eyes growing bigger. "Maybe that Post-it note really was a clue."

"Let's not get too hasty here. I'm not even certain the person over there is Brooke." Sam paused, hoping he wouldn't detect that wasn't entirely true. He'd be too eager to devise a narrative, to create a conspiracy theory connecting the deaths.

Kevin shook his head. "If that is her, that's a crazy coincidence. Two people, working at the same startup, dying just a few weeks apart. What bad juju. Why else would Dylan want to talk to you?"

"I don't know."

James pointed to the tarp-covered form on the pavement. "Well, if that isn't Brooke, then I think he wants to talk to you because he's not completely over you, even after all these years."

Sam looked down and muttered, "Oh, I'm pretty sure he's over me."

"How can you be so sure? Plus, he's certainly better than Alex."

Sam punched him lightly on the shoulder. "Need I remind you again that you're the reason I went out with Alex in the first place."

"Because you needed to move on with your life after Jeff." James shrugged. "I thought you'd just have a fling with him. I never thought it would become serious. But I'm definitely sure Alex is not right for you anymore."

"Definitely?" Sam asked. "The other night you said he was fine for dating, but not necessarily marriage material. Why do you say he's *definitely* not right for me now?"

"I have my reasons." James glanced across the street, at an upscale clothing store. "We just saw—"

Kevin cleared his throat. "Are you sure that's not Brooke?"

"I hope not." She peeked at the screen on her phone. "But she hasn't called me back, and I'm getting worried. Let me try calling her again."

Sam pulled up the number and dialed, not totally optimistic Brooke would answer. But there was always a chance another girl with a similar tattoo lived in this building.

The call immediately went to voicemail. She left another quick message, trying not to sound too freaked out. "Just checking to see if you still want to meet. Let me know if your plans have changed." Who knows? With all of the commotion around the building, maybe Brooke was trying to figure out what was going on too. Perhaps she'd come outside, and she'd left her cell in her condo.

When Sam looked up from her phone, James was still

distracted by something across the street. Kevin elbowed him, and he turned his focus back to her.

"What do you keep looking at?" she asked.

"Nothing," Kevin said, a little too quickly.

Although James faced her, his eyes darted to whatever was pulling his attention, so Sam followed his gaze. He was watching the store entrance across the street, and there, coming out the door, looking like a happy couple, was Alex with another woman. "What the—"

She started to leave, making a beeline for the store, but the police officer called out to her. "Ma'am, I'm sorry, but the detective asked that you stay here until he speaks with you."

Sam reluctantly returned to join the officer and her friends. When she glanced at the store entrance again, Alex and the other woman were gone. She scanned up and down the street, her view obscured by the crowd. She jumped up and down, trying to see over the heads around her, but she saw no sign of Alex. *Damn.*

Kevin put his hand on Sam's arm.

She shrugged him off, glaring at him, then at James. "Why didn't you tell me?"

"I was going to," James said.

"It might not be what it seems," Kevin said as he attempted to put his hand on Sam's arm again, but she wasn't having it. She'd thought Alex had evolved from his clubbing days. Apparently, he had not.

"Oh, I'm pretty sure it's exactly what it seems." She shook her head. "I should have known better. He was such a player when I knew him in residency. Men never change."

Sam pulled out her phone, fully intent on ending her relationship with Alex. She was done with him. And as much as she hated how people casually broke up over text these days, she felt that if anyone deserved it, it was Alex.

Kevin tapped Sam on the shoulder. "You can do that later."

"No," she snapped, "I'm doing this right now."

"But that detective is here."

Sam turned, and sure enough, Dylan stood with Miranda on the other side of the police line.

"James," Dylan said. "What are you doing here?"

Snaking his arm around Kevin's, James said, "My boyfriend lives here."

"So you all know each other?" Miranda asked.

James pointed to Dylan and Sam. "We went to high school together."

"What a small world." Miranda nodded to Sam. "Good to see you again, Dr. Jenkins. Although, I wish it were under better circumstances. Detective Myers said you may have some information."

Sam pointed to the tarp behind them. "Is that Brooke? Brooke Delaney?"

"Would you mind giving us a little privacy?" Dylan lifted the crime scene tape and motioned for Sam to come under it.

"Of course, Detective," Kevin said.

He started to leave, but James resisted moving, with an inquisitive look on his face, until Kevin finally pulled him away.

Once they were out of earshot, not only of Sam's friends, but of the other onlookers as well, Dylan said, "We cannot confirm that information at this time, but I still would like to ask you a few questions."

"It is her, isn't it?" Sam said.

"I'm sorry," Dylan said, "but we cannot—"

"C'mon, Dylan," Miranda said. "Dr. Jenkins is trust-worthy. She won't go blabbing to anyone."

"I told you, please call me Sam."

Dylan looked back and forth between the women. "You two know each other?"

"Yes, Dr. Jenkins—I mean Sam—has been answering some clinical questions I have about another case."

"Another case? What other case?"

"There was a death that I'd thought was a little suspi-cious, and …" Miranda looked at Dylan a little sheepishly. "I may have talked with Sam about it. But Dr. Duveneck allayed my concerns, and once the labs come back, he should be able to close the case."

Dylan gave her a stern look. "You've been talking to Sam about it?"

"She was the one who found the decedent."

He raised his eyebrows. "What? You found a dead body?"

"Well, he wasn't dead when I found him," Sam said. "I tried to resuscitate him, but he passed away shortly after arriving at the hospital."

They explained to Dylan what had happened to Erik, and why Miranda had reached out to Sam, with the detec-tive interjecting questions throughout. When they were done, Sam motioned toward the tarp behind them. "And Brooke—if that is Brooke—also worked at Redew. In fact, she'd asked me to come to her condo this morning to talk about something strange we'd found in Erik's notebook, and we'd been trying to figure out what it meant since his death. She'd indicated in her last text to me that she had an answer."

Miranda looked shocked, seeming like she wanted to ask Sam to say more, but Dylan, maintaining a poker face, put his hand up to stop her.

"Unfortunately," he said, "it appears that this was just an accident." He motioned to the body under the tarp. "The decedent had hanging plants on the balcony, and it appears she slipped on the stepladder she was using to tend to them and fell over the side."

Miranda gave Dylan a skeptical expression. "Really? You still believe that, after learning someone else who worked with her died recently?"

Dylan remained stoic. "I have to evaluate all the evidence and not draw any conclusions at this point."

"But you just said it appears to be an accident; that's drawing a conclusion," Miranda shot back.

He flattened his lips together before responding. "You're right. I shouldn't have said that. But, at this time, we haven't found any evidence to the contrary. The door was locked with the deadbolt engaged."

Dylan had a point, but Sam just couldn't believe Brooke's and Erik's deaths were not connected.

She looked at Miranda, and their eyes locked. Miranda gave a slight nod, and Sam knew they were on the same page.

23

James and Kevin stayed by Sam's side for the rest of
the day, mostly trying to distract her with movies on
Netflix, but, inevitably, they'd regress to replaying
the events that had unfolded that morning. She
couldn't believe Brooke was dead. Dylan had said there
was no evidence of foul play, that it seemed like it had been
a horrible accident. But was it really?

Now two people had met their untimely demise right
before Sam was supposed to meet to them. What were the
chances of that? She scolded herself for not being more
wary, for not understanding there could be consequences.
What if the email she'd sent had put Brooke in jeopardy?

Then there was the issue of Alex.

Sam had seen enough. Her mind kept reeling in the
image of him with the other woman, how he'd gazed at
her, how they'd appeared intimate.

Kevin cautioned again about other explanations, giving
James a side-glance as he said this. James had a cynical
look, but he didn't say anything.

So, Sam finally completed what she'd started, when

they'd been standing next to the crime scene tape, when Dylan and Miranda had interrupted her.

She sent a simple text to Alex: *We're through.*

He didn't reply immediately; Sam figured he really *was* working in the ICU at that point. But when he eventually did respond, instead of texting, he called.

Sam declined it, and Alex left a voicemail asking her what was wrong.

She felt bad about ending the relationship this way, but she was furious.

Even if Kevin was right, even if there was another reason for what they'd seen, Alex had been growing more distant lately. Sure, his board exams were coming up soon, which were certainly a huge source of stress for him. She'd wanted to have breakfast with him that morning, before she was supposed to meet with Brooke, but he'd told her he couldn't, that he needed to get a couple of hours of studying in before his shift.

Since he was downtown instead, with another woman, he obviously wasn't studying.

So whatever the explanation, at the very least, he'd lied to her.

On Monday morning, she found herself back at ObraCare, at the clinic that used to be her home base. The previous couple of weeks—in between days at Redew— she'd been at several of the other ObraCare clinics around Central Texas. Now she was back at this clinic, and it strangely felt like home. She fell into her routine, seeing patients, following up on labs and imaging studies, and when Jerry arrived midmorning for the start of his shift, he seemed happy to see her.

"It's been a while, Doc. Glad to have you here."

"Thanks, Jer. How have things been going around here?"

"Oh, the usual. Nothing ever seems to change much, other than the latest corporate gimmick to get patient satisfaction scores up."

How patients rated the clinic—which sometimes had more to do with the coffee in the waiting room than how well she'd managed their medical condition—seemed to be the only thing that mattered to the company. Healthcare was now a service business, and as far as ObraCare was concerned, it didn't matter which doctor each patient saw, just as long as the ratings stayed high. Higher ratings meant more returning patients, which meant increased revenue.

"What's their scheme this time?" Sam asked.

"Each patient gets one of these." Jerry held up a bright orange stress ball with the ObraCare logo on it. "And now we have timers on every exam room door. The MAs have to check on the patients every ten minutes and bring them a soda if we haven't started our visit with them yet."

"Really? How are the MAs supposed to get anything else done?"

"I don't know, but they figure it will decrease the perceived wait time, and get those ratings up." A timer beeped, disturbing the previously placid clinic. Jerry frowned. "And now it begins."

"I saw the timers on the doors, but I didn't know what they were for. None of them had gone off yet."

"It's not too bad in the morning, but once things back up in the afternoon, it seems like they're constantly going off." He shook his head. "Makes it hard to think around here."

Sam lamented with him as one of the MAs rushed by with a can of soda and silenced the offending device.

Although she didn't like how ObraCare was continuing to focus on superficial measures, she still wanted to find out if there was a remote chance of getting her old job back, especially now that Redew seemed cursed.

"Have you had a bunch of different docs working here?" Sam asked.

"Actually, no," Jerry said. "Dr. Cresswell has been here most of the time. She's an OB/GYN that just moved from Houston. She's great and seems to be picking up the nuances of workers' comp pretty quickly."

"I've met her before, on one of your days off." Sam was a little relieved because Anita was looking for an OB/GYN practice to join, so maybe Sam did have a chance of working here full-time again. However, if Dr. Taylor had been scheduling Anita most of the time at this clinic, then maybe …

Cynthia appeared from around the wall, interrupting Sam's thoughts. "Dr. Jenkins, there's a woman here to see you."

"Is she a patient?"

"No. I don't think so. She said you were meeting for lunch."

"Oh, that's right," Sam said. "I'd completely forgotten. Where is she?"

Cynthia pointed down the hallway behind her. "In the waiting room."

Sam glanced at Jerry, who gave her a shooing motion. "Go on, I've got everything taken care of. Have a good lunch."

She found Miranda in the lobby, sitting next to the coffee maker. "I guess we have a lot to discuss."

Miranda nodded as she stood. "Is it still a good time to grab lunch?"

"Absolutely."

They took Miranda's car to Jason's Deli, tucked into a cluster of restaurants in the shopping center across the freeway, and after filling their plates at the salad bar, they circled around for a bit, before finally claiming a somewhat private booth in a corner of the packed dining room.

"You didn't seem convinced that Brooke's death was an accident," Miranda said.

Sam figured she could speak a little more freely, now that they were alone, and because Brooke's identity had been released the previous day, with news reports parroting Dylan's speculation, that she'd fallen while tending her hanging plants.

"Well, what do you think?"

"I don't think it was an accident," Miranda said. "But there's no indication of foul play, or that she had suicidal ideation from any of the evidence we collected." She sighed. "However, sometimes people hide things pretty well. Did she seem down or depressed?"

"No. She was upbeat and had a bubbly personality. And she was excited about starting graduate school in the fall. She'd already picked out an apartment to live in."

"She was moving soon?"

"The program's at Northwestern, and I think she was planning on moving there this summer, so she could get to know the city."

"Chicago?"

"That's right."

"That's a long way from home. Do you think she was anxious about it?"

"No. Like I said, she seemed very excited."

Miranda nodded, then took a bite of her salad. Sam followed suit.

After a few moments, Sam ventured to ask, "What does Dylan think?"

Miranda waved her hand as she swallowed. "Dylan thinks it was a bad accident. He says there's no evidence to the contrary. The door was locked, so it appears she was alone when she fell. And if she wasn't suicidal, then it must have been an accident."

"But you think otherwise?"

"I'm like you; this seems too coincidental. In less than a month, two employees from the same small company suddenly die? There's got to be something else going on." Miranda sighed. "But I'm at a loss for what it could be. And even if I had a hunch, I have no clout—I'm just a nurse working as a forensic investigator."

They picked at their salads, but after a few bites, Sam couldn't resist asking, "Is Dylan your fiancé?"

Miranda instinctively reached up and ran her fingers over the ring on the chain around her neck, a broad smile expanding on her face, her cheeks flushing, making her affection apparent. "Yes, he is. How did you know?"

Sam didn't want to tell her how she'd observed their brief, secretive show of endearment as they stood next to Brooke's body. So she just said, "You seemed close the other day."

"Was it that obvious?" Miranda shook her head as she continued to smile. "Even though we aren't violating any policies about workplace relationships, especially since we're in different departments, we've been trying to keep it on the down low."

"How did you meet?" Sam shoved a loaded forkful of greens into her mouth. She really didn't want to know.

A wistful look came over Miranda. "While we were in

college, at Texas State. He was studying criminal justice, and I was in the nursing program." She laughed. "We were in the same forensic anthropology class, and we started talking during the field trip to the body farm."

Sam raised her eyebrows. "The body farm?"

"Technically, it's called the Forensic Anthropology Research Facility, but all the students call it the body farm. It's out west of San Marcos, and all these people have donated their bodies to let researchers study various aspects of decomposition, to help investigators solve crimes." She laughed again. "It's so romantic, right?"

Sam couldn't help laughing too. So it was perfectly natural for Miranda and Dylan to have an intimate moment next to a corpse.

"Anyway, we really didn't start dating until I took the job at the ME's office, and we kept running into each other. One thing led to another, and"—she touched her engagement ring again—"here we are."

Sam forced a smile. She was happy for Miranda, despite her own failed relationships. "But you disagree with him on the cause of Brooke's death."

"Well, Dylan's wonderful, but he's very pragmatic. He's always thinking about what might be used as evidence in court. So it's hard to convince him about something, if you only have a hunch."

"That makes sense."

"Wait a moment …" Miranda leaned back against the cushion in the booth, looking at Sam curiously. "You're the high school friend he mentioned, the one who helped out with those investigations last year."

"Guilty as charged."

"And now you're involved in these cases. It's like you have a black cloud over you or something."

"Yeah," Sam said, thinking about the situation she now

found herself in. Two deaths, plus even more uncertainty about her future. "Maybe I do."

"But you found the evidence to prove those cases were homicides—and you identified the assailants."

"I suppose I did."

"So maybe you can figure out what happened with these deaths."

"I don't know. I think I just got lucky."

Miranda looked at Sam appraisingly. "No. You've got a knack for this."

"But I don't even know where to begin."

"You're still working with the startup, right?"

"I am."

"So look for anything that might link these deaths together."

Sam sighed. "I'll try, but it's just not clear right now."

"I know. Often these cases seem murky—until suddenly, the right bit of information comes along, and then all the pieces line up."

24

Once Sam got back to clinic, she relieved Jerry so he could eat lunch, even though there was a rush of people trying to get their physicals done on their own lunch breaks. But Sam didn't mind. The physical exams required by the Department of Transportation for commercial drivers only took a few minutes each to perform, as long as the patient didn't have any serious chronic conditions. Fortunately, this was the case for all of them that day, and Sam cleared the rooms by the time Jerry got back from lunch.

They spent the afternoon seeing a steady stream of uncomplicated follow-up visits. On days like this, when the two of them worked in tandem and everything ran smoothly, Sam really liked being at ObraCare. Everyone was smiling and polite, from the staff to the patients, and in fact, she hadn't heard any timers going off at all. The team was meshing well together, and Jill noted how good it was to have Sam there again.

An idea hit Sam as she pondered her situation. If she

could stay at this clinic, she'd be instrumental in helping the team keep those patient satisfaction scores high. She could use this angle to convince Dr. Taylor to bring her back as a full-time employee. So, during a slight lull in activity, she pulled up her email, intent on drafting a message asking for a phone call, so she could lay out this argument to her boss.

Before she got started, she saw an email from Nicole, the undergrad she'd met in Dr. Galloway's lab. Nicole had written that she'd hate to impose, but she had a ton of questions. She wanted to know if Sam was available to talk.

Poor thing. She must be devastated after Brooke's death.

Sam quickly typed out a reply that it was no imposition at all and that she'd be happy to meet. It would be better to console her in person, rather than over the phone.

Then Sam sent an email to Dr. Taylor, asking him if they could set up a call. This was also a conversation that was better to have in person, but because her boss lived and worked in Houston and only visited the clinics in Austin for performance reviews or in the event of a crisis, she'd have to take what she could get.

No sooner than she'd hit the send button, the pace picked up again, and she and Jerry didn't have another break until it was time for her to leave.

Since Nicole lived near campus and didn't have a car, Sam met with her in the courtyard between the Texas Student Union and the Undergraduate Library that evening. The two buildings had starkly contrasting styles: the library with an industrial look from the 1960s, all sharp angles and concrete, and the union, with white stone walls and red clay roof tiles, incorporating the Spanish-style

architectural elements common to most of the older buildings around campus.

Nicole sat at one of the many wrought iron tables scattered in the courtyard, a stack of books teetering next to
her laptop. "Thanks so much for meeting with me, Dr.
Jenkins."

"Not a problem. I'll take any excuse to enjoy this
weather." Sam glanced around at the other students chatting and working at the tables around them. It was a lovely
evening, with twilight shading the sky a deep indigo and
pleasant breezes rustling through the oak branches above.
She spotted an isolated table away from the crowd and
motioned to it. "Maybe we should go over there."

"Uh, sure," Nicole said. "If you think so." She closed
her laptop, then began to gather her books into her
backpack.

"Here, let me help you." Sam picked up the stack of
books, and they relocated to the secluded table. Once
they'd settled, she lowered her voice and said, "How are
you doing?"

"Oh, fine. Just a little stressed about all these classes
and studying for the MCAT, but I'm managing."

This was not the answer Sam had been expecting, but
maybe Nicole didn't want to talk about Brooke's death just
yet. She'd let Nicole open up about the loss of her friend
when she was ready.

"Anyway," Nicole went on, "like I said, I have a ton of
questions, and I really appreciate that you're here. It's just
a little overwhelming. There's all the stuff I need for my
applications, to make them as good as they can be. Then I
need to decide which schools to apply to—those application fees sure add up! And why does Texas have to have a
completely different application system? Why couldn't they
participate in AMCAS like everyone else?"

Sam smiled as she remembered having all the same concerns. It didn't seem that long ago. Plus, in addition to the anxiety of applying to medical school, she had to go through the whole process again when she applied to residency programs.

"I mean, I'll probably stay in Texas if I can, but they say you should also apply to a few out-of-state schools just in case you don't get in."

Nicole continued to ramble on for a bit, and Sam let her. Then she started asking specific questions, like what she should look for in a medical school, what case-based learning was like, and the differences between didactic courses and clinical rotations. Sam answered what she could and directed Nicole to online resources for everything else.

After about half an hour, Nicole seemed to have run through her list, then she said, "I'm so glad I met you. Brooke was right; you are awesome! I'll have to thank her for letting me know how friendly you are; otherwise, I would have never worked up the courage to ask for your help when you came to the lab that day."

A pit formed in Sam's stomach. Nicole didn't know. How should she break the news?

"When was the last time you spoke with Brooke?"

The younger woman gazed at the branches above them for a moment. "I think it was Thursday last week." Then she looked back at Sam and nodded. "That's right. It was Thursday. She wanted me to go out with her on Friday, but I had to see my parents down in San Antonio over the weekend. I ended up staying through this morning, since my brother was my ride and didn't want to leave last night." She scrunched her nose. "Thanks to him, I missed my first class, but I got back in time for organic chemistry."

"So you haven't heard?" Sam asked gingerly.

"Heard what?"

Sam repositioned herself in the clunky metal chair, wrestling with it, turning it so she could face Nicole directly. She leaned closer, softening her voice. "I don't know the best way to tell you this."

There was never a good way to tell anyone that someone close to them had died. As a resident, she'd been thrown into tough situations without any guidance, where she had to notify family members in the emergency department that a loved one had passed. She glanced around at the other students. This was too public. In the hospital, at least there were small, private consultation rooms.

"What haven't I heard?" Nicole looked worried now. "Did something happen to Brooke?"

Sam took a deep breath and put her hand on Nicole's. "There's no easy way to say this. Brooke died on Saturday."

Disbelief filled the younger woman's eyes. "What? How is that possible?"

"I'm so sorry," Sam said. "That's why I wanted to meet with you in person. I thought you already knew." She'd assumed Nicole hadn't directly mentioned it in the email because it was too painful. She rubbed the girl's arm. "I thought that's what you wanted to talk about."

Tears streamed down Nicole's face. "I just can't …" She sucked in a ragged breath. "I just can't believe it."

"Neither can I." Sam glanced around as she let the younger woman weep, looking for a tissue or something to give to her. Then she remembered there was a restroom inside the library, and she spotted it through the wall of glass in the lobby. "Just a sec."

She ran inside the stark building, into the bathroom. Of

course, there wasn't any Kleenex, only paper towel dispensers, so she entered a stall and grabbed some toilet paper. When she got back outside to Nicole, she offered the scratchy tissue.

"Sorry, this was all I could find."

Nicole accepted it and dabbed her eyes.

"How did she…What happened to her?"

"She fell from her balcony."

"No. I've been there. The railing is pretty high," Nicole said, raising her hand to the height she remembered, at the level of her chest.

"It appears that she was tending to her hanging plants with a stepladder and slipped," Sam said.

Nicole gasped. "How awful." She burst into tears again.

Sam offered a hug, and they embraced for a moment, two strangers in shared grief.

"Is there anything I can do for you?" Sam asked. Through the windows of the student union, she could see the restaurants in the food court. "Do you want something to drink?"

Nicole shook her head. "No, I'll be…I'll be okay."

The other students in the courtyard seemed oblivious to the sorrow surrounding the two women.

After a few moments, when the latest wave of grief settled, no longer washing over Nicole, she said, "What if it wasn't an accident? That other guy at the startup …"

"Erik."

"Yeah, Erik just died too, right? That seems strange, doesn't it?"

Sam nodded. "It does. But I don't know what else to do. It seems, right now, that Erik had a severe asthma exacerbation. And now this …"

"They were both young, though. How could they be

dead?" Then Nicole sat up straight. "What if it was Greg?"

Even though she'd had the same thought, Sam didn't want to speculate too much. She needed more information. "Why would he want to kill Erik? And then Brooke?"

"Greg was mad Erik got the job at the startup."

This confirmed what Lisa had said, but Sam wanted to make sure. "I thought he wanted to finish his PhD first."

"Sure, that's how he is now. But when Dr. G started looking at options for using the prototype for screening drugs, Greg was all in. He still had a ways to go on his PhD at that point, and he really didn't care about finishing it, not if he could be a founder in a startup."

"And now that Erik's dead—"

"Greg has his job."

Sam frowned. "But why would he want to kill Brooke?"

"Because she wouldn't go out with him."

"Is that reason enough to kill someone?"

"It is for some men. You've seen how he is." Nicole pouted her lips. "Grumpy Greg."

Could this really be what had happened? Perhaps, but there could always be another explanation. If someone had killed Brooke, well, the most likely person would be someone she knew.

"Was Brooke dating anyone?" Sam asked.

"She was seeing a guy, but she wouldn't tell me much about him. I kind of got the notion he was a little older." Nicole shrugged. "But Brooke wasn't taking it too seriously, since she was leaving for Chicago in a few months."

"Did she indicate how her boyfriend felt?"

"She never called him that, never thought it was significant enough to officially call him her boyfriend. Plus, she said it didn't matter how he felt because she'd be gone soon."

Sam wondered if this man had thought the relation-ship was more meaningful than Brooke had. Even though the evidence pointed to her slipping and falling off a stepladder, and the door to her condo was locked from the inside, maybe the mystery man had been there that morn-ing. And maybe he had a key.

25

Toward the end of the following day, as Sam saw patients at her old clinic, Alex sent her yet another text message. She'd been ignoring them since that awful Saturday.

Can we meet? Please?

He'd added the hands-together emoji, as if praying.

He never used emojis.

Sam still felt a tiny bit of guilt for dumping him with a single text. That was not her style. She should suck it up and at least meet him in person to tell him it was over. But he should know perfectly well why she'd broken up with him.

They'd agreed to meet at the Whole Foods downtown after Sam got off work. She'd picked the location to prevent Alex from wooing her in any possible way. A grocery store was a neutral place, with plenty of people around to keep emotions from escalating. If things didn't go well, she could just leave.

Right after Sam parked in the underground garage, she got a text from Alex. He was upstairs, on the rooftop deck.

It took some navigating to get there, up the escalator, through the store, past the line of registers. She'd only been on the rooftop once before, and she couldn't remember how she'd gotten up there. Finally, she asked one of the employees, who pointed to a small door toward the front of the building. "They're outside."

Sam paused at the foot of the concrete stairs, running up against the building, the small surface lot behind her filled with cars circling like vultures. It was her last chance. She could just text Alex, tell him that something came up and she couldn't meet with him.

But she felt like a jerk for not ending it in person.

She took a deep breath and climbed.

When she reached the top, she looked around for Alex. The deck was a surprisingly bucolic setting, despite having the backdrop of the Whole Foods corporate headquarters rising up behind it. A grove of modern, metal, tree-like sculptures stood in front of the office entrance, presumably to provide shade, but they didn't do much at this time of day. Groups of tables under the sculptures were filled with people chatting and laughing, as they unwound after the workday, not caring that the lowering sun glared in their eyes.

"Sam!"

She turned around to find Alex had claimed a pair of Adirondack chairs on a green berm, like an island in a sea of concrete, away from the rest of the tables. When she got closer, she saw the grass on the berm was fake, but the trees forming a canopy above Alex were real. A half-bottle of wine with two glasses and a small cheese plate were spread out nicely on the table in front of him. On a small stage nearby, a singer strummed away on his guitar, lamenting love lost.

Damn it. Of course, even a grocery store in Austin could be romantic.

She sighed as she stepped up onto the grass. Alex stood and tried to give her a hug, but she rebuffed his attempt by turning away.

"Look," he said as they took their seats, "I don't know what I did to piss you off, but I want you to know you mean everything to me." He reached for her hand on the armrest, but she pulled away. "I know I've been distant lately; I've let this damn board exam take over my life. But it will be over soon, and I'll be there, to give you the attention that you need…that you deserve."

Sam didn't respond, and instead, folded her arms across her chest.

Alex picked up the bottle and poured wine into each glass. "I got your favorite riesling."

He knew her tastes so well. She picked up her glass and took a sip, and the dry yet syrupy wine coated her mouth, burning slightly as it traveled down her throat. Then it seemed to just evaporate off her tongue.

She put the glass down on the table, relaxing a bit, resting her hands in her lap.

Ignoring his own glass, he leaned forward with an earnest look in his eyes. "Please, just tell me what I did wrong."

Sam crossed her arms again. Was she ready for this? She might as well get it over with, just get to the truth of the matter.

"What were you doing on Saturday morning?"

He paused for a moment, then said, "Since I had the afternoon shift, I got to the hospital early and studied in the library. It's nice and quiet, especially on the weekends."

"So, you weren't on Second Street?"

"What?" He blinked. "Oh, right. I did go there, just for

a little bit, with a friend—Leslie."

Sam narrowed her eyes. "Leslie?"

"She works at the hospital. I ran into her while I was studying; the library is next to the administration offices where she works."

"She works in administration, and she was at the hospital on a Saturday?" This sounded rather fishy.

"Yeah, she had a couple of things she needed to pick up from her office, and then she asked my opinion about a gift she wanted to buy. It was for her husband's birthday."

All the anger that had been building up, the suspicions roiling inside Sam, deflated with the word "husband."

"So, you went shopping?" Something still didn't seem right.

"I'd been studying for a while and needed a break. Leslie had picked out a shirt, but she thought Gerald—her husband—might not like it, and since I still had an hour or so before my shift started, I went with her to check it out, then she dropped me back off at the hospital."

Should she believe him? She gave him a hard stare, trying to glean any information she could from his face. He returned her gaze with nothing but openness in his features; then his eyes flashed with understanding. "Oh, you thought—" He sat back and laughed as he shook his head. "No, no. It's nothing like that. She's only a friend. I was just helping her."

Either Alex was telling the truth, or he was the best actor in the world.

Sam really couldn't tell.

They sat for a moment without speaking, surrounded by the chatter of cheerful people unwinding after work and the giggling of children running around, chasing each other. The singer had moved on to a song with a more bubbly beat.

Alex leaned closer to her and said, "You have male friends, right? You've gone shopping with them, right?"

That was true. James was one of her best friends, and she had gone shopping with him numerous times.

"And I haven't been jealous of your friendships."

That, however, was not entirely true. Alex had seemed quite jealous of Dylan when their paths had crossed before. His jealousy wasn't completely unfounded, though. Sam had been—and still was—attracted to Dylan. Maybe because she would never know what might have been.

Dylan, who'd flirted with her in English class sophomore year of high school. Dylan, who'd seemed so awkward when he asked her to homecoming that year.

Dylan, who was now engaged to Miranda.

And they seemed absolutely perfect for each other.

Alex extended his hand toward her, over the gap between the chairs, his palm up.

Did she believe him?

James had told her to dump him, that even though he was handsome as hell, he was bad news.

But then she thought back to how he was the one who had encouraged her to go out with Alex in the first place. And how Kevin had warned her not to jump to conclusions, to always presume positive intent. She certainly hated when people made the wrong assumptions about her.

Alex wiggled his fingers, beckoning her to put her hand in his.

She finally relented. He gave her a gentle squeeze, caressing the back of her hand with his thumb.

"You know I love you," he said. "You mean the world to me. Once I get the boards out of the way, things will be better."

Perhaps, but then she had no idea what was going to happen to Redew. First Erik had died, and now Brooke.

What was going on?

Alex tilted his head. "Something's still bothering you, though."

She nodded as she tried to hold back tears.

"What is it? You can tell me."

"Brooke died."

"Who?"

"Brooke. She worked at Redew. That's why I was downtown on Saturday, when I saw you. I was supposed to meet her, but she fell ..."

Alex raised his eyebrows. "Was that what all the commotion was about? Was that why there was a big crowd with the police?"

"Yes. She lived in that condo building, and she fell off her balcony."

He shook his head. "Wow. And Erik too."

"And Erik too," Sam repeated.

"Erik was a good guy," Alex said. "I liked talking to him. How much bad luck can a company have?"

"A lot, it seems." Then she went on to explain all of her personal worries, most of which he knew already. She felt bad, because they seemed so minor compared to the fact that two people had died. But these were the thoughts that crowded her mind—how Dr. Taylor hadn't responded to her email yet. How she was defective because she still hadn't finished residency. How her plan to correct everything was all shot, since she'd had to drop those MPH classes when she'd had pneumonia ...

He continued caressing her hand, his support flowing through his touch as she let it all out.

When she ran out of steam, out of the need to release her distress into the open, he said, "Everything is going to be all right. As I've said before, once I pass the boards, I'll be on track to make partner in our practice. We've got some great candidates we're interviewing to join us, and that will make my schedule in the ICU much more tolerable." He put on a big grin. "We can get married. And you won't have to worry about what's going on at Redew or ObraCare or anything else."

She started to pull her hand away. "I don't want to be a housewife or a stay-at-home mom." She shook her head. "I have all of this education. I need to use it."

He held on tight, gently squeezing her hand as he said, "You can and you will. All I'm saying is, I'll take care of you. I'll be here for you. You can pursue your dreams, and you won't have to worry."

Was he proposing to her? Now? At a grocery store?

No. He was just planning their future together.

His phone buzzed. After he checked the alert, he gave her a pained expression. "My shift starts soon, but I'd love to take you to dinner tonight, so we can reboot our relationship."

She glanced at his untouched wine on the table. He'd been hedging his bets.

"Just say the word, and I'll call in sick. You mean too much to me." He gazed into her eyes. "Will you, Samantha Jenkins, go on a date with me?"

He looked so handsome, so sincere. Even though they'd had their ups and downs, she did enjoy their time together. And when he turned on the charm, he certainly knew how to make her weak in the knees.

But did she love him?

She still wasn't sure. However, if he was the right guy for her, she'd hate to throw it all away over a misunderstanding.

She smiled at him and said, "Yes."

26

After Alex had listened to Sam, had expressed how much he cared, she felt awful for assuming the worst about him. She should have spoken with him before she'd sent her breakup text. But she still felt— what was the right word? Tepid. She felt tepid about their relationship. Why was she so resistant to settling down with him?

Maybe James was projecting, placing his anxiety, his fears over his commitment to Kevin, placing all of his worries into his opinion of Alex. And as a result, he was influencing her, causing her own feelings to be tainted.

Sam spent the next day, her third clinic day in a row, at an older location on the north side of Austin, with cramped hallways and tiny exam rooms. But she fell into a rhythm with the physician assistant who worked there, and every follow-up patient she saw was improving. She even saw a few patients whom she released from care—their treatment course complete, their injuries healed, their function back to baseline. They could now move on with their lives.

As she kept busy managing other people's problems, she rarely thought about her own. Her unease was diminishing.

The night before had been wonderful, a refreshing of her relationship with Alex. They'd left their cars at Whole Foods and strolled down the street to have dinner at Clark's Oyster Bar. The seafood had been succulent and delicious, and as they shared key lime pie for dessert, he teased her a bit about her suspicions that he'd been cheating on her. He even told her that she and Leslie should meet sometime—that he thought they'd be great friends. Then he chastised himself for bringing up the subject of marriage a few weeks before, then running off to cover a shift at the hospital. He apologized, saying he realized it had signaled the wrong message to her. "Forget my career," he'd said. "You are the most important thing to me."

If she and Alex got married, and he helped with her school loans as he promised, maybe she could slow down a little bit. She never really knew what it was like, to not be pushing to excel all the time. The only real break she'd had was after her mother had died, and she had been too devastated to enjoy it.

~

THE FOLLOWING MORNING, Sam pulled up to the startup with a more optimistic outlook, mainly for her future with Alex, even though she wasn't certain how things would turn out with Redew. The first thing she did was stop by Matt's tiny office. He was startled to see her and quickly rubbed his face, as if he were smoothing the wrinkles out of a sheet. His bloodshot eyes made him look like he'd been up for days.

"Good morning, Sam," he said with a small sniffle. "I forgot you were coming in today."

She sat in the chair opposite him. "How are you holding up?"

Matt had sent out an email to the company about Brooke's passing. Of course, the company's employees now only consisted of Greg, Whit, and himself, but he'd also included Sam, Lisa, and Dr. Galloway. He'd kept the tone very professional, as if he were addressing a large organization.

This was the first time she'd seen him in person since Brooke's death, and she'd expected him to be like he'd been after Erik's death, upset, as everyone had been, but not really affected on a personal level. However, this time, he seemed much more distressed.

"I'm doing about as well as I can," he said. "She was so young."

Sam nodded. "I'm still trying to process it too." They both were silent for a moment; then she said, "Is there anything I can do to help?"

He sat up in his chair. "As a matter of fact, I have a proposition for you: Would you be willing to take over the work Brooke was doing? We're so close with some of these VCs, I think we'll be securing our series A here pretty soon. We're almost done with diligence for two of the firms, and all signals have been positive so far."

"That's why you look so run down," Sam said.

"Is it that obvious? It's been tough. And Whit has been with his family. He says his sister—Brooke's mother—is devastated."

"No doubt. How awful it must be to lose a daughter who had so much going for her."

Matt nodded solemnly, and after a short pause, he said, "Would you be willing to help out more around here?

Brooke told me you'd been doing a lot in the lab with her already."

Sam thought through her upcoming schedule at Obra-Care. The number of days she'd been assigned for the next couple of weeks had shrunk, but she still had her regular expenses—plus a rent increase—and loan payments due. She really needed to talk to Dr. Taylor.

Matt seemed to interpret her hesitation as reluctance, so he said, "We can pay you."

She let out a brief laugh since she wasn't getting paid by Redew right now. And the promise of the riches she'd receive from her stock allocation was years down the line, if ever. "How much?"

"I can pay you what we were paying Brooke. I'd offer more, but with these VCs combing over our financials, I don't want to make too many changes. And once we secure our series A, I can bump up the options we'd include in your package when you sign on as our chief medical officer."

That would mean Sam would make about a fifth of what she made seeing patients, even as a prn physician. While it was significantly less, the amount would be enough to cover her expenses—for now. Thank goodness she lived frugally. "I still have my commitments to ObraCare." She didn't want to let on that her schedule was much lighter in the coming weeks.

Matt held up his hands. "By all means, please keep seeing patients. It adds value to what we're doing here. But on your off days, could you help out?"

She wanted to do everything she could to make this startup successful. She would do it for the memories of Erik and Brooke, to continue the work they had started, to potentially improve the lives of thousands by discovering new treatments for their conditions.

She nodded. "I'll do it."

"Wonderful," Matt said. "I'll forward the details to Lisa so we can draw up a contract for you." He made his way to the door. "Let's tell Greg."

Sam hesitated before she stood up. "He's here?"

"Yeah, he's been here the last couple of days, after he defended his dissertation on Monday."

How did she feel about Greg? He now had Erik's job, the one he'd been wanting, according to Lisa and Nicole. And he'd been spurned by Brooke. Had he killed them?

She shook her head, trying to clear her thoughts. *Don't be silly.*

Even though Miranda had suggested Sam look for anything that could possibly tie the deaths together—and Greg certainly seemed to fit the bill—she needed to be careful. Before Brooke had died, when Sam had called Miranda and said she'd suspected Greg in Erik's death, Miranda had backtracked. Would she do that again?

Having noticed Sam wasn't with him, Matt leaned back into his office. "You coming?"

She nodded and followed him. As they made their way past the cubicles and through the lab, Matt carried on about how everything was going to be fine, how they'd only had a small setback—of course, these deaths were tragic, but they weren't related to the work at Redew, and they had a solid foundation for their platform technology. He glanced at her a couple of times to check her reaction, as if he were trying to give her a pep talk, but it seemed he was the one who really needed it.

When they entered the fly room, Greg was hunched over a microscope counting flies. The place had gotten much messier in the week since Sam had last been there. Bottles of reagents were strewn on the counters along with trays of flies, pipette tips, and assorted papers. And the smell of yeast was even more dank than usual.

Sam sighed. Maybe this wasn't such a good idea.

"She said yes," Matt announced.

Greg looked up and grunted.

"Well, I'll leave you to it," Matt said, glancing at his watch. "I've got just enough time to get ready for my next call."

He disappeared, leaving Sam and Greg alone.

"Congratulations on defending your dissertation," she said. "How did it go?"

Greg turned back to the microscope, ignoring her, and resumed counting and sorting.

Sam sighed again, then stood by quietly. *Maybe he doesn't want to lose his count, so he needs to concentrate*, she told herself. When he scooped up the separated flies into two vials, she said, "What do you need—"

He cut her off by holding up a finger, then he pulled another vial of flies out of the tray and began assessing them.

Sam continued to wait a minute more, but after he failed to acknowledge her, she left the lab, deciding to sit in an empty cubicle. She had several articles she wanted to read anyway—there was always more to learn—and if Greg was too busy to talk to her right now, he could come get her if she was needed.

She was deep into reading a journal article entitled "Drug screening in *Drosophila*; why, when, and when not?" written by a researcher at the University of Colorado, when she felt a presence next to her.

"Do you know how to handle the flies?" Greg asked.

And hello to you too, Sam thought. "Yes, Erik and Brooke showed me, and I took a genetics lab in undergrad. We had a similar setup to what you've got here."

Greg nodded, then went back into the lab.

She supposed he wanted her to help. Maybe he wanted her to read his mind as well. She marked her place in the article, stood, and returned to the fly room.

"Where are the flies you'd like me to count?" she asked.

Greg pulled a tray off the shelf on the far wall and handed it to her. He sat back down at his microscope and motioned to the free scope next to him. "You can use this one."

Of course she could use that one; what other microscope was she going to use? There were only two in the tiny room. She considered the irony of the situation, that she'd been working in this lab, with these flies, and on these experiments, much more than he had. But it was his show now, and she needed to follow his lead.

"How do you want me to record the results?" she asked. When Sam had helped Brooke, she'd written down the counts on Post-its and given them to Brooke to document. It just made things more consistent, since Sam could only show up to help occasionally.

Greg huffed as he put down his pen. "Just put it in Brooke's notebook. She should have the fly lots listed from when she did the cross. The phenotypes and linked genes should be in there."

"Do you know where it is?"

"Isn't it at her desk?" he asked, and then he turned back to his microscope.

Sam sighed as she got up and left the lab to search Brooke's cubicle. She stood there for a second, looking at the personal items she hadn't paid attention to before. Maybe she should box these things up and give them to Brooke's parents, as she'd done for Erik's.

One of the pictures on the desk was a group photo of the members of Dr. Galloway's lab, including the professor,

Brooke, Nicole, and several other people. Greg was at one end, not looking at the camera, but looking sideways—to the end where Brooke stood.

Sam didn't see a notebook sitting anywhere, so she started pulling open the drawers. No notebook, just various office-related items: pens, pencils, scissors, a stapler.

When she got back to the fly room, Greg was leaning over his microscope as before, ignoring her. She looked around and saw a stack of lab notebooks on one of the shelves. She picked up the one on top. It was Brooke's, and it appeared to be the most current notebook, based on the dating scheme.

It was organized just as Erik's had been and was just as neat, with the main exception that Brooke's handwriting was a little larger, with more loops, more feminine.

Sam flipped to the middle of the notebook, where the entries ended, and found documentation of the most recent crosses Brooke had performed with tables already set up to evaluate the progeny.

She returned to the available microscope, then picked up the vials in the tray Greg had given her, verifying the lot numbers matched what Brooke had written in the notebook. They did.

She sat down and wheeled her chair forward, flipping on the lamp for the microscope. She twisted the valve for the line connected to the fly pad, allowing a low flow of carbon dioxide to permeate through the ceramic plate, but then she remembered she was doing things in the wrong order. She disconnected the tubing from the plate, then inserted it into the vial, sliding it alongside the cotton, making sure to keep the vial sideways so the flies didn't drop into the goopy food at the bottom once they were knocked out.

"What are you doing?" Greg barked, causing Sam to jump.

"I'm anesthetizing the flies so I can count them."

"This is a better way."

Greg rolled closer, so she scooted back to give him space. He turned off the carbon dioxide line, pulled out the tube, and reconnected it to the fly plate. The flies in the vial had already been knocked out, so he turned on the flow again and dumped the tiny insects onto the white ceramic disc.

"Next time, use this to knock them out," he said, holding up a separate line teed off from the tank line strapped along the back wall. "That way, you don't have to keep disconnecting the line from the plate. It reduces fatigue on the tubing and prevents it from cracking and leaking."

Greg had a point. Even though he appeared rather sloppy and disorganized, it seemed he did pay attention to at least some important details. Sam hadn't known about the separate line; otherwise, she'd have used it.

He frowned at her. "Why were you doing it that way?"

"That's how we did it when I took my genetics lab, and that's how Brooke did it."

"Well, she isn't here anymore, is she?" he snapped. He turned back to his scope again.

Sam closed her eyes for a beat, taking in a deep breath. Then she gingerly scooped the unconscious flies back into their vial, placed it back into the tray, and turned off the gas and the microscope lamp.

She didn't have to take his horrible attitude.

Sure, she'd been excited when she'd agreed to be an advisor, and she'd hoped Matt would be successful securing funds so she could hire on full time. Erik had been nice, and Brooke had been pleasant. Sam would gladly have joined their team.

But Greg was…well, grumpy.

"Look," she said as she stood. "I don't need to be here. I'm just trying to help. If you're going to be an ass about it, I'll tell Matt that I'm out."

Greg didn't even look at her. He just kept looking through the optics on the microscope in front of him.

Fine. He can deal with everything by himself.

She went to the door and opened it.

"Wait."

Sam turned around.

Greg hunched his shoulders, like a schoolboy in time out. He looked down at his lap as he picked at the bottom of his shirt. "I know I'm not the nicest guy…or the easiest to get along with."

You can say that again.

"And I'm being thrown into the middle of this. Sure, I've been doing this type of research for years." He motioned toward the larger space on the other side of the wall. "And hell, I built most of that prototype out there. But now I'm trying to piece together what Erik had done, what he'd been working on, and what his plans were. Matt said it's very important that we keep moving forward with what Erik had started, at least until we get funding. Then he said I could start some of my own projects, as long as they look promising." He sighed. "And Brooke…she knew some of Erik's plans, but not all of them. She was going to …"

He hung his head and was quiet.

Sam came back over to the chair she'd been sitting in, amazed that Greg was opening up. This was more than she'd ever heard him say before. He seemed to be letting his guard down. At least a little.

She sat there, watching him, his profile fixed, hard to read. But she thought she could see pain, anguish.

After a few moments, he went on. "I talked to her last week, and she was going to help me figure it out, as best as she could. But now she's…gone."

He continued staring at his lap.

"You liked her, didn't you?" Sam said.

Greg didn't look up, but his ears turned pink.

"I'm sorry. I shouldn't have pried."

He shook his head slightly, muttering, "It's okay."

"Well, maybe I can help. I'm not a PhD, and all I had was a couple of genetics classes in undergrad, but I'm not just some random person off the street. We could work together to determine what we need to do."

Greg sat up, looking at her like a wounded dog, glad someone was giving him another chance. "That would be nice."

27

G reg and Sam spent the rest of the morning in the conference room, going over Erik's and Brooke's notebooks, putting aside the need to evaluate the progeny of the crosses that had already been performed for the time being. Sam gently convinced Greg it would be worth their while to gain a better understanding of where things were than to keep moving forward without a road map.

They used the whiteboard to organize their thoughts, making lists of the experiments that had been completed along with their results. They also pulled data from Greg's old notebook, comparing his results with those of the newer experiments, trying to decipher what Erik had learned.

Greg seemed quite grateful for Sam's patience with him, and when he asked her if they should get lunch together, Sam had to decline; she'd made plans to meet Alex for lunch at the hospital after their reconciliation. Greg looked crestfallen when Sam mentioned her boyfriend, and he nodded his head in a knowing way, the way someone who focuses too much on academics does, someone who doesn't think socializing is necessary, until, one day, they wake up and realize they're alone.

She was torn, because she thought they'd made a lot of progress, and if she were free, she definitely would have had lunch with him, especially since he was beginning to lower his always-angry facade. He knew what he was talking about, despite the rough and bedraggled exterior.

Sam arrived at the hospital garage and parked, and as she entered the building, she heard her name.

Miranda approached from the opposite side of the lobby, near the gift shop.

"Funny how we keep meeting, isn't it?" the investigator said with a smile. "Are you here for lunch with your boyfriend again?"

"Yeah. We'll grab a bite in the cafeteria."

"Sounds romantic."

They both laughed, then Sam asked, "And I take it you're here for a case?"

Miranda patted her satchel. "Yup. Just being thorough, gathering records and such." Then she looked more serious. "You might as well know; it looks like the ME is going to close the cases for Erik and Brooke."

"Then I guess it was just a horrible coincidence."

Miranda shrugged. "We're still waiting on the labs for Brooke's case, and even if anything shows up, the ME will just say she was impaired, and that contributed to her fall."

"And he still thinks the low IgE level in Erik's blood doesn't mean anything?"

"Dr. Duveneck said that's not always a reliable indicator. And he said the whole duck thing."

"Duck thing?"

"You know," Miranda began, "if it walks like a duck and it quacks like a duck—"

"Then it must be a duck," Sam finished.

"He complained that young people are always looking for zebras."

Sam knew that old adage in medicine was often true: When you hear hoofbeats, think horses not zebras, meaning that common things are common, like horses, and rare things are rare, like zebras—here in the US anyway. So the most likely diagnosis is usually the actual diagnosis, not the rare condition that medical students and residents have only read about in a textbook.

"Regardless," Miranda said, "Dr. Duveneck gets the final say. The extra tests he ordered on Erik's blood should be back soon, but he doesn't think it will have any impact on his determination. It will only provide a definitive cause if the level of one of the compounds is elevated, that it was the one that triggered his asthma attack."

"Well, I guess that's it, isn't it?" Sam said.

Miranda nodded. "But I enjoyed having lunch the other day."

"Me too," Sam said with a smile. "Let's do it again soon."

"What about Saturday? If you're free, that is. Dylan will be working."

"That's funny, so will Alex. What do you have in mind?"

They hashed out plans to go kayaking before saying goodbye. As Miranda walked away, Sam saw Alex's familiar figure down a side hallway. There were plenty of doctors in scrubs and white coats bustling around, but she knew it was him from his sandy blond hair. She hurried to catch up to him and was about to call his name when she realized he was not alone. He was with the same woman he'd been with the day Brooke died.

It was just a work friendship, he'd said. He was helping her pick out a gift for her husband, he'd said.

She was dressed for the office, wearing a cream blouse with a navy pencil skirt and matching pumps, her hair up in a twist. The glint of a diamond wedding ring flashed on the woman's left hand as Sam got closer.

So, he was telling the truth—at least the part about her being married.

As they approached the stairwell closest to the ICU entrance one floor above, Sam expected Alex would leave the woman to go upstairs. Instead, he kept walking down the hallway with her.

Sam followed.

She stayed a safe distance behind, trying to blend in with the other hospital staff and visitors, tracking them through a few turns, until, on a less-crowded corridor, they entered through a door. Sam approached as the door closed, and she caught a glimpse through the door's window of Alex and the woman entering an interior office behind an admin sitting at a desk. Stenciled on the window was the word "Payroll."

So Alex was telling the truth about that as well.

Sam walked past the office suite, then stopped. What should she do?

Maybe nothing. Maybe Alex was being completely honest with her, and she was just being paranoid.

She could act like she hadn't seen anything. Just go upstairs and wait for Alex.

Maybe she would mention it. Maybe not.

As her mind raced through what she should do, what the possible consequences of each action would be, she heard the door open, and she jumped. It was the admin she'd seen in the office.

"Can I help you?" the admin asked.

Sam smiled and stepped closer to the woman, who seemed pretty no-nonsense. "I think I'm lost. I'm trying to find the ICU." She could now see through the window into the office suite. The door behind the admin's desk was closed.

The admin pointed down the corridor, toward the direction from which Sam had come. "These hallways can be like a maze," she said, and she gave Sam instructions, telling her where to turn and where not to turn, making things more confusing if Sam had actually been paying attention.

Instead, Sam's concentration was on the interior office door.

It opened, and Alex appeared.

The woman's hand snaked up his shoulder, wedding ring gleaming, and caressed his face.

The admin stopped talking when she noticed Sam wasn't listening to her anymore. She followed Sam's gaze into the office and sighed.

Alex moved around the admin's desk toward the hallway, keeping his focus over his shoulder on the woman, who now appeared in her office doorway, slightly disheveled, her blouse untucked from her skirt on one side. Once she noticed the admin and Sam, her face flushed.

Alex registered the woman's look and turned around.

Anger flashed on his face when he saw Sam.

He opened the hallway door and said, "What are you doing here?"

Sam narrowed her eyes, fury rising in her chest. "I should be the one asking *you* that question."

The phone rang on the admin's desk, and she excused herself as she squeezed past Alex through the doorway. She looked relieved, and Sam didn't know if it was because she had a reason to remove herself from the situation or because now she wasn't the only one who knew of the tryst.

Perhaps a little bit of both.

"You wanted me to meet Leslie sometime. I'm sure this isn't what you had in mind."

Alex blinked a few times, the initial anger in his features melting into contriteness. He stepped closer to her, holding out his arms. "It's not what you think."

"Of course it isn't." Sam glanced through the window as she backed away from him. Leslie had tucked in her blouse and smoothed her hair, but the blush of embarrassment remained. "You always have an answer for everything."

"Can we just talk about it?"

"There's nothing to talk about," Sam said and walked away.

28

When Sam got back to Redew, Greg was sitting in one of the cubicles, eating tacos.

"Back so soon?" he asked, his voice muffled by a mouthful of food.

"Yeah." She walked past him to the empty cubicle where she'd left her things.

He rolled his chair back so he could peer around the fabric wall, a curious look on his face. "Everything okay?"

"Not really."

"Want to talk about it?"

What, does he think we are best friends now? "Not really," Sam said again.

"Did you eat?" He held up a foil-wrapped bundle. "I've got an extra taco if you want it."

"No thanks. I'm not hungry." She glanced over at Matt's office, hoping to find a distraction, anything to avoid conversing with Greg, but the door was closed.

"Well, I'll save it for you just in case," Greg said as he gathered up the remnants of his lunch. "I'll put it in the fridge."

"That's okay," Sam said. "Really, you can have it. You don't need to save it for me."

He shrugged. "I got it to eat later, but it's here if you want it." He went into the breakroom.

Why is he being nice to me?

She watched him through the doorway as he put the taco away, rinsed out his mug, and brewed a cup of coffee with the Keurig machine.

As he turned to look at her over his shoulder, she quickly swiveled her chair to face the desk and began flipping through her pile of papers.

Even though Miranda had told her there was no evidence to indicate foul play and the ME was closing the cases, it just seemed unlikely for the deaths of two people who knew each other, who worked together at a small company, who died only weeks apart, to be a coincidence. There must be a connection. In her mind, Greg still seemed to have the strongest motive for Erik's death, and there was always the possibility that his yearning for Brooke may have turned into a deadly obsession.

Maybe it hadn't been pain she'd seen in his face when he'd spoken about Brooke earlier that morning. Maybe it was anger.

The machine spewed out the last drops of steaming brew, filling the whole office with the scent of java.

"Want a cup?" Greg stood in the doorway of the breakroom, holding his mug up with an earnest smile.

Of course, maybe he was nothing more than a bashful, geeky guy who was socially awkward, and Sam's mind was looking for conspiracies where there were none.

Why was she expecting the worst in everyone?

Because of Alex.

She needed to move on from everything that had happened. Since Matt had told her he was close to getting

a term sheet from at least one VC, she could end up
working a lot more with Greg. What a great way to start a
working relationship, believing Greg was a murderer.

"Sure." She returned his smile. "Thanks."

He went back into the breakroom, grabbed a mug
from the cabinet above the machine, and popped in
another capsule.

Sam stood and went to the doorway as the machine's
pump wound up to brew another cup. "So, I was thinking
about Erik's notes. It seems the results from the Huntington's compound are somewhat inconsistent."

"Yeah, Brooke was saying something about that last
week. And I think that's probably true. I know Matt and
Whit are keen on finding a treatment for one of these rare
neurodegenerative disorders, especially since we could fast-
track everything through the FDA with an orphan drug
status." He shrugged. "But if they don't work, they don't
work. I'm confident, once we get my prototype working
again, that we'll find other drug candidates for other
diseases."

They took their cups into the conference room to
continue poring over the notebooks. They had a pretty
good tag team going, with Greg reading out the disease
model and drug used in each experiment, and Sam adding
the information to the growing table on the whiteboard.

After about half an hour, as they were pausing to go
over the data listed in front of them, looking for patterns to
elucidate what, if anything, Erik had discovered—and ultimately, whether or not he'd been on the path to replicating
Greg's results—she could hear Matt through the wall.

He'd seemed so exuberant that morning, but now his
voice was raised and had a hint of urgency in it.

Sam couldn't make out the exact words he was saying.
She glanced at Greg, but he seemed oblivious.

She closed her eyes for a moment, taking in a deep breath. *Stop expecting the worst.*

Matt was probably talking to someone about an issue completely unrelated to the business.

Greg flipped through Erik's notebook, looking back and forth between it and the whiteboard. "Okay, I think we've got all of the stocks listed. And all of the drug candidates."

He compared everything with the spreadsheet on his laptop. "And, of course, Erik was meticulous, so everything is documented correctly here as well. But I'm not seeing—"

Just then, a thump came from Matt's office. His door banged open, and he stormed out, rushing past the cubicles.

From where Sam sat in the conference room, she couldn't see where he went, but she thought he'd gone down the hallway to the restroom because she heard a door slamming shut.

Sam and Greg looked at each other.

"What's that about?" Sam asked, a pit forming in her stomach.

"Dunno," Greg said. "Bad taco?" He turned back to the spreadsheet. "Okay. The list of conditions Erik eliminated includes ALS, spinal muscular atrophy, and Batten disease. But there's a comment next to Huntington's made by Matt. It says to follow up with the Huntington Foundation."

They were discussing what this could mean, when Matt materialized at the door. It appeared he had scrubbed his face while he'd been in the restroom, his face pink, his hair slicked back, and he wore a smile, but it didn't come up to his eyes.

"Everything okay?" Sam asked.

"Uh…well …"

"Hey, Matt," Greg said, clicking on his trackpad, "what's this about a grant from the Huntington Foundation?"

Matt sucked in a breath, then nodded. "Yes, Whit suggested we apply for one of their grants."

"But, based on these results," Greg said, "it appears that the studies using the Huntington models did not yield hits from any of the drug libraries. Not even the one candidate I thought I'd found."

"Erik told me about that. He updated the foundation with those results, and we had to withdraw our application." Matt slumped his shoulders. "It was a shame too. The award would have given us more time to raise funds… and it looks like our time might be running out." He mumbled the last part, but it perked up Sam's ears.

"What was that?" she asked.

Matt sighed and shook his head slowly, as if he wanted to be anywhere else but here. "They passed."

"Who did?"

"The VCs."

"All of them?"

"All of them," Matt confirmed. "Apparently, they got wind of Brooke's demise, and they got cold feet—so they passed."

Greg looked up. "But she was leaving in a few months anyway."

"I know," Matt said, "and I told them that, but they almost seemed superstitious. As if we're cursed." He looked directly at Greg. "It took everything I had after Erik died to convince them that we weren't dead in the water, that you were the perfect replacement for Erik, that you came out of Dr. Galloway's lab and were practically a co-founder. And the *only* reason you hadn't joined us full-time is that you wanted to complete your PhD."

Greg's chest puffed up a bit when Matt said he'd practically been a co-founder of the company, but Sam's mind raced to figure out what this all meant.

"They're skittish," Matt said. "With two deaths…even though they weren't directly related to our company …"

"So, are you telling us that this company has to shut down?" she asked.

"Not immediately," Matt said. "We have enough runway to last through the end of summer, but the lead time to convince another VC to invest in us is considerable." He ran his hands through his hair. "I don't think it's possible."

Greg muttered to himself, something about post-docs and recruiters, and the first thought in Sam's mind was that she should call Dr. Taylor.

From his office, Matt's cell phone started playing "Eye of the Tiger," and his face brightened a touch. "I left a message for Whit—that should be him. Maybe he'll have some ideas."

He disappeared from the doorway. His voice sounded hopeful as he answered, but then it became muted as he closed the door to his office.

Sam tried to steady her breath. It would be okay. She would just call Dr. Taylor and explain the situation. He'd been supportive of her in the past, but would he be again?

Greg tapped away on his laptop, lost in a fugue.

She stared at the whiteboard. They'd figured out a lot that day, and some of the results were promising. It was too bad it would never come to fruition.

After a few minutes of silence, she heard the door to Matt's office open, and he appeared at the doorway again, this time looking a little less pessimistic.

"What did Whit say?" Sam asked.

"Well, he said that's just how things are in the startup world." He took a deep breath. "But he also said there are always options, and when he gets back from Dallas tomorrow, we'll come up with a strategy." He nodded as if he were trying to convince himself more than anyone. "Whit said, 'Don't lose hope.'"

29

The mood in the conference room remained dour, despite Matt's attempts to cheer Sam and Greg up. He repeatedly reminded them that Redew still had some cash in the bank and to remember that Whit had successfully helped other startups in similar situations. He eventually lost steam, however, as if he'd not even convinced himself to remain optimistic, and retreated to his office.

Greg had returned to his grumpy state, all traces of the more positive side of his personality vanishing, which was fine by Sam. She didn't feel like talking much, either, and they spent the rest of the afternoon in the lab, silently counting flies.

The next morning, Sam showed up at her old clinic as she had done earlier in the week, bright and early at 8:00 a.m. She was surprised when she got to the work area. Anita Cresswell was also there.

"It's good to see you again," Anita said, "but I thought you were covering Jerry's shift."

Sam shook her head. "No, I usually come in first."

"Huh." Anita checked her email, clicking and scrolling for a few moments. Then she said, "Yeah, the schedule has me here now, and you're supposed to come in at ten."

Sam peered over the other doctor's shoulder to look at the screen, and sure enough, she'd gotten the times mixed up, which was annoying. That meant she'd be staying until 7:00 p.m., and she'd promised Greg she'd help him at Redew after work since they didn't process as many flies as they'd needed to the day before. She'd just have to let him know.

"Okay, no big deal," Sam said, even though she was mentally kicking herself. If she'd known—and it was really *her* fault for not double-checking the schedule—she could have gone to Redew before her shift directly from her apartment. But it was all the way on the north side of town, and with traffic, by the time she got there, she'd have maybe fifteen minutes in the lab before she'd have to return to the clinic in time for her shift. Hardly worth the effort.

"Why don't you go chill out for a while?" Anita said with a smile. "No need to be here if you don't have to be."

Sam took a deep breath. "Yeah, I suppose I can do that."

There was a Starbucks on the other side of the freeway where she could hang out. And there were always more research articles to read, so it wouldn't be a total waste of time. But her enthusiasm for learning had diminished the day before—if Redew went under, what was the point?

She gathered up her purse and stopped by the front office before she left. Jill sat at her desk, typing away on her computer, with a window looking out over the lobby just behind her monitor.

Sam rapped on the doorframe. Now was her opportunity to get Jill's take on whether she had a chance of getting her old job back.

"You got a minute?"

Jill looked up. "Hey. I thought you weren't coming in until later."

"Yeah, I didn't check the schedule, so I came in too early. I'll just hang out at Starbucks for a bit."

"Sounds like a plan. But you seem like you need something—how can I help you?" As the clinic operations director, Jill always had an upbeat attitude. It helped when dealing with angry patients.

"Well, I was wondering—" Sam began.

"Sorry to interrupt," Cynthia said as she appeared next to Sam, "but there's a patient on the phone who wants to talk to you. He's upset about the results of his drug test. Says we screwed up and cost him his job."

Jill closed her eyes and took a deep breath. "Okay. What line?"

"Line 3," Cynthia said.

"Got it." Jill punched the appropriate button on the phone next to her monitor, then hesitated before she picked up, giving Sam an apologetic look. "Can we talk later?"

"Of course," Sam said.

She turned to go out the back door, but Cynthia stopped her. "Dr. Cresswell asked if you wouldn't mind staying; there are three new injuries who just checked in."

Sam nodded. "Sure." At least taking care of these patients would keep her mind off all her worries.

She made her way back to the work area, tucked her purse in a drawer next to her computer, and donned her white coat.

Anita came around the corner from an exam room, stopping at the whiteboard to note that X-rays were needed for the patient she'd just seen. She glanced over her shoulder and said, "Oh, good. The MA found you. Thanks for staying. It looks like we're about to get slammed."

"Not a problem," Sam said.

Anita hurried off to the next room just as Cynthia brought back one of the new injuries. He was a middle-aged man who was limping and had his left foot wrapped in a towel. Another man, wearing tan work clothes that matched the patient's, supported him as they followed Cynthia into one of the procedure rooms.

"Hi, I'm Dr. Jenkins," Sam said as she joined them in the room. She peered over Cynthia's shoulder to see her new patient's name on the face sheet of the chart. "And I take it you're Mr. Toffler?"

The patient winced as he nodded, then settled down into the procedure chair.

Sam bent over his injured foot as Cynthia adjusted the controls to raise his legs. "Tell me what happened."

"I was using a pressure washer on a job this morning, and the damn thing slipped. Cut my shoe and right into my foot."

"Okay, let's take a look," Sam said as she gingerly removed the towel. "Are you allergic to any medications?"

Mr. Toffler shook his head.

"Any issues with drugs like ibuprofen or Aleve? And would you have any concerns about receiving an injection?"

He shook his head again in response to each question.

"Let's start with a shot of ketorolac for your pain," she said as she nodded at Cynthia.

She returned Sam's nod and left the room.

Once Sam had removed the towel, she found Mr. Toffler's foot was swollen and red with a small, round puncture wound just above his third and fourth toes, as if someone had stabbed him with an ice pick.

"Those pressure washers can be pretty powerful," Sam said.

"I'll say," Mr. Toffler's coworker said. "Strip paint off a car if you ain't careful."

Sam spent the next couple of hours working up Mr. Toffler along with the other new injuries, while Anita saw the regularly scheduled patients. Finally, right before lunch, there was a lull, and they could stop and take a breath.

For once, Sam was glad she'd made a mistake. If she'd actually checked the schedule the previous night, if she'd come in when she was supposed to, she'd have arrived only an hour before, with Anita trying to juggle everything herself. They'd be scrambling to catch up, dealing with angry patients and complete chaos.

"Thanks so much for staying this morning," Anita said. Then she lowered her voice. "Honestly, I'm not always sure what to do with some of these new injuries. I'm glad you were around."

It made sense. Most of the occupational injuries they saw were musculoskeletal in nature, along with a few lacerations and injection trauma, like Sam had seen that morning. Not the usual types of cases for obstetricians.

Fortunately, Sam had started working at ObraCare in Houston, where most of the clinics were larger, with multiple physicians scheduled regularly to support the patient volume. She learned a lot of what she needed to know from them; plus, she'd always had backup. But even then, some of the other docs hadn't known what to do.

In fact, on one particular Monday morning, a patient had come in with a subungual hematoma, a big blood blister under his toenail. He'd been seen by a semiretired family doc the Friday before because he'd dropped a gas canister right on his foot, smashing it. While the other doctor had at least taken X-rays to make sure the toe was not broken, he'd done nothing to relieve the buildup of blood under the toenail, allowing the throbbing pressure to swell.

So, the poor guy had suffered the entire weekend, until Sam relieved his agony. It had only taken a few seconds— she'd burned a small hole in the nail, releasing the blood and abolishing his pain.

"Why the hell didn't the other doctor do that?" her patient said with a mixture of relief and frustration.

Sam didn't have an answer, but she knew that some doctors could be skittish about these types of injuries and were loath to perform even minor procedures like this.

Anita was an OB, a surgeon, so she'd be fine.

Sam smiled at her. "Don't worry, most of these injuries aren't very difficult to treat. And if anyone is seriously hurt, they go to the ER first. It's not like you're dealing with complicated pregnancies. By the way, how are your interviews going?"

Anita's eyes lit up. "I guess you haven't heard; I've been offered the job here."

Sam blinked a few times. "Oh," was all she could say.

Anita didn't seem to notice Sam's reaction because she went on. "After I interviewed with a few OB practices here in Austin, I thought about it for a long time. Of course, they all need new docs because there's a big influx of patients. But I'd be low man on the totem pole, so I'd have to take more call than the senior partners. Then it hit me last week—I realized I kind of like working here."

Sam could certainly see how practicing at ObraCare would be much better than the stressful life of an OB.

"So I talked it over with my hubby. We'd love to start a family soon, and if I kept practicing OB…well, that would be…difficult. And then, once we have kids and they're in school, being an OB would make it really hard for me to be around for all those important moments, you know?"

"Makes sense." Sam forced a smile. "Congratulations."

Anita was right. For a doctor, the hours for seeing occupational medicine patients with no call were ideal. It was pretty much like working a corporate job. Unless, of course, you got sick. And they told you there was no one to cover for you.

Sam had half a mind to warn Anita off, to let her know that things weren't as rosy as they seemed, but then would she be doing this for purely altruistic reasons?

"Thank you," Anita gushed. "Since you used to work here, is there anything I should watch out for?"

Sam shook her head.

30

Sam worked through the rest of the day, truly focusing on her patients, more so than usual. She was a hollow shell, filling herself with her patients' concerns, helping them find the resources they needed, so she wouldn't have to face her own difficulties.

But as the number of patients churning through the clinic dwindled, and most of the staff left to go home, leaving a skeletal crew, Sam's turmoil resurfaced.

The full impact of her decisions over the previous two months slammed into her, with the last blow coming when Anita cheerfully said goodbye, along with "Thanks for all your help!"

Thanks for all your help! Sam ruminated on this line. She was the help, just filling in. This was not her clinic anymore.

The final two hours dragged on. She wished a flood of patients would come in to distract her. But there was only one—a man who needed a respirator fit test. Something the medical assistant didn't need a doctor for, and so Sam had all too much time to herself.

Things were definitely over with Alex. And his promises of marriage, of taking care of her, which would solve her employment issues—those were gone. But she didn't really want that anyway. What he'd wanted was a kept woman, someone to take care of him and provide him with offspring just like him.

She texted Lisa, asking if they could talk, and her friend replied that she was tied up for a few hours, but she would give Sam a call later that evening. Since Lisa had floated the idea that Sam could be an advisor to a portfolio of health-related startups, maybe that was an avenue she should pursue more aggressively.

Plus, she could just keep working as a float for Obra-Care and get back to her MPH studies. There was no reason why she couldn't continue on the course she'd been on before she'd gotten pneumonia. Heck, she should also look into applying to family medicine residencies, especially since she'd seen so many articles about the need for primary care doctors.

Every year, numerous family medicine programs had residency positions that went unfilled, mainly in rural parts of the country. When possible, these spots were gladly taken by foreign medical graduates, looking to get a start in the United States. American medical students, on the other hand, usually sought out residency training in larger urban areas, along with all the conveniences of city life. And many of them wanted careers in specialties with the potential to make more money, specialties with training only available at large academic medical centers, specialties like dermatology or plastic surgery.

But Sam didn't need any of that, and family medicine, maybe being a true country doctor, suddenly seemed appealing to her. Seeing patients from birth to death, through all the ups and downs of life, being a doctor who could treat anything. Why hadn't she considered it before? She spent the remainder of her shift researching these programs, and by the time she left the clinic, she was feeling a little more optimistic about her future.

She needed to talk to someone, though, to make sure she was doing the right thing, to make sure she wasn't just acting out of despair.

James. He was always there for her, always looking out for her, always providing clarity when her mind was muddled. After she drove home and parked her car, she went straight to his apartment, something she'd done a thousand times.

He welcomed her in, and they plopped down on his couch, with Sam turning toward her dear friend, tucking her legs under her. Then she let it all spill out. The uncertain future of the startup, her own certainty that she'd lost her old job for good, and, finally, what had happened with Alex.

"I hate to tell you I told you so…but …" James said.

Sam hung her head. "I know, I know."

"Sure, I nudged you into going out with him, even though you were reluctant. I thought it was just because you were still skittish after what happened with Jeff."

The mention of Jeff sent confounding waves of emotion through her, a mixture of anger, frustration, and heartbreak. He'd been her fiancé until…well, until she realized he didn't respect her.

"You're right, I was skittish because of that," Sam said, "but I also knew Alex's reputation, and I could have kept things more casual with him."

"No." James patted her arm. "I should have listened when you told me, not teased you and pushed you."

"That's okay. You thought he'd changed. It's what I'd thought too." She picked up her phone and scrolled through her texts. "Get this—he sent me a long message trying to justify his actions, saying 'a man has needs,' that he was just 'getting it out of his system,' and he really does love me and still wants to marry me. Like that's supposed to win me over." She tossed her phone aside. "Scumbag."

As she balled herself up on the couch, James leaned over and embraced her protectively. "I'm so sorry."

"It's not your fault."

"But I'm a man"—he leaned back and took her hands—"so I'm apologizing on behalf of all men; we *can* be scumbags sometimes. However, not all men are as scumbaggy as Alex. Some of us can be a little more sensitive." He squeezed. "Plus, I'm just sorry you went through this and you're feeling this way."

"Thanks, James." She squeezed his hands back and took a deep breath. Enough moping. She untucked her legs and sat up. "Now I need to figure out what to do with my life."

"Don't we all?" He smiled. "But you've always got options. I mean, look what I've cobbled together."

"That's true," Sam said. And that's when she looked around the room and noticed the boxes.

She'd been so absorbed in her own problems that she hadn't paid attention to her surroundings.

James's apartment was in a transition state. The shelves under his TV were bare, save for a few straggling cables, and brown cardboard boxes were stacked in the corner.

She slumped back on the couch, the trace of enthusiasm she'd captured escaping from her like air from a balloon. "You're packing."

"Yeah. Gotta get out by the end of the month. They've already leased this place to someone else."

"Figures. Everything's going to hell, and my best friend is leaving."

"I'm not leaving. I'll just be a few more minutes away. We can still hang out."

"But it's different," she said. "Because you and Kevin are more serious now." She stood and moved toward the door. "I should go."

"No, don't." He followed her, then gently grabbed her hand to stop her. "You know, I could use some help packing. Kevin's coming by to take some of these boxes to his place. Then we can all grab dinner together."

"I'd be a third wheel."

"You're never a third wheel." James looked directly at her, his eyes full of concern. "I don't think you should be alone right now. What will you do if you leave?"

"Go home and mope."

"Exactly. Help out a friend instead." He smiled. "That's what you do best."

She sucked in a deep breath and nodded. "Okay. I'll stay."

They worked for a while, loading up boxes, occasionally pausing to share a photo or trinket, relishing the memories they brought back from childhood, when times were much less complicated.

After they'd been at it for about half an hour, Sam's phone buzzed. It was Lisa.

She went out onto the balcony to get some fresh air and rehashed everything all over again. Lisa listened as she ran through her concerns about the startup and the situation she was in, about to be unemployed.

Her friend, in her practical way, calmed Sam a bit when she said, "I've seen startups in similar situations, and you never know when things will turn around. It's a rollercoaster ride, so it's not over until it's over. Those guys are right; don't lose hope."

"Okay, but I feel so out of control. And what do I do if a miracle doesn't happen?"

"Well, I agree that putting all your eggs in one basket has great risk, but if you don't give it a chance, you can miss out on the reward. That's why our law firm looks for many baskets. I do know of a couple of other startups that may be interested in having you advise them. However, it will take time to set up some meetings. Can you hang in there?"

"I guess."

"Good."

Suddenly, Sam felt selfish. Here she was, worried about things that seemed minor compared to Lisa's loss. How was she doing?

"I'm okay," Lisa replied to her inquiry. "But I heard the ME is closing the case, that his final determination is that Erik died from severe asthma. Does that make sense to you? And then that poor girl's death. How could those not be related?"

"Yeah, it seems highly unlikely that they aren't. But I happened to run into the ME investigator yesterday, and she told me the same thing you heard. In fact, she said he's closing both cases. There's just no evidence to support anything other than Erik's death being a result of asthma complications and Brooke's death being an accident."

"Well, if there's no evidence, there's no evidence," Lisa said in her very pragmatic way.

Sam wished she could deal with life as easily as her friend seemed to.

There was movement inside James's apartment, and through the sliding glass door, Sam could see that Kevin had arrived.

"So, I'll get back to you with some options on those startups," Lisa said. "And don't discount Redew. Whit is well-connected, and I'm sure he'll find a way to keep things going. At the same time, however, don't drop your clinical practice. There's no reason for you to stop working part-time, right?"

"Right." Sam then said goodbye and went back inside.

Kevin appeared animated, and his excitement seemed to have rubbed off on James.

"You won't believe what Kevin just told me!" James said.

"What?" Sam asked.

"Go on." James nudged his boyfriend.

"Well, the morning that girl died—"

"Brooke," Sam said.

Kevin nodded. "So, the morning that Brooke died, this guy rode up in the elevator with me. I figured he just lived in the building since I'd seen him before. But after Brooke died, I found out that she lived on the sixth floor—the same floor that the guy got off from the elevator."

"Okay," Sam said, wanting to pull whatever he had to say out faster. She glanced at James, who wasn't helping, looking like a kid who couldn't wait for a surprise party.

"So today, I was looking through the *Austin Business Journal*. There was a bit about up-and-coming CEOs in the area. And there was a picture of that same guy."

"The one from the elevator?" Sam asked.

"Yep. And then I saw his name in the caption."

"And ..." She couldn't take it anymore. "Who was it?"

"Matt Purcell."

31

"What?" Sam couldn't believe what she'd just heard. "Are you sure?"

"Well...pretty sure," Kevin said. "I mean, the picture in the journal was just a thumbnail." He looked up at the ceiling. "Yeah, I'm pretty sure it was Matt."

"But you said one of your colleagues had worked with Matt on another startup—and James even talked to her. You didn't mention you'd seen him in your building before."

"That's true. Katie didn't have many nice things to say about Matt, but I only knew his name. I'd never met the guy, so I didn't know what he looked like. But when I saw his picture in the *Austin Business Journal*, I knew I'd seen him before. And then it hit me; I'd seen him in the elevator getting off on Brooke's floor the morning she died."

This was all too much for Sam to take in. Did Kevin really see Matt that day? And what did it mean?

James piped up. "Okay, so say you saw Matt. There could have been any number of reasons he was there.

Maybe he was meeting someone else. Are you sure he got off on Brooke's floor?"

"Yeah, that I'm definitely certain of. He followed me into the elevator on the ground floor, and he had a coffee in each hand from Houndstooth. I asked him which floor he was going to so I could push the button for him. It was the sixth floor—Brooke's floor."

"Huh."

Just then, pizza arrived, and Kevin put it on the coffee table while James grabbed a few beers out of his refrigerator. They all grabbed slices out of the box and sat around munching while they talked through what this new information meant.

"The ME is going to close Brooke's case, though," Sam said in between bites. "There's no evidence of foul play. It looks like it was just an accident."

"But what if it'd been staged?" Kevin asked.

"That's always a possibility," Sam said, "but I remember Dylan mentioned the deadbolt was engaged. If it was Matt, he'd have to have a key to get in." She shook her head. "Plus, her death is the reason these VCs are pulling out, and that's Matt's biggest goal right now: to get funding to keep the company going. So why would he kill her?"

"Was she an integral part of the company?"

"No. She was supposed to leave in a couple of months anyway, for grad school in Chicago."

"Then it doesn't make sense that they'd balk because of her death," Kevin said. "There's probably another reason."

"Matt said they're just superstitious, especially after two deaths, because he had to persuade them everything was moving forward after Erik died. When he convinced Greg to join, the VCs were okay with that, especially since Greg had done some of the groundwork that was the basis for founding the company."

"So, everything is back on track?" Kevin asked between bites.

"Well, kind of. I've been helping Greg figure out what Erik had accomplished. But from what we found, it seems Erik had problems replicating Greg's early experiments. The drugs that had looked promising for a couple of neurodegenerative diseases might not work. And that would set back the company's ability to bring in revenue by years." She sucked in a deep breath, her heart starting to race. "And I was meeting Brooke that morning because she'd figured out what Erik's Post-it note meant."

Kevin's eyes grew bigger. "What if Matt killed both Erik and Brooke because they were jeopardizing Matt's fundraising? Katie told me he's notorious for over-promising."

James had been watching the two of them pick apart these ideas while chewing on a pizza crust. "This is interesting and all, but how do we prove it? How do we even know if it was Matt that Kevin saw, that he was there that morning?"

Sam picked up her phone, pulled up a picture of Matt from his LinkedIn profile, and showed it to Kevin. "Is this him?"

Kevin studied the image for a moment. "Maybe, but that picture is so formal. He wasn't wearing a suit that morning, just jeans and a T-shirt. And his hair was different."

She took her phone back and looked at the picture a little more closely. It was a studio portrait, and Matt did seem a little stiff, like he'd been apprehensive, maybe trying to impress someone. She then pulled up the Redew website, where she knew there were photos of Matt that were more casual and taken from different angles. "How about these?"

Kevin took the phone again, and this time he immediately said, "That's him. I'm pretty sure."

"Okay," James said. "What do we do with this information? How do we prove he was there that morning?"

Sam shook her head. "I don't know."

But Kevin sat, staring at the empty pizza box on the coffee table for a moment, then he spoke up. "I have a friend who knows how to find the location of any cell phone from data collected by the cellular network. He could find out if Matt was there that day."

Sam squinted at him. "Can he do it legally?"

Kevin shrugged. "I've never asked. But let me give him a call." He stood with his phone and slid open the glass door to go out onto the balcony.

Crisp spring air buffeted in, and Sam filled her lungs hungrily, clearing her mind. She secretly hoped Kevin's friend would shoot the idea down.

"Who is this guy?" she asked James.

"Dunno. Kevin knows lots of people with various skills. It's all above my head."

"I just don't want him doing anything that's not legal."

"I'm sure he wouldn't," James said. "But, you know, there are a lot of things that aren't completely black and white. So what if we let Kevin do his little spy thing with his friend, and then it turns out Matt wasn't there that morning? There'd be no harm in that, right?"

Kevin came back inside with an excited look. "Okay, my buddy Ethan can do it," he said, then grimaced, "but we need the data from Matt's SIM card, so we'd have to get access to his cell phone."

Sam shook her head. "I'm not going to steal his cell phone."

James sat up. "Ethan only needs the data from the SIM card, so we could copy it, right? And that should only take a few seconds."

Kevin nodded enthusiastically. "Yeah. Sam, if you distract Matt, one of us could pull the data off of it. Then we'd have what Ethan needs."

She protested, "But I'd be an accomplice to something that's possibly illegal." She was torn. She really wanted to know if Matt had anything to do with Brooke's death. However, even though the fate of the company was still a long shot, if Matt or Whit pulled through and got funding for Redew, then they'd surely be offering her a full-time job.

And how could she work with Matt with any doubt in her mind that he could possibly be a killer?

She'd had this same thought process only a few days before, but about Greg instead of Matt. She really needed to stop overthinking things.

But her curiosity nagged at her. She wanted to know.

She reluctantly said, "And even if I decided to distract Matt so one of you could access his phone, how would we set this up? I only see him at the Redew offices, so how would we explain either one of you being there?"

James's expression brightened. "I know exactly how we could do this. I'll pitch to *ABJ* that I want to do a profile on Redew—you know, just like I did on that solar company? It would be a lot better than all these rinky-dink profiles I'm doing of the next food delivery startup or dating app."

Kevin laughed. "Yeah, there are way too many of those—college kids create apps to solve the problems they have. They don't have enough experience to solve bigger problems that could change the world."

"Exactly," James said. "And Redew is doing work that could benefit people who need it the most, right?" He turned to Sam. "I mean, you still believe in the technology and the approach Redew is taking, right?"

Sam nodded.

"Okay, then. I shouldn't have a problem pitching the idea to *ABJ*. And even if they don't bite, I can still go there under the guise of writing a profile."

"That'd be dishonest, though," Sam said.

"No, not really. If *ABJ* doesn't want it, I can sell the piece to someone else. And then we'd know for sure if Matt was really at Brooke's condo that morning. And if he wasn't, like I said, no harm, no foul."

Kevin smiled in agreement.

She hoped that would be the outcome. Then everything would be fine. It would still be awful that Brooke's death was an accident, but if Sam had a future with the company, she wouldn't always wonder about Matt. However…

"Suppose he was at Brooke's condo," she said. "What if he was there at the time she died?"

"Then," James said, looking grim, "he might just be a killer."

When Sam entered Redew's offices several days later, Matt called to her across the work area, from the door of the conference room, with excitement in his voice. "Come, come." He motioned for her to join him, as if she were taking too long, even though she'd just arrived. "I've got some news for you."

She set her purse and bag down in an empty cube, then went to the conference room and settled into a chair at the large table. Greg and Whit were already there, chatting like old friends.

"I don't know how Whit did it," Matt said as he tipped his head in admiration, "but he convinced Mundy to stick with us. We signed the term sheet this morning."

"Strike while the iron's hot." Whit beamed. "That's what my father always told me."

"Really? That's great!" Sam said. "No, that's better than great. That's fantastic!"

She looked around, and everyone, including Greg, had huge grins on their faces, their bodies all charged up, as if they'd just won a championship game.

"We've agreed," Matt said, "along with Dr. Galloway, that we'd like to extend an offer to you to be our chief medical officer, starting as soon as the deal is finalized."

"When will that be?" Sam asked.

"We should close in the next thirty to sixty days."

"We hope you'll accept," Whit said. "Just think of all the lives we can help with the work we're doing here."

"Will you join us?" Greg asked.

She took in their faces, and despite the ups and downs of the last couple of months, the highs of South by and the tragedies of Erik and Brooke, she saw optimism. She could think of nothing other than possibilities—how she would now be part of something affecting the lives of thousands, possibly millions, more people than she could've hoped to help as a single doctor, seeing patients one at a time.

Sure, she'd miss the individual interactions, along with the patients who'd held her in high regard, attributing their improvement to her capabilities, when sometimes, she couldn't fully explain their outcomes, and sometimes, she'd felt like an imposter.

But this job would allow her to use all of her skills and compassion. And it didn't require additional training, finishing residency, and obtaining board certification.

These men didn't care about those accolades; they only cared that she could guide them, to interpret the results they got from their work, and to find the groups of patients who needed the most help, whose lives were defined by their illnesses. This job offered her the chance to truly make a difference, not only for them, but for society as a whole.

Sam nodded as she grinned. "Of course I'll accept."

"Wonderful," Whit said. "We'll work out your specific requirements and have Lisa draw up a contract."

Then he turned to Matt, his expression stern.

"However, I do want to point one thing out." Whit paused, glanced over at Sam and Greg, then focused on Matt again. "The reason Mundy got nervous is that they found out about Brooke's…uh…accident from the media, and Redew's name was mentioned. In the future, it's always best to fully disclose anything that could reflect poorly on the company as soon as possible to investors. I was able to smooth things over by letting them know that Brooke was not an integral part of our operations—"

"I told them that," Matt said.

"Yes, I know," Whit acknowledged. "Of course they were also quite concerned after Erik's passing." He nodded at Greg. "But you did a great job showing how Greg is just as competent and capable, if not more so, than Erik."

Sam wasn't so sure; she hadn't really seen any evidence to support that statement, yet, but then again, maybe she was wrong.

"However," Whit continued, "I don't anticipate we'll have any other tragedies like this. But one of the very first things you must do when an event happens, even if it seems minor, is call all your investors. Transparency and honesty are of the utmost importance."

"Understood," Matt said, looking properly admonished. "I'm glad you're much more influential than I am."

"I can be." Whit smiled wryly. "Of course, doubling my initial investment also improved my powers of persuasion."

Matt's eyes widened in understanding.

"Yes," Whit said. "One way to be convincing is to show how committed you are. VCs are more likely to go in with you when they know you have a lot of skin in the game."

After the exciting announcement, Sam and Greg retreated to the lab to continue working with the flies.

"I'll be so glad when that money comes through," Greg

said. "I can't wait to work with Trotman, to turn my prototype into a solid system, so we can automate all this sorting and counting. This is definitely not my idea of a good time."

"I hear you," Sam agreed.

They'd spent the first few days of the week working like robots, counting, sorting, crossing. All to be repeated time and time again. She was beginning to develop a kink in her neck and stiffness in her back from bending over the microscope. And before today, they'd done this work without hope, without any motivation other than it was just a job they were being paid to do.

It was the only thing she had. Although she'd finally gotten on Dr. Taylor's schedule for a phone call, he'd canceled on her twice, and now they had an appointment to meet in person the following week, during one of his quarterly visits to the clinics in Austin.

But with the term sheet signed, there was hope. More than hope—a pathway to future success. And she couldn't wait to tell Dr. Taylor, to his face, that she would no longer be working for ObraCare.

As she prepared her workstation to begin analyzing flies, her mind drifted to the plan James and Kevin had concocted the previous week. She'd almost all but forgotten about it. And they hadn't brought it up with her again, even though she'd spent the rest of the weekend helping James pack. She hoped her reluctance to commit a possibly illegal act had convinced them not to go through with it.

She and Greg worked side by side, processing batches of flies and recording results, until lunchtime, when he asked, "Wanna grab something to eat?"

Sam's stomach grumbled. She'd been so focused on her work that she hadn't realized she was hungry until that moment. "Sounds good."

They stopped by the outer offices to see if the others wanted to join them. Matt was at his desk, staring intently at his monitor, with Whit looking over his shoulder.

"Thanks for asking," Matt replied, "but we want to work through these numbers again, to make sure we have a good plan to meet Mundy's milestones, before Whit leaves in a few minutes. He needs to get back up to Dallas for Brooke's funeral."

They all remained still for a brief moment, as if they were having a tiny vigil.

Whit broke the silence when he sucked in a deep breath and looked at Sam. "Anyway, I want to get this done before I take off, so we can get that offer to you as soon as possible." To Greg, he said, "And we can give you a raise so you're earning something more commensurate with your potential."

"Plus," Matt said, "we'll need to lock in a budget for a larger office with a bigger lab space so we can increase our head count to make good on our promise of delivering new medicines to patients."

Since the others were still working, Sam felt guilty about going somewhere for lunch, so when she opted to go to a small sandwich shop located two buildings over, Greg agreed. They exchanged small talk while they waited for their sandwiches, since the shop was takeout only with no tables. Three people worked behind the counter, an older man, who appeared to be the owner, along with a young man and a young woman, all sharing a strong family resemblance.

As a stream of office workers from the neighboring buildings came in to pick up their online orders, Sam learned that Greg had grown up and went to college in North Carolina before coming to Texas for grad school. He didn't seem interested in reciprocating her questions, in learning more about her. But she didn't mind, and the conversation moved on to Redew. They were both excited to have more certainty in their futures, with the caveat that the certainty would only last as long as their funding. "Or," Greg said, "until we start making money to support the company. Which is why these results are so frustrating."

The young woman behind the counter announced that their sandwiches were ready, so they grabbed their orders and left.

"What's frustrating about them?" Sam asked.

On the return trip to Redew, Greg went into detail about the different experiments and crosses, many of which she was familiar with, having been involved with counting the progeny. But for her, all of these bits of information had been like pieces of a puzzle, scattered about and not forming a coherent picture. Until he said, "So, basically what I'm saying is, Erik's results look pretty good for Alzheimer's, but it's just not consistent for Huntington's."

Sam stopped outside Redew's front door and turned to him. "Do you think the Post-it we found in his notebook might explain things?"

"Which Post-it? What are you talking about?"

"The Post-it I showed you. Remember, the day I came to Dr. Galloway's lab?"

"What did it say?"

"Here, I'll show you again." Sam pulled the door open and made her way to the cubicle where Erik's notebooks were stacked in a corner. She set her sandwich down, pulled out the right notebook, and flipped to the page with the Post-it.

Greg read it aloud. "'Verify counterselection.'" He stared at it for a moment, as if the cogs in his mind were churning. Then his expression darkened.

"Good. You're back," Matt said as he came out of the breakroom, holding two cups of coffee. "Come with me. I'd like to introduce you to someone."

They followed him to his office, and sitting in the guest chair in front of Matt's desk was James.

At first, Sam tried to act like she didn't know him, as did he. But then she remembered what Whit said about being transparent and honest, about the need to fully disclose everything.

"Hey, James," Sam said. "What are you doing here?"

James gave her a curious look. "I'm doing a profile of Redew for *ABJ*."

Matt smiled. "You two know each other?"

"We went to high school together," Sam said.

"How wonderful!" Matt's smile blossomed into a grin. "What a small world." He went on to introduce James and Greg to each other, with both men exchanging curt nods, and Greg's expression remaining gruff.

Greg held up his sandwich. "Gotta eat so I can get back to the lab." He turned and left.

Sam excused herself so Matt and James could talk. Maybe her friend really was only doing a write-up on Redew and nothing more. Matt was certainly happy about it—he had good news to share, and the *ABJ* would be more than willing to publish an announcement about the latest startup getting funded in Austin.

Sam scarfed down her sandwich—she'd noticed Greg had left his lunch on his desk, uneaten—and then she returned to the lab to continue working with the flies. Greg was hunched over his microscope and didn't acknowledge her, but she didn't want to disrupt him with his counts, so she just went about her work quietly.

After a few minutes, Greg said, "Damn."

Sam looked up from her microscope, rubbing her eyes, allowing them to adjust. "What is it?"

"We're out of vials." He looked at his watch. "Nimbus Scientific closes early on Thursdays, but if I go right now, I can be back in time to get these crosses done and keep our schedule." He stood. "I have to get the company card from Matt."

She followed him, and as they approached Matt's office, laughter from the men inside spilled out. They seemed to be getting along pretty well.

Greg tapped on the doorframe. "Sorry to interrupt, but we're out of vials. If I leave now, I can get to Nimbus Scientific before they close."

Matt frowned. "It's only 1:30."

"They close early on Thursdays."

"I could have sworn we just ordered several cases of vials."

"We haven't received any since I've been here," Greg said.

"I'm pretty sure Erik bought some—I remember signing off on a purchase order…Let's go check the supply closet." Matt glanced at his visitor as he stood. "Please excuse me."

"Of course," James said, a little too enthusiastically, probably for the opportunity to execute his plan.

"Don't forget your phone," Sam said.

Matt glanced at his phone on his desk, then back at Sam, a question on his face.

"Uh, you know, since Holly's at 36 weeks," she said. "That's technically full-term, so the baby could come at any time—you wouldn't want to miss any calls."

"Oh, is your wife pregnant?" James asked.

Matt's face brightened, unable to contain his excitement, but slightly tinted with a touch of apprehension. "Yes, we're having a boy."

"Congratulations!" James said.

Matt picked up his phone and slid it into his pocket. "Right. I'll only be a minute, but you're right, Sam—I don't want to miss any calls."

As Matt and Greg wandered toward the lab, James gave Sam a strange look. She shrugged.

She would just have to patch things over with him later. It was ridiculous they'd even come up with this scheme in the first place.

S am moved into the office and perched on the edge of Matt's desk, her arms crossed. James gazed up at her in defiance, as if he was a schoolboy unwilling to admit wrongdoing.

"Look, I think this whole thing is a bad idea," Sam whispered. "I just don't want to do anything—"

She didn't get a chance to finish, because Matt reappeared at the doorway. "Hey, James, since I'm headed into the lab, why don't we give you a tour?"

Flashing a smirk at Sam, James stood. "Sounds like a great idea."

They followed Matt into the lab, where they found Greg searching the cabinets, looking for the cases of vials Erik had supposedly ordered.

"No, no," Matt said to Greg. "Check the supply closet —you know, the one that's in the back corner of the fly room?"

Greg nodded and went into the smaller space. Sam wanted to join the search, but she couldn't leave James alone with Matt. She was worried he would find some other opportunity to snag Matt's phone.

"So, here it is." Matt nodded at the prototype, his hands shoved into his pockets. "I know it's not much to look at, but we've got a contract engineering firm lined up to build the next-generation system for us."

He quickly stepped over to the easel, blocking James's view of the janky prototype and becoming more animated as he showed off the renderings of the new system. "Here is the future of our company," he said with a flourish. He went on to explain to James how flies would be automatically counted and sorted based on images processed by proprietary machine learning algorithms.

As Matt was going through his explanation, Greg came back to the room and proudly said, "I helped develop those algorithms. It's the foundation of my dissertation."

"Wow," James said. "That's great. So, I take it you just graduated?"

"I will next month, now that I passed my defense."

"Congratulations!" James leaned around Matt to peer at the door where Greg had just emerged. "And what's back there?"

"That's where we store the fly stocks," Matt said, giving Sam and Greg a look indicating he didn't want them to elaborate any further. "Did you find the vials Erik ordered?"

"Yup. You were right; they were in the supply closet. I just hadn't noticed them before."

"And who is Erik?" James asked, playing dumb.

Matt sighed as he put on a grim face. "I might as well tell you, as you'll probably find out one way or another. He used to work here." He moved toward the door to the office space, gently directing James to follow. "Tragic situation, really. He had some health problems that got the better of him."

Sam tagged along behind, still not wanting to let James out of her sight. As she neared the door, Greg said, "Since we have more vials now, we can keep working."

"All be back in a sec," she said to him over her shoulder, then hurried to Matt's office.

She got to the doorway just in time to hear Matt say, as he sat back down behind his desk, "So, where were we? Right, I was just about to tell you the good news: we're about to close on our series A funding."

"That's fantastic." James nodded and scribbled in his notebook. "How much did you secure?"

"It will be just over five million. I know that's not huge compared to some of the other startup companies, but it will get us closer to bringing some of the candidate therapeutics we've identified to market. And it will help us de-risk our offering when we approach strategic investors."

"So, you're possibly looking for a larger pharmaceutical company to partner with down the line?" James asked.

Sam was impressed. He'd done his research. Maybe he really was here for the interview and nothing else.

"Yes, that's a possible avenue for us," Matt said. "It makes sense because we couldn't possibly replicate the distribution channels the larger companies have established. Not to mention paying for the marketing campaigns to get these drugs to the patients who need them." He paused for a beat. "It's too bad Whit isn't here. It would be great for you to talk to him."

"And Whit is"—James flipped through his notebook— "your acting CFO?"

"That's right," Matt replied. Then his eyes lit up. "You know...Whit is having a get-together at his house this weekend to celebrate." To Sam, he said, "I was going to tell you and Greg as soon as I was done with this interview." Then he looked at James. "Would you be willing to join us? It'd allow you to get a little more color for your profile, and you'd get a chance to talk to Whit. He's supported us from the start. Gave us the seed funding so we could lease this place. Plus, he convinced Mundy Capital to go in on our series A."

James smiled. "I'd be honored to join you."

THAT SATURDAY AFTERNOON, Sam and James pulled up to a Mediterranean-style home that was so wide, it appeared to be a whole village in and of itself. They parked amongst the other cars on the circular drive and approached the massive front doors, almost big enough to drive through. While they waited for the door to be answered, they took in the manicured landscaping, lush with junipers and mountain laurels, along with patches of bluebonnets.

Whit opened the door himself, which surprised Sam. With a setup like this, she'd expected him to have a full staff.

"So glad you could make it," he said to Sam. Then he looked at James. "Is this your boyfriend?"

She flushed. "No. This is James Lewis."

"Ah, the reporter doing the profile on Redew. Matt said he'd invited you." He looked back and forth between the two friends. "So, you know each other?"

"We went to high school together," James said.

Whit nodded. "Very good. It's great to maintain those lifelong connections. In fact, those connections have given me the edge in many situations." He extended his arm inside his home. "Welcome."

The view blew Sam away as she entered. Just beyond the foyer was a living room that could have been in *Architectural Digest*. Beyond that, picture windows looked out over a pool lined with limestone coping, filled with water the deep turquoise of the Mediterranean, sparkling and glinting in the bright sun. And finally, beyond that, was the skyline of downtown Austin, beautifully framed by Italian cypresses on either side.

"Wow, this place is fantastic!" James said.

"Thank you. Good thing we bought this place a couple of decades ago; there's no way we would be able to afford it now."

Sam found Whit's attempt at modesty surprising. Usually, these types wanted to show off their wealth as much as possible. And this place certainly did that.

Whit led them to a game room, with a bar on one end, a massive TV on the other, and in between sat a billiard table alongside French doors opening out to the pool deck.

Matt was on the couch by the TV with his wife, Holly, who looked every bit of being full-term, filling out her knit maternity dress. Greg sat nearby, wearing a T-shirt and cargo shorts with his knobby knees and pale legs extending out below. The trio paused their conversation to acknowledge the new arrivals with brief waves and nods before resuming.

Sitting at a poker table next to the bar was a woman Sam recognized from a family picture in Whit's office. But she appeared much more frail than she'd been in the photo, seeming to have aged at a faster rate than her husband.

Whit introduced his wife as Eleanor. "Please forgive me," she said. "I would stand to greet you, but I'm afraid I'm not as spry as I used to be."

Sam wanted to ask what was wrong, but she also respected Eleanor's privacy.

James, on the other hand, had no qualms and asked what was affecting her anyway.

"Oh, the usual," Eleanor said, waving her hand. "Getting old and various health issues."

"What type of health—" James began.

Whit cut him off. "Can I offer you something to drink?"

Despite her personal and professional curiosity, Sam was glad to end the awkward situation, understanding from Eleanor's vague answers that she didn't care to discuss it. Sam figured, once she got to know Whit and his wife better, if they wanted to share her ailments, they would.

Whit went behind the bar, motioning for them to join him around the front. Sam thanked Eleanor for hosting before she and James moved over, squeezing between the barstools. Whit asked what they wanted, listing various libations, both alcoholic and non, and then he patted the taps mounted on the wall behind him, his chest puffing out a touch. "I also have my own brews—a Hefeweizen and an IPA."

James looked at Whit appreciatively. "You homebrew?"

"Ever since college."

"I'll take your IPA," James said.

"And I'll try your Hefeweizen." Sam didn't drink much beer, but she did like the citrusy flavor of the German style.

"I'm on it." Whit placed a pint glass under the spigot of one of the taps and pulled the lever toward him.

It sputtered and spewed out a few drops of amber-colored beer, followed by a trickle of foam.

"Damn it. I need to replace the keg, and the CO_2's probably low." He put the glass down. "No worries. I've got more. Just need to switch it out." He left the room.

After a few moments, Sam could hear bumping and scraping behind the wall with the taps, probably from Whit changing out the keg.

Instead of waiting, James wandered over to the others sitting in front of the TV. As Sam followed, her phone buzzed. It was Miranda.

Dang! She'd completely forgotten about their plans to go kayaking.

She excused herself and went out into the hallway to take the call. The first thing she said was, "I'm so sorry."

"No worries," Miranda said. "I'm flexible. Things come up."

"You wouldn't believe where I am right now." Sam looked across the game room at the view of the skyline through the French doors. She went on to explain why Whit had thrown his impromptu party.

"That's funny, I'm not far from you—I'm already at the Rowing Dock."

This was true. Whit's house was one of many elegant homes perched on the cliffs above Lady Bird Lake, where, a few hundred feet below, the kayak rental business floated on docks next to Zilker Park.

"Now I feel really bad," Sam said, "since you're already there." She watched as Whit's daughter Allison came down the hallway, smiling briefly at Sam as she walked past, before going to her mother in the game room. "I could always leave early and come meet you."

"Don't be ridiculous—it sounds like everything's working out for you, which is great!"

Allison came back through the door to the game room after retrieving her mother, supporting the frail woman as they shuffled by. Sam smiled at the women before they disappeared down the corridor.

"Really, it's not a problem." Miranda laughed. "I'll just go solo. We can get together some other time."

"How about lunch tomorrow?" Sam asked.

Miranda agreed, with Sam profusely apologizing again and promising she would be there, no matter what. As soon as she hung up, Lisa appeared, and they went into the game room to join the group by the TV.

Greg looked awkward in his cushiony seat, as if the chair might swallow him. Matt and Holly, on the other hand, looked every bit the perfect couple on the couch. And James stood by, slightly removed, observing.

Lisa said hello to everyone, then leaned over to give Holly a brief hug before perching herself on the armrest next to her pregnant friend.

"So, when are you due?" James asked.

"A couple of weeks," she said as she rubbed her protuberance. "I'll be so glad when this is over. I feel like a beached whale."

"And this is your first?"

"Yes." She beamed, looking over at Matt, who returned her smile.

"Say, Matt," James said, "I thought I saw you downtown a couple of weeks ago, at the Second Street Condos."

The color drained from Matt's face as he froze, like a deer in headlights. He recovered quickly, though. "You must be mistaken."

"Isn't that where Brooke lived?" Greg asked.

Sam and James both flipped their heads toward him.

Matt seemed curious now. "How did you know that?"

Greg shrugged. "Well, it was in the papers. But I gave her a ride home one time. Pretty nice place for a college student to live."

"All set," Whit said from across the room, so Sam and James went back to the bar.

Whit put a pint glass under the tap again, tilting it at an angle, and this time, it filled as expected. He stopped just as the fluid level neared the top, allowing the foam to rise right to the edge. Then he turned and placed the beer in front of Sam.

"You've done that a few times," James said.

"Yeah, it takes a deft hand." Whit started filling a glass for James. "Although, at the airport lounge in Narita, they have a beer-dispensing robot that does this automatically. A perfect pour, every time." He shook his head as he set the full pint in front of James. "Leave it to the Japanese to build a machine just for that one purpose."

Whit pulled an IPA for himself, then held up his glass. "Cheers."

Sam and James followed suit, and they all clinked their glasses together before they took their first sips.

James then began questioning Whit for his profile, asking the older man about his background and how he'd become involved with Redew, so Sam joined the others in front of the TV again. She claimed the overstuffed chair next to Greg, who kept darting his eyes in James's direction, with what appeared to be a jealous look. "What was James doing at the Second Street Condos?"

"Oh, he just moved in with his boyfriend, who lives there," Sam said.

Greg visibly relaxed, and he smiled as he repositioned himself to face Sam. "Oh, I see."

He then filled her in on the work he'd done the day before, since she'd been in clinic. He was starting to explain how he thought he'd figured out why some of their results seemed inconsistent, when James appeared by her side.

"Hey, I need to show you something." James tipped his head toward the door. "Come with me."

"Can it wait? Greg was telling me something important."

"Well, this is *more* important." James gave Greg a fake smile. "Could you excuse us?"

Greg nodded sullenly.

Sam rolled her eyes as she followed James out into the hallway.

"Kevin just sent me a text," he said, holding out his phone. "Matt *was* at Brooke's condo the morning she died."

"What? How did you—"

"Even though you attempted to sabotage our plan, I'd already carried it out when Matt offered me something to drink after I arrived at your office. Turns out there's plenty of time to copy a SIM card while a cup of coffee is brewing." He looked back down at his phone. "Anyway, I got the data to Kevin, who sent it to his buddy, and Matt was at the Second Street Condos that morning."

Just then, Matt appeared at the doorway. "Gotta take a leak. I'm afraid Whit's beer just goes right through me." He turned to go down the hall.

"So, Matt," James said casually, "what were you doing at Brooke's condo the morning she died?"

Matt halted in his tracks, pivoted back to them, then grabbed James's arm. "How—" He stopped himself and gave James an indignant look. "What are you talking about?"

34

J ames coolly removed Matt's hand from his arm. "You *were* at Brooke's condo the morning she died."

Matt squinted at him, his face turning red. "No. I wasn't there."

"I have proof."

"How?"

"I have my ways," James said slyly.

Suddenly, Sam realized what was going on. Nicole had said Brooke had been seeing someone older, someone she didn't want to talk about. Now it all made sense. She wasn't certain if Matt had killed Erik—she couldn't think of a good motive—but he might have had a reason to kill Brooke. "You were having an affair with her, weren't you?"

The anger on Matt's face melted into anguish, his shoulders slumping as he hung his head. "Yes," he mumbled. After a brief moment, he looked up at them, imploring them to believe him. "But it didn't mean anything. It was just a fling. She was leaving Austin soon, and I was …" He straightened up, now seemingly filled with righteousness. "My life is about to change, and a man has needs."

Sam and James both shook their heads in disgust.

"So, did she change her mind about this fling?" James snarled. "Was she going to expose you for the creep you are? Did you push her off the balcony?"

"No, no." Matt held up his hands. "I left before she died. We'd agreed it was the last time, before the ..."

"Before the baby arrives," Sam finished.

Matt nodded pitifully and lowered his eyes. "If only I'd stayed a little longer...then she might still be alive. She wouldn't have slipped, if only I'd been there."

"I hope you three aren't talking about work," Holly said from the doorway to the game room. She came over to take her husband's arm. "I know we're celebrating the funding round, but it looks like you're being interrogated."

Matt instantly transformed into the savvy CEO and put on his winning smile. "James is just asking some tough questions for the profile he's working on." He bobbed his head as if admitting he'd just been caught. "So, yes, you're right, honey. In a way, I am being interrogated." He glared at James, then patted his wife's hand as he gave her a peck on the cheek. "You know how all-consuming running a startup can be. And now that we've got a VC involved, I'm going to be their whipping boy if we don't deliver on our promises." He glared at James again. "Thank you for giving me a preview."

Holly flinched. "Ah! He's kicking my bladder. Where is that restroom?"

"This way, my dear." Matt escorted her down the hallway.

Once they were out of earshot, Sam whispered, "Do you believe him? It's pretty disturbing how easily he can switch personas. Maybe he was lying to us about leaving Brooke's apartment before she died."

James pulled out his cell phone again. "He may be a scoundrel, but it appears he's telling the truth." He tapped the screen, bringing up a text message. "The data shows Matt did leave Brooke's condo about an hour before she died"—he nodded—"so it matches what he told us."

"Why didn't you say so?"

"Because I wanted to see what Matt had to say. And the data could be wrong, or he might not have been with his cell phone the whole time." James shrugged. "In any case, we were able to get him to confess to the affair and have him reveal how vile he is."

"So Brooke's death was just an accident," Sam said, but then she remembered something from earlier. "Or maybe it wasn't. Greg just admitted to knowing where she lived because he'd given her a ride home."

James considered this for a moment. "Perhaps he's been there more than once."

ould it really be Greg? Sam thought back through her interactions with him since they'd first met. Most were not positive, and she still didn't really trust him. She had started warming up to him recently, after working with him closely for a few days, but only moderately so. He was more competent than she'd expected from her initial impression of him, but he sure was moody. It was always hard to tell what would trigger a downturn in his attitude.

She peered through the doorway next to James, into the game room. Greg and Whit were deep in discussion, while Lisa was looking at her phone.

"How should we handle this?" Sam whispered to James.

"Some of Greg's research led to Redew's creation, right?"

"Right."

James shrugged. "So, I can ask him about that. Then I'll steer the conversation toward how well he knew Brooke, since she was also in Dr. Galloway's lab during that time." He nodded. "If these deaths were not accidents, it makes sense that Greg killed both Erik and Brooke. He had a reason to kill Erik: Erik stole his job. And he had a reason to kill Brooke: she spurned him."

"If that's the case, Greg could have pushed Brooke off her balcony," Sam said. "But how would he have killed Erik?"

Then she noticed they were standing in front of an odd-looking door next to the game room entrance. It appeared to be wood, but it was just a facade covering a steel panel underneath. It was hanging from a rail, and it had a strange handle. She tugged on it, and the door rolled to the side. A seal let go with a soft swack, releasing a wave of cool air, and a light flicked on. The new doorway revealed a room containing several kegs and small tanks, along with a tangle of tubes connecting a few of the silver cylinders to the wall. They must be feeding the taps in the bar on the other side.

"Wow!" James said from over Sam's shoulder. "This place is decked out. He's got a keg room!"

As she slid the door closed, an idea struck her. "What if…?"

She'd started thinking aloud, but she stopped when Matt and Holly came back down the hallway. Holly smiled as she rubbed her belly, with Matt escorting her like a gentleman. As they walked past, when his wife wasn't looking, Matt scowled at them. Then he followed her into the game room.

"You were saying?" James prompted.

Sam blinked to clear her mind. "It's kind of a crazy idea, but Greg would know enough about physiology to pull this off: what if he flooded the fly room with carbon dioxide, causing Erik to die of asphyxiation?"

He raised his eyebrows. "Do you really think that's what happened?"

"It's possible. The section of the lab where we count flies is not very big, so it wouldn't take much carbon dioxide to suffocate someone. The door was locked when I found Erik—whoever did this probably trapped him inside. Plus, his keys were missing."

"What? His keys were missing?"

"Yeah, when I helped Lisa move his car, they weren't with his things at Redew. We never found them."

"Huh," James said. "Another clue."

Sam continued talking through her theory, trying to decide if it was even plausible. "There's a large CO_2 tank to knock out the flies so they don't move around, and usually when we're counting, we're hunched over the microscopes." She tapped her chin. "If I remember correctly, CO_2 is heavier than air, so it would settle toward the ground, be more concentrated there. If Erik was hunched over his microscope, he'd only be a few feet from the floor...I'd have to do some calculations to be sure, but I think it's possible."

"But wouldn't that also kill the flies?" James asked.

"Well, the ones that Erik had been looking at under the microscope had died, but Brooke and I just thought it was because the CO_2 continued to run after he passed out. A little CO_2 puts the flies to sleep, but too much will kill them. However ..." She thought for a moment. "The rest of the flies are stored on shelves above the benches where we use the microscopes, so the concentration of CO_2 would be less up there. Maybe that's why they survived."

"So the flies under the microscope died the same way as Erik."

"Yes." Then Sam remembered something else. "And

that would explain the cool air I felt around my ankles that day. It was the CO_2."

"Like a fire extinguisher," James said.

"Right, just like a fire extinguisher, one that uses carbon dioxide, anyway. They put out fires by displacing the oxygen fires need, smothering them."

"Got it. Let's go talk to Greg."

Before Sam could say anything else, James ran off into the game room. She stayed in the hallway for a second, thinking through her logic again. It seemed like a far-fetched concept, but that's why there are warnings on fire extinguishers and dry ice—because too much carbon dioxide could kill.

She turned to follow James, but Matt stood in the door-way, blocking her. Over his shoulder, she could see James looking back to see what had happened to her. She waved him on. She'd catch up with him once she dealt with Matt.

"Look," he said as he maneuvered them away from the game room entrance, "I know what I did wasn't right, but you've got to believe me. I really did care about Brooke." Defiance crept into his face. "Frankly, she was the one who started it. And she's the one who kept it superficial. It wasn't a big deal for her."

"What about Holly?"

Matt grimaced. "She'd be devastated if she found out. But it's over." He lowered his eyes. "It's out of my system now. I'm going to be a father."

Sam didn't know what to say, which seemed to make him nervous. Was that really the reason he was upset? That Brooke was dead? Or was it that being a father gave him another barrier to philandering? She couldn't tell, and she didn't care.

"So, can I trust you not to say anything?" Matt asked meekly.

Holly peered around the corner. "What are you two up to?"

On cue, Matt switched on his charm. "Just talking about plans for Redew, honey."

His wife advanced on them, her previously rosy glow replaced with incredulity. "Are you really?" She narrowed her eyes. "Or is it something else?"

"Of course, babe. Now that we've secured funding, we're extending Sam an offer to work for us full-time." He turned to Sam. "And we hope she'll accept it."

"You'd like that, wouldn't you?" Holly spat. She sneered at Sam. "Another floozy to have around the office, where you spend God-knows-how-many hours. Someone to hang off your every word."

Sam stifled a laugh. The thought of throwing herself at Matt seemed ridiculous.

"Holly, are you okay?" Lisa's voice came from the game room, heralding her appearance. "What's going on?"

"I think Matt's found another one of his conquests right here," Holly said.

"Sam?" Lisa scoffed. "I don't think so. I've known Sam for years. Plus, she's got a serious boyfriend."

Sam cringed inwardly—she hadn't had the chance to update Lisa on the state of her love life. But for now, the inaccuracy kept Holly at bay.

"Then it's you!" Holly turned on her friend, causing Lisa to stumble backward into the game room. "You're the one that Matt's been spending all his time with, making silly little excuses for why he needs to be away."

"How can you say that, Holly?" Lisa shook her head. "You know I'd never do that. And I was with Erik before he ..." Her gaze fell to the floor, her shoulders slumping.

Suddenly, Holly broke down in tears. "I'm so sorry." She tried to embrace Lisa, but her belly made it difficult. "I don't know what's gotten into me. It's this damn pregnancy." She buried her head into Lisa's shoulder, muffling her voice. "My emotions have been all over the place...I feel so jealous and resentful sometimes...my mind keeps playing tricks on me."

Matt put his arms around her as she released Lisa. "It's okay, my love." He steered her to the couch and helped her sit down, lifting her feet up on an ottoman. "The baby's coming, and all this torment will be over soon."

"Is she going to be okay?" Sam asked Lisa. "And are *you* going to be okay?"

"I think so. She's always been the suspicious type, but this pregnancy has really affected her." Lisa gave a brief nod. "She'll be fine. And so will I."

Sam looked around. No one else was in the room. "Have you seen James?"

"Yeah, he and Greg went outside. They were having a deep discussion about something—for that piece James is writing for the *ABJ*, I guess."

Sam nodded, but her stomach tensed. She looked through the windows and couldn't see anyone outside. "I'll be back. I need to talk to them." She exited through the French doors to the pool deck.

36

O nce Sam was outside, she looked around, but she still couldn't see anyone. A wide, curvy pool with a spa, lined with limestone coping, filled most of the space in front of her. A few loungers sat on the pavers around the pool, with a table and an outdoor kitchen off to the right. And then there was the view.

It was breathtaking. She paused for a moment, soaking it all in. Amongst the cluster of buildings and construction cranes downtown, she could see the Frost Bank building. If she'd had a telescope, she could probably see the conference room where she'd first met Matt.

Greenery surrounded the pool deck, and when she walked to the edge, there was a small drop-off to a lawn below with a forest of trees down the hillside.

Where did they go?

"Have you come outside to enjoy the view?"

Sam heard Whit's voice, but she couldn't see where it was coming from. She turned around to face the house and saw his head poking up between the grill and a potted plant. He stood below the pool deck, on the lawn as it extended around the side of the house. He climbed a stairway up and into the outdoor kitchen, complete with a sink and a small refrigerator next to the grill.

"It's lovely," Sam said. She turned to take in the open expanse again. "You have a wonderful setup."

"Eleanor and I used to have quite a few parties here. And our daughter, Allison, too, when she was in high school." Whit smiled wistfully, and then sadness over-whelmed his face. "But we've slowed down a bit, now that Eleanor's good days occur less frequently."

"She's not well?"

He looked down. "No. She has Huntington's. And we might have been better prepared for it, if we'd known."

"I'm so sorry." Now it made even more sense why he'd recommended Redew apply for a grant from the Hunt-ington Foundation.

"Thank you." He opened the grill, picked up a squirt bottle, and sprayed the grates. As white clouds of steam plumed up, he swapped the bottle for a wire brush and began scraping. "We'll be okay, though. We've got help around the house and good doctors."

"You said you didn't know, that you could have been more prepared. Was she adopted?"

He smiled. "Yes. You're a smart one, aren't you?" He set down the metal brush on the counter and closed the grill. "But let's not dwell on this. We're here to cele-brate." He picked up his beer. "Let's go back inside to gather the others. I'll grab the meat and get you another drink."

"I'm fine, thanks," Sam said. "Actually, I was looking for James and Greg. Do you know where they are?"

Whit swallowed the gulp he'd taken. "They went on that trail." He pointed to an opening between a couple of trees down below. "If you follow it down a ways, you can see the lake." He set down his pint glass, then motioned to the stairs. "Here. I'll show you."

Sam followed Whit across the lawn and into the woods. With the sun sinking in the sky behind them, the clouds had a pink hue, and bird songs filled the air.

As they walked along the trail, Sam asked, "Is that why you invested in Redew?"

"Hmm?" Whit said. He seemed distracted.

"Once you found out about the research Brooke was doing, is that why you decided to invest in Redew?" Sam repeated. "Because your wife has Huntington's?"

"You know," he said, as if he hadn't heard her, "you spend your whole life creating products, building your career, accumulating wealth. Finally, you reach a point where you decide you can slow down and enjoy the world, then life reveals a card you weren't expecting, one that's already been dealt to you. How cruel it can be." He turned to her, a strange look on his face. "But with Redew, I found hope. And it seems to be working."

"What do you mean?"

"The drug we've identified—it's helping Eleanor right now."

"What?" Sam was alarmed. Even if everything went perfectly, it would still be another ten years before patients could take any of Redew's repurposed drugs. "You're giving it to your wife?"

"We're here." Whit extended his arm to show off the view.

But Sam didn't look. She focused on Whit's face. "How can you give a drug that hasn't been fully tested to your wife?"

"Matt promised me that we would get the drug approved for Huntington's eventually. She's just benefiting from it a little early."

Then it hit Sam. The reproducibility issue that Erik had talked about. And the Post-it note. "Erik was trying to replicate Greg's results…but he was having problems, wasn't he?"

"Those were just hiccups. Greg's work was solid. Dr. Galloway assured me."

"And Brooke figured it out, didn't she?" Sam backed away from him. "You had a key to her apartment because she was your niece." She stumbled over a tree root, catching herself before she fell. She didn't dare look down, keeping her eyes on Whit, in case…in case, what?

"You'd better watch out," Whit said menacingly. "You're awfully close to the edge. You might fall."

She saw a movement from the corner of her eye right before he charged at her.

Sam was only a few inches away from a drop-off. There was nowhere to go. She grabbed onto the sapling beside her, hoping it would be enough to keep her from going over the edge.

Greg leapt from behind an elm, rushed at Whit, and knocked him to the ground. The two men tussled in the dirt and leaves. Whit ended up on top of Greg, wrapping his fingers around the younger man's throat.

Sam jumped on Whit's back, trying to pull him off, but he was too strong.

She looked around for something, anything, to give her an advantage. She grabbed a large stick and hit Whit's back with a crack. But it broke, and Whit continued his assault.

Greg sputtered below Whit, his arms flailing.

Sam reached around, trying to find another stick or branch…something…anything. In the moist earth behind her, she felt something smooth, cylindrical. It was a pair of binoculars.

She hefted them up and slammed them on the back of Whit's head.

He slumped forward onto Greg, who sucked in a huge breath, now that his airway was no longer compressed.

A moan drifted up from below the ledge—the same one Whit had tried to push her over.

She scrambled to the edge and peered over the side.

It wasn't a sheer drop-off. Fifteen feet below, on a small outcropping jutting from the face of the cliff, lay a familiar figure.

"James!" Sam shouted. "James! Are you okay?"

He groaned, then twisted to his side and vomited.

"James!" she yelled again.

His eyes fluttered open, but he seemed confused as he looked up at her.

"Don't move. Stay right there. We'll get some help."

Sam turned to Greg. "And how are you?"

Greg nodded as he continued sucking in air, his hands rubbing his throat.

Sam crawled over to Whit and began to assess him, but he started to stir, so she backed away.

"We need to tie him up or something so he doesn't hurt us," she said.

Greg just nodded again. He looked dazed.

"Take off your belt," Sam said as she looked around. Tying Whit's hands up wouldn't be enough; he could still try to attack them. "Let's move him over to that tree so we can secure him better."

She stood and leaned over to grab Whit's arms at the wrists. Greg had pulled off his belt, but he just sat on the ground with it in his hands, like a toddler who didn't know what to do next.

"Get his legs, will you?" She motioned with her head as

she started to pull on Whit's wrists, inching him closer to the tree.

Greg pushed himself up, then bent over to grasp Whit's ankles awkwardly.

The older man was more awake now, and he started to pull his arms away from Sam. She squeezed tighter as she yanked.

Whit thrashed, kicking Greg, who fell backward and let go of Whit's legs. Whit rolled his body, twisting and pulling his arms away from Sam. She couldn't hold on any longer and released him.

She pitched backward and landed on her rear. She scooted away.

He crawled through the leaves and twigs toward her, leering at her as he closed in.

Sam butted up against a tree. She felt blindly behind her, pushing herself alongside the trunk, trying to keep moving. Rough bark scratched her arms, spindly wooden fingers tugged her hair.

Whit's hand, covered in mud and leaves, was only inches from her leg.

A branch came into view, right above her head.

She reached up, pulled herself to her feet, and ran.

After a few yards, she came to a fork in the trail, with one path down and to the right, the other up and to the left.

Which way?

Footsteps pounded behind her, growing louder.

She didn't dare look back. No time to think.

Just run.

Sam went left, but it didn't look familiar.

A branch snapped behind her. He was getting closer.

But then, after scampering up a small hill, she could see the house through the trees.

As soon as she reached the clearing below the pool deck, she yelled, "Help!"

Matt appeared moments later as he opened the French doors, a curious look on his face.

Sam could hear Whit's ragged breathing behind her as she scrambled to the steps.

"What's going on?" Matt said, his face now filled with astonishment. "Whit? Why are you chasing—"

Allison was there now, pushing past Matt to get a better look at what was going on.

Once she could see her father, she looked surprised. "Daddy? What are you doing?"

Sam finally allowed herself to look behind her as she approached Matt.

Whit had stopped in the clearing. He looked stunned.

Allison rushed by Sam, down the steps, to her father.

When she got to him, she touched his arm and spoke softly. He mumbled a response, then crumpled to the ground.

Lisa and Holly were outside now. "What's happening?" Lisa asked.

"I don't know, but we can figure that out later," Sam said. "We have to go back down there. James needs help."

37

L isa called 911, and the ambulance arrived within minutes. By then, Sam, with Matt's and Greg's assistance, helped James climb up the ledge. He was banged up and a little woozy, possibly from a mild concussion, but he seemed to be okay. When the paramedics asked if he wanted to go to the hospital, he refused —he didn't want to get stuck with a huge ER bill.

Sam promised she would stay with him for the next day to watch for any neurological changes. He told her she didn't need to, but she said it wasn't an option.

The police, however, took a little longer to arrive.

The only thing Sam knew for certain was that Whit had attacked her and Greg. It also seemed likely that he'd pushed James over the cliff edge, although his memory was a little fuzzy on the details.

Of course, Allison reasoned that maybe James had just slipped. Whit wasn't responding to anyone's questions as he sat in a chair next to the poker table in the game room, his daughter holding a cold pack to the back of his head. She'd wanted to take him into another room, but everyone else held firm. They didn't want Whit to leave their sights.

While they waited for the police, Sam went over to Greg, who was sitting in a chair by the TV. "You saved my life. Thank you."

He gave her a small nod. "You're welcome."

"Did you see Whit push James over the side?"

"No. I wasn't there."

"But you were there when Whit charged at me."

He gave her another small nod.

"Wait," Sam said. Things weren't adding up. "But Whit said he saw you and James go into the woods, that he'd told you there was a view of the lake."

Greg slowly shook his head back and forth. "He did tell us that, but I was never there with James."

"Okay, let's back up because I think I missed something here," Sam said. "Lisa said she saw you and James go outside and that you were pretty deep in conversation."

"Yes. James was asking me questions about my research. He said we should go outside, so we wouldn't disturb everyone."

Sam thought that James had actually wanted to confront Greg without anyone around. But it was a bone-headed thing to do if he really thought Greg was a killer.

"Then what happened?" she asked.

"James started asking these weird questions about Erik and Brooke, and then Whit showed up. He said we should check out the view of the lake, that he'd show us the path."

Drawing the details out of Greg was like pulling teeth. "But you didn't go down the path with them?"

"Well, I started to, but then Whit snapped his fingers and said it would be better if we had binoculars. He told me there was a pair on his desk in his office, that I could get to it from a side door."

Based on this, it seemed Whit was worried James was getting too close to the truth—she wondered if Whit had been warned by the questions James had been asking about Erik and Brooke. But it seemed he hadn't wanted to hurt Greg.

Sam looked over at Whit, slumped in his chair, with Allison rubbing his arm, saying over and over, "Daddy, please talk to me." But he still wouldn't respond.

She turned back to Greg. "So, you got the binoculars, and that's how you ended up being there right when I needed you. It's a good thing you surprised Whit; otherwise, he'd probably have pushed us both over the edge."

"Well, that's the thing. I had come back outside when I heard you ask Whit where James and I were, and when he said he saw both of us go down the trail, I was curious because that wasn't exactly what happened. Whit lied to you, and I wanted to know why. So I followed you."

"You thought something was wrong."

Greg nodded yet again.

"Well, thank you. I'm really glad you were there to stop Whit." She stood up to go find James. He'd disappeared, and she wanted to keep an eye on him, to make sure he didn't vomit again. Maybe he'd gone to the bathroom.

"And I'm sorry for everything," Greg mumbled. "All the trouble I've caused."

"What?" She sat back down. "What do you mean?"

"The results," he said, hanging his head. "My wonderful results that started everything." He used air quotes when he said wonderful.

"The results that identified the drug targets that Redew was formed to commercialize?"

"Yes."

"Erik was having trouble replicating your results, so

…" A thought suddenly struck Sam, about the stories she'd read, stories of scandals where researchers had fabricated their data. "You didn't make everything up, did you?"

"No, no. I'd never do that. But Erik figured out an error I'd made. I think that's what got him killed."

"You also think Erik was murdered?" Of course, she hadn't shared her theories with Greg—especially since she'd suspected him—but it was interesting that he'd come to the same conclusion.

"It makes sense. He couldn't replicate my results for the Huntington's drug, but his results were close to what I'd found for Alzheimer's. Turns out, I'd messed up my counterselection protocol, and the Huntington's drug seemed like it had worked because most of the progeny from my initial crosses didn't actually carry the Huntington's gene."

"They were normal flies."

"That's right. Well, mostly normal. There was a mix of normal and Huntington's carriers, and that's why the data didn't look right. Yesterday, after you told me about the Post-it, I figured it out from his notes. And I was looking through Brooke's notes too …"

"So she'd figured it out as well."

James appeared at the door to the hallway just then and motioned for Sam to join him. She excused herself, telling Greg she'd be right back, and stepped out.

"Where were you?" Sam asked, looking at his pupils, trying to see if they were equal. They appeared to be, but it was hard to tell without better light. "How are you feeling?"

He waved his hand. "I'm fine. You don't need to worry about me." He touched her arm, directing her down the hallway. "But you've gotta see this."

"What is it?" She followed, but she really wanted to go

back and ask Greg more questions. "I was just learning why Erik was—"

"Come with me." He went down the hallway, past the restroom and the kitchen, through the foyer, where they'd first entered the house, across from the extravagant sitting room with the glorious view, and finally turned into a home office. Whit's office.

It was filled with what Sam would expect for a man who'd spent most of his life in corporate America. A wide bookshelf under the window housed volumes of business books, books on finance, managing teams, market strategy. Memorabilia filled the walls, including plaques, framed certificates, and small shelves with mini trophies, along with pictures of Whit with various people. She had no idea who they were, but they looked important. Above the credenza behind the desk were Whit's diplomas—his undergraduate degree and his MBA. Pictures of his family sat on the credenza behind the opulent desk, pictures from happier times, when Allison was a child and Eleanor was younger and healthier.

James walked behind the desk and used the bottom of his shirt to pull open a drawer. "These didn't look like they belong to Whit." He pointed at a set of keys nestled amongst pens and paperclips. On the ring was a silver double helix. "Are these Erik's keys?"

"I think so. We can ask Li—" Sam stopped herself. Should they get Lisa to confirm these were his? Did they want to cause more heartache right now?

Greg had also figured out that Whit had killed Erik and Brooke, so it was all going to come out at some point.

They should wait for the authorities.

"What? Why'd you stop?"

Sam pushed the drawer closed with her knee. "You

need to quit snooping around. This is evidence. We should leave."

Out in the hallway, James said, "But those are Erik's keys, right?"

"I think so."

They headed back to the game room, but James stopped before entering. They were standing in front of the walk-in refrigerator again.

"So Whit killed Erik," James said, placing his hand on the refrigerator door, with kegs and CO_2 tanks on the other side. "He's the one who killed him with CO_2, not Greg."

"That's what it looks like," Sam said. "And he was going to kill us and make it look like an accident."

"Yeah, but why was he doing all of this?"

"I just found out from Greg that the promising drug candidate for Huntington's wasn't so promising. Erik couldn't replicate Greg's results, and then Brooke figured it out. I think that's what she was going to tell me before she died."

"But I still don't understand. Why would Whit kill them?"

"Because he believed Greg's initial results. His wife has Huntington's disease."

James's eyes widened. "She does?"

Sam nodded. "I'd asked Whit about his wife's condition right before he—"

"Tried to kill you."

"Yes, right before he tried to kill me. He'd revealed she has Huntington's and that he'd started giving her the drug Greg had identified." Sam shook her head. "But, unfortunately, once the signs of Huntington's manifest, the treatment options are limited." Then something dawned on her as she watched Allison sit with her father through the game room entrance. "But his daughter—she's still young. If she has inherited the condition from her mother, she won't be exhibiting any symptoms for another couple of decades, the amount of time it would take to fully develop these drugs. He must have done this for his daughter."

38

Ohne week later, Sam's whole life was flipped upside down. She no longer had a steady job—at Redew or ObraCare—and she no longer had a home. When she'd finally had her call with Dr. Taylor, he confirmed there wasn't a full-time job for her. All he could promise is he'd keep her on the list of floating physicians and would reach out if he needed her. She'd asked him when that would be—he didn't have her scheduled anytime in the next month. He'd replied that the schedules for all of the clinics were filled, but if anyone got sick, he'd call. How ironic was that?

With no guaranteed source of income, she contacted the *locums* agency she'd worked with after her mother died. They gave her a few options, most of which were in rural towns around Texas. That was fine; she couldn't work in any of the big cities due to her contract's noncompete clause. She'd almost told Dr. Taylor she was going to quit working for ObraCare completely, since that would eventually free her from the clause—after a whole year—but she hadn't. She had no idea what she was going to do.

She let her apartment complex know that she would not be renewing her lease, which would have happened the following week, with a twenty percent increase. Fortunately, the manager gave Sam some leeway, since he already had a list of people waiting for units to open up, letting her break the lease on short notice without the penalty of a month's rent.

So, Sam was now packing up her stuff to put in storage —something she could afford—and then accepted a short-term *locums* assignment in North Texas, between the Dallas–Fort Worth area and the Oklahoma border. It would be at a small family practice clinic, and the only doctor working there needed someone to fill in during her maternity leave. The compensation included an allowance for a stay at a local motel.

Sam figured this would give her time to regroup. Maybe reenroll in the classes she'd dropped for her MPH, just in time for the summer session, and then she could start working on those residency applications. She would apply to them this cycle, and if all went well, she could finish up her MPH, if she really just focused on that and nothing else ridiculous—like another startup…or philandering boyfriends.

Lisa was disappointed Sam didn't want to pursue any of the other startup opportunities she'd identified, none of which could pay Sam except in equity. She was done with that. She needed to be paid what she was worth, and she was surprised her friend even wanted to keep dealing with early-stage companies. Lisa didn't seem phased much by what had happened at Redew, telling Sam she'd seen some pretty crazy things in the startup world, and the risk was worth the reward. But was it worth it if everything was built on false promises and people died?

Sam was almost finished loading up the U-Haul she'd

rented. James and Kevin had helped her load the big items—her mattress and couch along with most of the bulkier furniture—and now she was just packing up various other boxes to finish filling the cargo hold. They were going to meet her at the storage facility to help her transfer everything into her unit that afternoon. And then she'd make the five-hour drive to her new, temporary position.

Miranda stopped by around lunchtime, so Sam took a break. They walked over to Taco Deli, just down the street, directly across from one of the trailheads for the Barton Creek greenbelt.

"Man, I'm going to miss this place," Sam said wistfully as they waited for their order.

"You aren't leaving forever, right? This is just a stopgap for you."

"It is, but last week I thought I was on a completely different trajectory with my life. And now ..."

"And now, you're okay. You didn't become another victim to Whit Chapman, and you didn't stay clueless in his delusional world."

"But did he really kill Erik?"

"I think your theory holds water. The last of the testing came back, and there were no significant levels of any compounds from that list in Erik's blood."

"But?"

Miranda sighed. "But Dr. Duveneck says that doesn't mean anything. He's still sticking to his initial assessment that Erik died as a result of an asthma exacerbation."

"But didn't they find Erik's keys in Whit's—"

Sam stopped herself.

Miranda squinted at her. "Were you snooping around before the police arrived?"

"I wasn't, but...someone else found keys with a silver

double helix and showed them to me. They were in a drawer in Whit's home office."

"Was that someone else your friend James? The wanna-be investigative reporter?"

Miranda locked eyes with Sam, but Sam didn't want to tattle on her friend.

After a moment, Miranda waved her hand. "Don't worry. It's not important. Anyway, Mr. Chapman's attorney claims he found the keys after Erik died and kept them because he didn't know who they belonged to. It doesn't matter anyway. Dr. Duveneck and the police aren't going to pursue it any further, since there's really not any solid evidence, and the parents are satisfied with his determination."

Lisa had been as well. Some people were more accepting of bad outcomes.

Sam didn't think she ever could be if she were in their situation. "But aren't there ways to prove Erik was killed by CO_2 asphyxiation? I'm sure he was acidotic."

"He was, and I pointed this out to Dr. Duveneck, but he said patients become acidotic during asthma exacerbations too."

"But if he had excessive levels of CO_2 in his system, his pH should have been really low, and—"

Miranda held up her hand to cut Sam off. "I know, I know. But the reality is that several hours had passed between the time you found him and when he'd been pronounced dead. By then, he'd received bicarb at the hospital during resuscitation, so it just muddies up the picture."

"Well, there's also the CO_2 tank. Brooke said Erik had ordered a new one before he died, but the tanks were empty when she and I were working. There have got to be records, purchase orders—"

Miranda stopped her again. "I agree. I would love to dig into this and find definitive evidence to show Whit killed Erik. Your theory really does make sense. But there's no interest, so it's out of my hands." She shrugged. "On the other hand, there is some evidence pointing to Brooke's death being a murder. Whit had access to Brooke's apartment because he was Brooke's uncle. Dylan's getting the records from the parking garage to see if he parked there." She leaned closer to Sam, lowering her voice. "But he's already received security footage from the condo management. Whit was there that morning."

"Did he admit to anything?"

"No, but based on your statement about what he told you—right before he tried to push you over that cliff—it seems he truly believed Matt's overexaggerated claims that the drug Greg had identified really would help his wife, and possibly his daughter."

"So, does his daughter carry the gene?"

"I don't know. The testing is still pending. But at a minimum, we have assault and attempted murder charges based on how he attacked you and James."

By then, their tacos arrived, and they dined while continuing to discuss the case. Sam asked about fingerprints in Brooke's apartment, but as soon as the question came out of her mouth, she realized Whit's attorney could claim they'd been there previously, which is exactly what Miranda confirmed. Then Sam had an idea. "Whit wouldn't have had a reason for being in the lab or for touching the CO_2 tanks—he's a finance guy. Has anyone checked for his fingerprints on the tanks?"

Miranda slowly shook her head as she gave Sam an appreciative smile. "I love your tenacity, but no, that hasn't happened. However...in light of everything else, maybe I could convince Dylan that these cases are connected."

Then she set her taco down and leaned closer to Sam. "You know, I'm going to tell you something that I haven't told anyone except Dylan; I've applied to the FBI Academy."

"Congratulations!" Sam said.

"Thanks, but I've only just applied. Who knows if they'll accept me. But, with your intuitive skills, maybe you should consider applying too."

"What? A doctor in the FBI?"

"They accept people from all different backgrounds. I don't know how many doctors, but there are certainly nurses, like me, who work as special agents." Miranda shrugged. "Just a random thought. But it would be kind of fun going through the academy with someone I know."

"What does Dylan think?"

"He's totally supportive."

"Even though you might have to move?"

"Well, it wouldn't be permanent. And—if I'm accepted—I could request to work at a field office here in Texas after I graduate."

Sam was truly happy for her friend. They finished up their tacos and walked back to Sam's apartment. Miranda helped Sam with the last of her boxes and hugged her goodbye. "Keep in touch."

"I will," Sam said. "If nothing else, I'll probably be back at some point for Whit's trial—the prosecutor says she might need my testimony." She smiled. "And let me know what you hear from the FBI Academy. I'll keep my fingers crossed for you."

She watched as Miranda drove away. Then she turned to the U-Haul, pulled down the back door, and secured it. She checked her watch. She had just over an hour to get this hulking vehicle to the storage unit, unload it, and return it. Then James would bring her back to do one last sweep of her apartment before she started the long drive north.

As she ground the gears, inching the truck forward, she thought about what Miranda had suggested.

A doctor in the FBI. She laughed. Well, she'd already started bucking the trend when she quit residency. Maybe she should look into it.

ABOUT THE AUTHOR

Stephanie Kreml writes mysteries and thrillers after working as an engineer, a physician, and a life science consultant. She lives with her family in Austin, Texas. This is Stephanie's third book in the Dr. Samantha Jenkins Mystery Series.

Sign up for her newsletter and receive a FREE copy of *Accidental Truth: A Dr. Samantha Jenkins Novella.*

Go to
www.stephaniekreml.com/signup

ALSO BY STEPHANIE KREML

Truth Unveiled

Neglected Truth

Coming Soon

Misguided Truth

Made in the USA
Las Vegas, NV
22 March 2023

69470560R00173